HOTEL BELLEVUE

Thomas Shapcott is an eminent Australian poet and writer, winner of numerous awards, including the Canada/Australia Prize. Born in Ipswich, Queensland, in 1935, he practised as an accountant for twenty-five years and is now the Director of the Literature Board of the Australia Council. His novels include *The Birthday Gift* and *White Stag of Exile*. He is married and lives in Sydney.

Author photograph by Regis Lansac

HOTEL BELLEVUE

Thomas Shapcott

PRINTING HISTORY

A BLACK SWAN BOOK   0 552 99330 1

Originally published in Great Britain by Chatto and Windus Ltd, London

PRINTING HISTORY

Chatto and Windus edition published 1986
Black Swan edition published 1988

Copyright © Thomas Shapcott 1986

Conditions of sale
1. This book is sold subject to the condition that it shall not, by way of trade *or otherwise*, be lent, re-sold, hired out or otherwise circulated in any form of binding or cover other than that in which it is published *and without a similar condition including this condition being imposed on the subsequent purchaser.*
2. This book is sold subject to the Standard Conditions of Sale of Net books and may not be re-sold in the UK below the net price fixed by the publishers for the book.

Black Swan Books are published by Transworld Publishers Ltd., 61-63 Uxbridge Road, Ealing, London W5 5SA, in Australia by Transworld Publishers (Australia) Pty. Ltd., 15-23 Helles Avenue, Moorebank, NSW 2170, and in New Zealand by Transworld Publishers (N.Z.) Ltd., Cnr. Moselle and Waipareira Avenues, Henderson, Auckland.

Printed in Australia by Aust Print Group

At every moment of our life we are the descendants of ourselves, and the atavism which weighs on us is our past, preserved by habit.

Marcel Proust, *Letters*

PRELUDE

In the Park

'When you die what will you give me? Grandma, are you going to give me anything? You promised . . . '

'Boyd, you greedy little cockroach! You must not ask; I have no intention of dying. I will live until I am one hundred and twenty-seven. And then – crash – I shall disappear suddenly so that nobody will ever *really* know, and my last will and testament will be fought over for another seventy years.' She looked stern, but he knew her. 'By that time you will have grown up, done whatever it is in life you are going to do, you will be older than I am now. *You* may be dead and gone long before me. So you see, cockroach, there is no use making plans beforehand.' Her very fast stride. He had to skip to catch up. 'No point in setting those surprisingly greedy little eyes on anything. Now, what do I possess that could possibly interest you?'

They were walking in the Brisbane Botanical Gardens. The December stormclouds were beginning to build up, low, burly presences heavy as dolomite but always scuffy like the edges of surf. Boyd had let go his grandmother's hand but she relented at the last (she always did). She was not going to have him sulk. She knew all the tricks.

'Well? What do you want to take from me?' she repeated, pausing to let him catch up.

'Nothing.' He knew some of the tricks, too.

'How so? And is that the tone to speak to your grandmother? I think we'd better examine the matter. What am I going to give you? Well,

Boyd Kennedy, son of my son, sole heir of my hopes and whatever twist of genes got thrown in along the way? There, you like that, don't you?'

She tousled his head. Her hands on him were always soft, caressive. He adored her.

'Last night I heard you saying to Miss Bennett you were going to give her everything, all your things; you said . . . '

'You heard me, Boyd? I'm ashamed of you. You surprise and hurt me. Listening, spying. I never thought that of you.'

The giving hand now snapped against her handbag. She was fumbling for a handkerchief.

'You were so loud.'

'How old are you now, Boyd?'

'Eleven.' Contrite.

'What you heard, whether it was loud or soft was . . . I said to Eve . . . what I said to Miss Bennett was . . . To barge in like that last night just after our little party tea, well it had been very frantic. I tried not to show it, of course. I hope you too will learn that. You must learn, Boyd, to control your baser and more passionate feelings.'

'She kept staring at me.'

'That is her way. She is myopic.'

'What's that?'

'Never mind. It could mean money-mad, sex-mad, but it does not. Eve, sex-mad? Well, there we are. I've presented you with a conundrum haven't I? I am sure you cannot imagine that shall I say *grim* person not endowed with conspicuous graces hiding grand, grand passions.'

Boyd relaxed, the crisis was over.

'Myopic means near-sighted. Remember that.' But her eyes flew heavenwards, all was well. 'Where's your vocabulary? When you're up here with me I will at least drum some sort of language skill into you.'

'She scared me.'

'Eve did? Wait till I spring that on her! She will be flattered. She will be boosted beyond measure.' She gripped him firmly by the hand. 'She will be astonished.'

'What were you drinking?'

'Cockroach!' His grandmother looked him over, then spoke with deliberation. 'There is always the time for port, after a meal. It is a digestive. Or else,' she sighed, 'the brandy.'

'Dad said he was worried.'

'About me? The boy's a fool, I am ashamed of him. Ashamed for him: setting my own grandson like a tracking dog. Did he ask you to measure the decanter each morning? Did he?'

No. Say nothing. You could always tell when Grandmother had been warming the cockles. He liked her then. Except last night.

'Will you really give her – Miss Bennett – everything? Even the mirror-glass vase in the hallway?'

'Silly boy. So anxious; I keep forgetting. Security. Dear Boydie, I have no means of selling the place under your eyes, giving away anything. You must understand metaphor, rhetoric. I was not speaking of real estate. Poor Miss Bennett wanted comfort, I am the only thing she has in this world – isn't that almost frightening? You will learn to say the right sophistries in your time, Boyd. Now, look at that over there: what do you think it is? You see it, that circle of very tall palm-trees? I think that is a sacred circle. Shall we go over and examine?'

She was ahead of him, as always.

'Do you feel it? I think I feel it. Look up at the sky. Boyd, hold my hand, this is exciting and mysterious. See, we are sharing some deep impulse; if we are patient we will feel it, let it sink into us.'

Her chatter stopped. Dark clouds pushed seaweed fingers in to the space of sky marked by the tops of the palm circle. Within those few moments there was no blueness: none. The shadow was not cold, but Boyd felt its difference.

'Yes,' he whispered, 'I feel it, yes. Something.'

'Only those who move out of themselves become part of the vision.' She was moulding his back and shoulders, she was standing behind him.

'A sort of tingle.'

She agreed. 'A sort of change, it's the way you see things, Boyd, you know what I mean? Yes, I believe you do.'

Her hands on him. The clouds scudded over. Struck by sudden claws of sunlight, he blinked.

'Now. I will sit over there. I'm really quite tired. Go and explore by yourself, Boyd, you will be quite safe if you keep to the paths. Along that drive you will pass all the yachts moored on the river. Some people actually live on water. You see their washing out and sometimes catch them fishing or sunbathing. They come in by tiny dinghy to get their provisions in town. Splendid, carefree lives.'

But when Boyd saw the yachts moored just as his grandmother promised they looked tiny, cramped, there was something unstable. Bobbing and dipping in endless ripples. Three of them displayed laundry, but that was only scraps.

He ambled further on, scuffing his feet. All the trees in this part of the Gardens were immense; the original town gardens, convict times. Under such trees only small, scatty shrubs were possible: garden beds, but pretty ragged, not like Melbourne with herbaceous borders and the straight hedge windbreaks you had to prune.

He crossed under a huge jacaranda. Blue flowers littered the ground, they became a mauve shadow. He rubbed his feet among them. Had he expected the stain to be blue?

'Nothing to do?'

He looked up.

'Yes, you.' The man on the bench gave a sudden grin, big white teeth. His face, though, was gritty and unshaven. Not too old, he was not an old man. Twenty, perhaps. He had sandshoes with football socks and a dirty old pair of khaki shorts. His chest was smooth, very tanned. There was a big grease mark on his shoulder, did he know that?

'Just walking.'

'Can see that. Want a piss?'

Boyd stopped in his tracks. He had been warned about strangers asking questions: Got a few pennies? Got a light? Got some money for a tram fare? He did not smoke, but he knew kids who did. He never carried money, but lots of kids did that and someone always cadged.

'There's a big tree up further, bet you've never seen anythink like it. Prickles all over. Even the trunk. And the branches. Nobody could climb that tree, betcha.'

The stranger had joined him and they began walking together. He did not seem to want an answer to his questions. Boyd knew enough of people who just wanted to talk, no answers.

The far end of the gardens grew thick and tangled, lots of canes and rain-forest clumps. But there was a glass greenhouse, and you could make out the red terracotta roof of a gardener's cottage. They went round the river path, skirting the thickets.

'You ever been round here before, huh? This your first time?'

Boyd nodded. The other kept looking at him.

'What are you staring at?'

'You. Any law says it's forbidden?' He grinned again now, and pulled his hand from his pocket where it had been playing. He tousled Boyd's hair in a rough parody of Boyd's grandmother. Boyd ducked.

'Don't do that.'

The other feigned sparring with him, danced around him, a tease. 'I won't hurt you . . . tell you what, though. I'm just bursting for a piss.'

That's what people did privately.

'Over here. Behind this clump. Come on, see who can piss the most.'

Of course a really big kid could do more, Boyd had to grin. This one was not really that old: sixteen, seventeen.

'Come on. Betcha.'

He followed in.

On the way back from the rain-forest Boyd discovered the pond with lotus plants. Huge, unreal flowers. There was a sign which warned how deep it was. He stood at the edge, dazzled by the waxy, pink flowers and pods of the old plants. Under that warm, pink softness, these raw, urgent nozzles; as they matured they grew darker and more rigid. He had left the big boy back there. He had not seen the thorn-tree. The big boy had not wanted to piss at all.

Staring at the lotus flowers Boyd saw him come out of the thicket wiping a hand on his shorts. Boyd ignored him.

But it was true, something had changed. Not the skin, but under the skin. Some thrashing, lean creature ate through the nerve ends. He had felt the same tingling in the palm-tree circle. That ripple.

Touch was part of it, but not really it. His grandmother's touch, moulding and massaging. That big boy, with his thick, rough hand: no wonder Boyd stumbled off like a startled creature. He watched, from the corner of his eye. The other boy paused beyond the jacaranda. Boyd looked down.

As he approached his grandmother's bench he could see it was empty. He felt a stab of panic.

She was further on, talking to a man under the weeping-fig avenue. She gave a wave. Then impulsively she reached out her hand to the other. Boyd could sense the sudden, electric tightness of her grip. Panic? Urgency? By the time he drew up the man had tipped his hat, formally, and strode off.

'Where have you been?' They both asked the question together.

Later, she took him up to the Bellevue Hotel, her favourite place for treats. In the dark inner lounge he fingered the frost on his glass of ice-cream soda. In here, everything seemed again permanent and comfortable.

MONDAY MORNING

Marie

Even before she pushed open the door with her knee, Marie felt the change. The pile of books under her arm spilled on to the carpet. Marie stooped to pick them up, half in, half out of the doorway.

'Are you there?'

Four p.m. Nobody in the block of units would be home. Each day the building emptied; at night the muffled lights of television flickered in darkened rooms, behind curtains. In some, a lamp shone mid-centre of the picture-window, not to look out, but to prevent others looking in. To Marie it had always seemed an interim measure – agreeably so – but they had been here ten years. Boyd did not want to change. No, Marie had pointed out the usefulness of the location. Their rooms had become inhabited in that time, they had achieved a certain smugness. Smugness or snugness?

To unlock their own door from the impersonal passageway was like opening a private treasure-trove hidden in a public thoroughfare. Even the kitchen declared her personality: its cheerful rumpus of cards and notes and reminders stuck on the refrigerator with little magnets, the red and white checkered curtains, the little Viennese clock. Marie had made her claims. Yes, and why not?

But something had altered.

Puzzled, Marie set down her belongings on the Laminex bench.

'Boyd? Boyd, you home already?' Her voice cut against corners and hard surfaces, seeming to sharpen in the process.

Marie strode into the living-room. Exactly as she had left it this morning, in her rush to get the school tram. Boyd would have gone shortly after. The wing-back armchair in the corner looked, almost with reproof, as if no one had occupied it for decades. She picked up a cushion and threw it into the seat. She shrugged, then went back to the kitchen. Marie's eyes were large and expressive in her taut face. Her long fingernails clicked against surfaces. She did not like surprises.

Why did she always crave coffee as soon as she came in? Silly habit, bad for you. Her throat felt dry. She reached for the percolator.

The note was centre-balanced on the refrigerator door, the door to the freezing compartment. Other bits and pieces had been removed, repositioned in the lower section. Boyd again, making his point, rubbing it in, trying to prove she was the untidy one. Framed like a picture, the little message, one fruit-magnet in each corner.

Marie turned on her heel, and with some deliberation rifled for matches, turned on the gas, rifled again, struck sharp downward, breaking the little tip of compacted dust into its shock of flame. So that the fire could begin to consume the wood of the match itself she held it up in her long fingers. Then she put it to the invisible power source of gas.

A small whoosh, then the whole ring of fire. She liked that, the little delay, then the gentle fanning of flower flame. Boyd of course always reproved her: don't keep the gas running so long, light up quick, quick.

Damn! Out of percolator coffee. Just enough to squeeze one cup. Marie knew she would want two.

She turned again to the refrigerator, opened the door, took out the carton of milk and – another habit, another little defiance – poured herself a small glass which she drank quickly, eagerly, like a school-child. Then she put the carton on the bench beside her coffee-mug.

That little sip of milk somehow increased the flavour of the coffee. With creamy lips, Marie had savoured the coldness and the soft richness, draining her glass. She could wait now, the two or three minutes for the percolator to brew. Boyd drank only black. Air bubbles began to cling inside the glass. They were forced off, released, vanished upwards in a sort of vortex. Faster, faster.

Her mother had once said to her, in that over-indulgent Viennese emphasis that Marie rasped back at, 'Darling, it is through suffering that you will discover your soul.' And Marie, at eighteen, had retorted: 'Masochist. Even your Dr Freud could have told you, *Mütterlein*, that you are a glutton in your masochism.' Her mother believed that communication meant embraces, hugs, eyes swivelling. Marie could not bear to hear those old stories of outrage, the war, wholesale destruction. Nothing to do with her. She would not be got at that way. When she and Boyd married, she accepted the Viennese clock and nothing else from her mother; she did not want to live with endless souvenirs. She idolized Boyd. She made her life around him, they made their lives around each other and were determined. At first they did not need anyone else at all. 'Another outsider' Boyd would grin if the bell rang. Later . . . but Boyd's demands were not at all like her mother's. Marie was not going to give up her independence lightly. Her mother could still scald and lay waste. Marie's hair, pulled back tight, emphasized high cheekbones. The other teachers thought she was elegant, infinitely sophisticated, all those languages, that innate sense of style. Marie took the first gulp. Boyd, too, placing her on that pedestal, at least initially. Was there no balance between puffy self-indulgence and endless self-control? She had feasted on Boyd, big, sometimes boisterous, sometimes moody. It was an addiction.

Marie turned to the refrigerator. She took down the note at last. So. What did Boyd have to tell her this time?

Boyd

'As a simple test, Mr Kennedy, just tell me the first words that spring to mind from this list: mirror? . . . '

'Vase.'

'Vase?'

'Grandmother.'

'Grandmother, Mr Kennedy? That is an interesting one. Perhaps you might tell me something about your grandmother?'

'Who said it was *my* grandmother?'

'And is it?'

'As it happens, yes. But it might just as easily be . . . '

'Then *you* said it was your grandmother, Mr Kennedy.'

Without the slightest attempt at secretiveness, Dr Steiner clearly jotted down the word 'aggression'. Left-handed. Why did mollydookers make him squirm? It had only been at Marie's insistence that Boyd made this appointment.

The mirror *was* the vase. A vase in what Boyd now realized was 1930s Art Deco style, probably worth a fortune today. He did not know what had finally happened to her vase, where it had got to. It had come to lodge in his secret recesses. No reason.

A vase of mirror slivers, that never held flowers – not that Boyd could remember. It had been the most precious thing in his memory of Grandmother's Brisbane house. Until he was fifteen Boyd went up every year to Queensland for his Christmas holidays.

He had been ten the first time. The mirror vase sat on top of a white crocheted antimacassar on the hallstand. It reflected itself only, though as a small child Boyd would gaze at each sliver in turn, to catch hints of the pinkness in his own face, the blueness of his eye, his dark brown hair. A proper mirror behind, on the hallstand, made the reflection game infinite, an endless splintering off and slicing apart, the promise of some tantalizing incompletion.

His grandmother's house had seemed infinite – in its variety, its large high-ceilinged timber rooms, the thousands upon thousands of tongue-and-groove boards that, to a small child, offered endless exploration and were so different from his own home's smooth plaster: there was a groove where a procession of little black ants always got in and scurried up some invisible but precise roadway. Their track wavered and detoured meticulously. That groove where a timber knot had been broken to reveal a strange wizard's nose and chin and eye and Einstein moustache; the groove where cream paint had missed, revealing a sandy pine base. Once, on those sweltery hot, sub-tropical days, when it was too intense to go outside, Boyd worked his way right round the grooves of his bedroom. 'His bedroom' – always kept aside for him, year after year. One of the delights was to return and discover toys, books, even lollies, discarded from the previous visit. An excuse every time to feel so much older. Only once had Boyd felt a sense of invasion, when he discovered a screwed-up cigarette packet – Camels – under the bed. The bedlinen, though, each year had its special, fresh odour from his grandmother's linen closet with its spicy pomanders. 'I never mind Boyd coming up,' Grandmother had said. 'He can amuse himself alone for hours.'

Grandmother's house *was* the tropics: unreal, intense in everything. The intensity of the heat, and then the intensity of cool sea-breezes that made you really discover, each afternoon, what physical pleasure coolness could be. Boyd would race out onto the front verandah once the breeze was up, just to feel the sensation of his sticky shirt loosening again and drying out on his body.

Even the intensity of colour itself: orange hibiscus flowers near the iron gate, colour of egg-yolks you could fry on scalding bitumen. Frangipani, that leaned over the grey-mottled paling fence from next door, with its cooling white petals and, when you looked close, a yellow throat more vivid than barley-sugar, with perhaps a small insect inside. Boyd learned to thread frangipani on grass-stalks; as propellers. Allamanda creepers with longer throats still; they always sprawled over that fence-line of Grandmother's big rambling garden, yellow as kitchen linen. Boyd's midsummer visit became the time Grandmother decided the allamanda needed pruning: he would wreak havoc, then scoop up the short-living flowers to take upstairs as trophies. Petals soft as butter. Grandmother never used her mirror-slice vase for them. Boyd had to place them on the kitchen table in that big, starched and golden room. She would use one of the broad china containers. She would cram them in.

And of course the smells. At night a tingle of smells. Odours entered the house, invading Boyd's bedroom: from the gum-trees and from the big weeping-fig out the back – even it had its own rain-forest smell. He had never smelled insects before. They had a compost-and-bark tang here. Sometimes there was a wilder, stranger smell: possums, his grandmother said. At first he thought it unpleasant, but each year when he encountered it again, it taught him something of its wildness, and he grew to love it, as a farm child might be reminded by smells of stored hay or cattle-dung. That unused, clean smell of bedlinen; after the first night it seemed moister, more sticky: sweat.

Cupboards that only Boyd opened: magic cupboards full of unexplained relics – bottles of buttons, cards with dress-hooks and poppers, unused hand-tools, sealed letters bound with silk ribbons that must never be opened – all with their mildew and dust smell, smells of having once been handled, fondled. Under-the-house smells: husks of unbelievably large spiders (he almost never saw them alive), the cone earth-traps of the elephant ants, bundles of old newspapers and *Bulletins* – the smell of them, later, in library archives almost had Boyd crouching, in short pants, back under the creosote-blackened stumps of that holiday refuge.

Hours, days, weeks, each year, every summer. And always, when he arrived, that pause at the mirror vase in the hallway. Even the very last time, when Boyd was nearly fifteen, he stooped down to see if his slivers of self were really visible, if they could fit their magic together. It was a habit, a ritual, by then. His grandmother expected it.

Anything chrome, glass, mirror-shiny, in fact, could certainly press that remembering nerve.

His grandmother lay over a week in the house, dead.

She had been indulgent, witty, garrulous. To others, it seemed, she could also be quite aloof.

It was this aloofness surely that Marie hated in Boyd. Splinters had grown between them.

Boyd's father had flown up to the old house from Melbourne and when he returned the funeral was over, the inquest, and everything in the old Brisbane house – the house itself – got rid of. Just like that.

But you can't shut the doors to a treasure-house, just like that. The next Christmas, Boyd had gone with his parents to Tasmania. The holiday was a disaster.

Boyd did not make his second appointment with Dr Steiner. Marie would call it running-away. The latest running-away. But it might be better termed a running-towards. It was absolute necessity.

The plane was circling over Moreton Bay preparatory to the touch-down. Boyd had never flown into Brisbane before: in the old days it had always been by train. The city was surprisingly close to the ocean. Why had he never realized that? His grandmother never took him to the beach. He had, perhaps, lived a remarkably confined life up here. It had seemed a revelation. His memories of it were crammed with the sense of endless discovery, endless confirmation of life's strangeness and unexpectedness. If she had set rigid boundaries, Boyd had blossomed and expanded within them. One p.m. This was precisely the hour Boyd had promised to see that shrink. 'You have some heavy disturbances, Mr Kennedy. I suggest we should undertake a series of therapy sessions. When you told me your wife accuses you of creating a barrier – a brick-wall you called it – I think you did touch on a problem. We must try to find techniques to diminish that barrier. I am confident of ultimate success. I have helped people in greater trouble than you.'

Not even a difficult patient! But, as he checked out dates with the secretary, Boyd knew he was playing a farce. His co-operative smile, Uriah Heep.

Marie, getting him into all this. Even this morning, as she was gulping coffee and late as usual, the ditherer behind-scenes who could leave home the cool, groomed and glistening Science Teacher – even then Boyd had turned away, inventing games with the toaster.

He had, finally, written only a note:

Have flown up to the Brisbane Conference early. I agree I've got to sort myself out, but Dr Steiner is not the way. Don't blame this decision on last night. It takes two to make a failure. I'll contact you when I can communicate. Don't know when that will be.
Boyd.

No, he wasn't angry.

Marie

Marie had shoved the inconvenient metal trolley along two aisles of merchandise before she realized the coffee section of the supermarket was back there. Coffee was her only excuse.

No, not her only excuse. Dagmar had phoned. She told Dagmar about Boyd's cruel note. She had to. She had sobbed. Dagmar had been brusquely concerned.

'Wait. Wait, do not do a thing. Hold on there, Marie, I am halfway down Cardigan Street already. Don't *do anything*.' As if Marie intended to cut her wrists?

As she put down the phone, the only thing Marie could think of was that second coffee and that she was out of percolator mix. The Viennese clock seemed intent on filling the emptiness with her mother's clicking tongue. Boyd knew evey turn of the screw. She had groped for her money-purse. She scrawled a note to Dagmar and stuck it on the door of the flat. She strode quickly, high heels clicking with deft precision.

She would not let Boyd throw her.

What had he written? Their decade together had always been the present. Suddenly the continuity of her world had buckled. This morning was an unreachable past.

Excuses about Brisbane. She was not wearing that, why should she? Last night: if she had known, would she have been different? The past is the first act of blackmail.

These trolleys never move as you want them to.

Dagmar would either wait outside the flat or come after her to the supermarket. Boyd would have let Dagmar in, offered tea, then retired to his corner. Damn Boyd.

Dagmar, wonderful Dagmar. She knew almost before you did yourself if you had disaster feelings. Little Dagmar, there was something about her absolute exaggeration in everything that lifted the spirit. A sort of well of generosity.

Marie caught her own eye in a mirror plastered with commercials. That brutally self-possessed stranger. Dagmar pined for such apparent control. Dagmar, her hair cut short these days, and putting on weight furiously: no, not a soothing visual presence. But, under the busy, buzzy body, she was balm and honey. Marie looked critically at rows of canned pears. She had no intention of buying canned pears, not now, not ever.

Her trolley was still empty.

Something bullying about supermarkets; they crowd you in. As if sheer multiplicity proved something. Why be bullied by six competing brands of pears if you don't want pears?

Her own mother hoarded towels and satin sheets, pieces of string in the kitchen drawer. Her mother was a glutton for supermarkets. Marie's eyes scanned more racks and shelves. The housewife loitering ahead, trolley jammed with merchandise and a small daughter bullying. Yes, canned pears for Mummy. Marie gripped cold chrome. Her neck was long, delicate. Beneath the sheen, something could snap at the least collision. She skilfully navigated past the intruders.

This entire hall of produce was not a hall of produce at all. No relationship with that wonderful harvest cornucopia that had, once in girlhood, made Marie open her eyes with wonder. Her mother had taken her to the Agricultural Show, insisting she look carefully at the big displays of wealth from each district. Her mother, Elena Maria Adriana, blossomed in those years. She cornered bluff farmers that time, she opened her huge eyes even wider, she admired the produce. Her heavy accent used to drench the young Marie with extravagant

ice. 'Look, *Kinderlein*, look, this is the very country its
she had promised. 'Do you not understand all these riches us
unding . . .'

How inappropriate. Marie learned, soon enough, how to squirm. She caught the amused glint as well as the interest in the eyes of those lean, tawny landholders of the Western Districts. They had played into her mother's schemes, everybody had been conned. Elena Maria Adriana swamped everything, everybody with the same indiscriminate warm pleasure. Marie had learned to resist. She had to.

Bottles of preserves; immense pumpkins, gourds and cabbages, maize and a hundred samples of sorghum. How her mother's excitement could sweep her up, those days. Marie must learn tolerance, she was no longer threatened. The War years gulped up breath, her mother's life affirmation despite everything: of course, Marie admired that, of course, there had been suffering, deprivation.

Not to be overwhelmed.

Marie reached out her hand: decision. A can, yes, but from a higher shelf. Lychees.

'Marieeeee!'

The scream was in high decibels. 'Marie, darling girl, you are all right? No wait, I am coming!'

Supermarkets were not fitted for the likes of Dagmar. As well think of each pear, each apple, as unique. The neighbour women, pushing trolleys, moved sideways. Dagmar was already upon her.

'Marie, hold tight, Marie!' Dagmar was a bearhug, even though she was too short.

'Dagmar, no. You're being a panic merchant. You see: I'm perfectly all right.' Marie's voice ripped up like stretched plastic.

'You are not all right, girl. Your voice on the phone . . . but not to worry, not to mind. Now I am with you, we must think new thoughts, plot new things. You'll see.' Dagmar reached imperiously. She snatched up a can of beetroot and slammed it decisively into the trolley. 'We will be on top of it. Now. What are we looking for?' Dagmar had seized the trolley and was clearing a path that even small children knew not to challenge. Small children hid behind the knees of mothers.

'Right! I tell you what this is, Marie. This is a First Day. Like the First Day of Creation. Forget Boyd, hah! We'll show Boyd. Your very first day solo. So. We will allow ourselves to create a new world. We, Marie, we are like God.'

Another can: spaghetti. 'No, not that dreadful stuff!' Marie, asserting herself again. Dagmar beamed encouragement.

'Silly me, I wasn't looking. It is the spirit of the thing that matters. Do you prefer baked beans? Sweetcorn in mush?'

'Dagmar, idiot, nothing like that. Here, if you must be crazy, let's go to the gourmet. Just my luck that you caught me in the Heinz lines.'

'Heinz lines. Heinz lines. Wonderful. Darling.' Dagmar stretched with another kiss on her cheeks. Marie chuckled. Nothing was solved, but at least, with Dagmar, something seemed possible.

'Wait.' Dagmar held up her palm, a traffic signal. 'First Day Of Creation, did I say? We must consider our sciences then. Look around. This is the unformed future, the raw material of our creation, the foodstuffs of our universe. Just as God must have stockpiled the foodstuffs of his creation before setting it all in motion and stirring the bowl to create his earth. Correction: *her* earth.'

'Dagmar, God did not have to rely on cans and packets.'

'You think not? Well, you are such a practical monster. Still, First Day means heaven and earth and the seven layers between, as the old scholars believed. What we should do is look for sevens. Seven days of creation, seven heavens, you see: the numerology works.'

'It was six days of creation, Dagmar. On the seventh, God rested.'

'That's costed in. Seven, I say. Now, let's see. Work by numbers. Every sort of food that has seven brands competing, we take one. How about that?'

'And if there are more than seven trade lines . . . ?'

'I insist. Seven. Neither more, nor less. Let's see what the Tarot pack of the supermarket turns up for us. Well, come on.' And Dagmar was off again, the trolley seeming light as fibreglass.

They ended up with bread, a cheese, coffee and some yoghurt. 'You see? Staff of life. From all the welter of this storehouse we have selected, by numbers, the essentials. Now you see how God felt at the end of her work.'

Marie gave her a hug and fumbled for her purse.

It was only when they spread themselves out with the purchases on her kitchen bench that the hollow place reformed under her ribs. Boyd's note still restated its declaration on the refrigerator door. Marie restrained Dagmar from ripping it off.

Some things even Dagmar could not know about.

Boyd

The plane bumped heavily on ground contact. Someone once told Boyd the most dangerous moment is not the landing itself, it is when the motors commence to brake, that reverse-thrust. A fraction too strong or too sudden and the whole plane might turn arse over turkey. Over-reaction. Boyd gripped his seat arms.

As the plane taxied to the terminal Boyd could make out ground staff, mechanics, signallers, drivers. Some of the men's overalls were unbuttoned revealing dark tans, bushy chests and swollen bellies. Melbourne had been chilly.

Packing had been perfunctory. As if spur of the moment indicated in him the capacity to be decisive. Only his briefcase. In it, toiletries, cheque book, the notes for his paper on 'White Collar Crime in the Computer Age'. It was an excuse.

The conference was less than three weeks off. Boyd did like to be prepared well in advance, no cracks in his mirror. Marie's constant stream of friends and phone-calls: hopeless to work at home. In their first years this did not bother him; indeed, he had prided himself on the capacity to retire to a corner and 'get on with it'. Marie's friends in those days accepted him like that, perhaps even envied that.

Later, well, so many things. The law lectures – long since predictable. When she insisted he join her encounter groups or her yoga parties or her theatre workshops, Marie only provoked him. Uptight, that became her word for him, in the new jargon.

There had been the matter of the wing-backed armchair. The only time of complete bitterness. Perhaps not the only time. Boyd could leave Marie tight with fury when he would not fight, or would refuse to engage in raw shows. Throwing plates, Boyd said with reproof, was such a TV sitcom way to demonstrate aggression. Once, very deliberately, he had crushed a wine-glass in his fist. The guest, a simpery young man who had been showing Marie Ikabana flower arranging, had whispered urgently with Marie for ages, later, before departing. Because Marie was so conscious of her many tight repressions she had willed herself to her theatrical extravagances, her yoga, her conscious expulsions of feeling. Hah!

Then the time he returned from a fortnight legal conference in Perth and discovered Marie in his corner wing-chair; converted by her needlework and her little table for correcting kids' assignments. It was as if she wished to possess some part of his most private being.

'You have the other chair, Boyd. I thought a bit of a shift around would do you the world of good. Would do us both the world of good. We're stagnating and I decided: this is the perfect location for marking essays and you don't study here any more. Look how I can spread myself around with them. Over there is just as good for your purposes. Whenever you sit in this chair lately you only start tippling.'

When they had first gone out together, to the theatre, she clutched her programme, twisting it to shreds.

He was last off the plane. Boyd looked with distaste as others around him shuffled and pushed to be first up, first in the aisle, first off the aircraft, first into the terminal. The need to be terminally first.

So this was Brisbane. Where was he to stay?

Marie so chirpy this morning. As if last night had been no burden. As if his hidden decision somehow charged her, too, with warmth and energy. Of course it had. Marie responded electrically in that way. She took from his every mood something for her own benefit. From his calmness she took safety, confidence, the security of a home base. And from his tensions she gave to herself some greater elasticity of feeling. The more tense he was, the more ebullient she became. If something pleased him she took that too. Energy is conveyed, if not always by directly obvious means.

He had not spoken to her for a week after the chair incident. She refused to be humbled, she insisted it was true therapy — always the bloody amateur psychiatrist. Her own little mannerisms: the way she chewed on her right side. The way she drank coffee too quickly. The way she always began phone conversations, 'Why, hello, Dagmar . . . ' 'Why, hello, Peter . . . '

A week without speaking. By the end he thought everything irreparable. She surprised him out of it with a party, all his third-year students. They thought her marvellous. She sparkled with energy, and indeed she flirted irresistibly. That night, Boyd recalled, made up for everything.

Wasn't it true she had always been there, central, the pivot, ever since he first met her?

'It's not me at all, it's just your idea of me,' she accused him that first quarrel.

Dr Steiner had helped her uncover, then absorb, childhood traumas: the need to be centre-stage, to claim attention. The hidden anxiety, the hidden anger behind those needs. The need for control. It was she who began to initiate their lovemaking. Boyd said she was wonderful.

The anonymity of a motel. There must be one somewhere. Brisbane held no trace-elements of Marie. He hailed a taxi.

'Where to, digger?'

'Into the city.' Then Boyd paused. 'No. Out to Toowong. MacGregor Street.'

It had been twenty years.

. . .

The cab twisted through hilly suburbs by some devious route (did the driver detect a stranger?).

Old sprawling streets had been tidied up. Rigidity. Their only perfection was in some illusion of anonymity. Token shrubs – hibiscus, abelia – were allowed if they could survive stern pruning.

The older back yards were a riot of flowering jacarandas, poincianas, frangipani, bougainvillaea, largerstroemia, rhondoletia, hoop pine, silky oak, poinsettia – Boyd could string out his grandmother's lists still. Along back fence lines, street after street: the familiar (again) mango-trees, papaws, macadamia. Straggling clothes lines and vegetable beds. She had taught him a certain willing untidiness. She had taught him style.

There was still Brisbane. Boyd had no conscious part in it, but it was there, resurfacing.

Mid April; he was drenched in sweat. He could feel runnels catch in his chest hair, and across his shoulders. His suit coat would be stained, now, under the armpit. He wound down the window as the taxi passed a football field, shouldered by huge weeping-figs.

On the slope above the Botanical Gardens he remembered the State Parliament House, ornate, a bit like the old Exhibition Buildings in his own Carlton Gardens, but with that warm soft sandstone almost unknown in Melbourne, and always those immense jacarandas. Blue carpets of blossom.

Across from the Parliament building was the Bellevue Hotel, and on the other corner the white grandeur of the Queensland Club. Boyd's grandmother always took him into the Bellevue, to the Ladies' Lounge. She bought him fizzy sodas. Tall glasses, with stems. His grandmother would sip a brandy-lime and soda. Years later Boyd could shudder at the abomination. She and Grandpa had stayed at the Bellevue for their honeymoon, just the five nights before Grandpa had gone off to be killed in World War One. The little outside area beyond the Lounge – full of tables, umbrella trees and scraping young students – was the first, the very first, *Biergarten* in Queensland. At the time he had no German and was impressed. Grandmother spoke three languages

(Marie knew six). Grandmother was quite special.

Grandpa had been Someone. So, too, was Grandmother; that was why she ended up isolated. The only little boy allowed over to play, at Grandmother's house, had been Handley Shakespeare. Every year Boyd and Handley would make their ritual tram-ride out to the Museum. The Museum was a strange building of red and cream brick stripes, with turrets and silver-capped towers and loggias, and with an old captured German tank among the rose gardens.

As they got towards puberty, Boyd and Handley would go through the Art Gallery in the Museum building to stare closely (if an attendant was not near) at the Gustave Doré and Norman Lindsay etchings upstairs. Handley also enjoyed showing Boyd the New Guinea artefacts in the Museum itself, all phalluses and cunts. He refused to be ruffled by attendants and screwed up his eyes behind spectacles to speak loudly about Anthropology. By that last year they had become old friends, only the first few days were spent in connecting up again, finding the links and the contacts. Whatever had happened to Handley Shakespeare?

Brisbane indifference. It had been there, always, in the untidy backyards, the unmanicured suburbs. That part Boyd had grown to love for its decision against pretension and its comfortable adjustment to its own environment.

Sometimes indifference disturbs. His grandmother once told Boyd her own family begged her to return to London. She had taken him to the back fernhouse in her garden. She could not endure her own family, she said, they meant nothing.

She made him love Brisbane so deeply he had fretted in Melbourne.

What was her Brisbane, then? Heat, torpor, lazy architecture, cupidity. It was a place, a city.

Yet he felt strangely elated. He was noticing things. His focus was sharp, colours were bright. Everything looked rinsed, the sky seemed rubbed with oil, it was so polished.

. . .

Number 73. The old timber house on its large slope of overgrown garden had been raped. The wide front verandah, where he had played with his father's ancient lead soldiers, was torn off. French windows opened nakedly onto tiny balconies of imitation Spanish wrought iron. There was a grotesque terrazzo-floored porch, merely a cage for more wrought iron columns. Someone's idea of 'improvement' in the early 1960s? That original front verandah, with its old broomstick-thin rails and panels, had been a greenhouse of maidenhair fern tumbling, ledge after ledge, in dozens of varieties, out of terracotta containers. In the hot summer it had been a wonderful, cool entry, preparing you for the high, clean hallway with its mirrors and light, and then into the spacious living-room, or right on to the huge golden kitchen at the end with its deal table and smell of rich larder secrets — more shelves of surprises and recognitions than Boyd could climb up to. Bottled preserves, chutneys, pickles, biscuit tins and barrels going back to the beginning of the century, jams, conserves, knobs of ginger, dried statice behind the larder door, bay leaves, rosemary, unnamed herbs knotted into posies or ground and seeded into bottles. Sugar and flour in big hessian bags: later, Boyd had wondered why his grandmother bought them in such quantities, as if this were some Station homestead, or a boarding house.

Boyd should have turned angrily away, right then. He could have hailed the cab before it completed its U-turn, moved off to some blank motel.

He stood on the paspalum grass of the footpath, put down his briefcase and unbuttoned his waistcoat. He took off the coat. This burden of heat: could he endure that? How could he have endured that?

Hayman Island and their honeymoon. 'The initiation' Marie once called it. That crazy rush from Reception to Essenden and the laughing. Marie more beautiful than he had imagined. He had worshipped her. The long, long flight, secret giggles, shared. They straightened their faces and acted at being old. Ah, dear jaded spouse, can I pass you the flight-map? Hostess smiles. So many chainlinks and shared jokes. Forget Hayman Island.

In the distance a train wailed and left the station. Boyd had spent years, out on the green garden chair near the back fernhouse, listening to the trains pull in and out of Toowong Station or the Auchenflower Station, gather speed for the straight stretch, then he would glimpse them as they crossed, with their hollow rumble over the Sylvan Road Bridge. He had learned from his grandmother the different sounds of particular trains: passenger trains, goods trains, solo locomotives, the railmotor to Ipswich with its nervous, rattly jangle. This was a new train sound – diesel. It hit the nerve.

Boyd pushed open the gate. The old shove, the old iron-rust squeak. Who was the present owner? He would have to explain to the lady of the house why . . .

That first swim at Hayman. How pale Marie's skin was. Her red bathers were the wrong colour. By dusk that was the colour of her own skin. Sandy sheets. Salt taste. 'I love you, I love you,' Boyd had wanted to make up for the sunburn. The abrasiveness of his hairy body. The amazing white and tactile fascination of the unburned parts of Marie's skin. Teach me, teach me. Unable to keep his hands from her, stroking, discovering, caressing, wondering and unable to stop. Hours. All night.

Buffalo-grass lawn. As a boy he had eagerly mown it every second day in the fecund summer heat and storm weather. A mess now. Rats' tails and knots. Someone had planted fast-growing native shrubs. Great tangles of cobweb – a dozen individual nests or colonies. In each a large spider hung, full centre. Boyd looked. Instead of a disorganized tangle, the struts and frets of web were part of the support system for an intricate inner structure, a fine parachute of quite miraculous design. It was under this handkerchief-sized cup of web that the large spider hung, in each case. Long, thin legs, smooth, rich body, fat with summer. And with eggs?

The determination of Marie, insisting next morning she go out in the sun again. 'That's why we came, isn't it?' That second night she'd had blisters. How tenderly Boyd had ministered. – Her skin flinched to his touch.

'Forget those,' she hissed later. 'I want you to teach me lovemaking. We're in this together.' His fingers thick and nerveless, then.

With a sudden burst of anger Boyd picked up a fallen twig and tore down the first web.

Why hadn't she said anything then? In this together.

'Hey, you, you there! Cut that out!'
Boyd looked up, caught in the act.
'You leave those spiders alone!'
The girl was young. Long hair in squaw plaits. Boyd brushed away sweat. She slapped back the front door as if it were not fine, old cedar. He shrugged, defensive.

She was wearing only a thin tight singlet (nipples, breasts surging as she thumped down the steps). Her thighs were gripped into a cut-off pair of dirty blue jeans.

'What the hell are you doing?' she challenged, coming right up to him. He shrugged again. He should have matched her anger.

'That big cobweb. Sorry, I suppose it was an impulse . . .'
'Look what you've done already.' She snatched the branch from his hand and for a moment he thought she might use it. She tossed it aside, into a pile of old rubbish. 'For your information, mister, I have an affinity with those spiders. I have. They've a name and an identity. Each one.'

She had bent to make sure of her specimens. The front of her singlet hung open.

31

'Those monsters? Yuk. They're all poisonous.' His fixed grin.

'I'd like to set it loose on persons like you!' She jerked her head back as if her hair kept falling across her face. 'You're just lucky. This one, the Golden Orb it's called, is deadly enough. But its biting structure isn't built for big flat things like people. You're lucky.'

'Okay, okay. Just spur of the moment. Can't stand spiders.'

She shrugged. 'That's a maternity case, that one. I've been watching it. Well, I have; you'd better believe it.'

'I believe it.'

'And there's another, there.' Eager, now, she pointed them out to him. 'No look. Higher. A week ago that one was big as a bopplenut. Now look. Well, look. You see them don't you? All those dots. They're spiderlings. Baby spiders. Yes, well, *look* at them, will you . . . '

Boyd loosened his collar, was he entirely sodden? 'I think you are trying to spook me, just a little.' But he looked.

'That's your problem.' She was twisting a twig to neat threads. 'Those spiders have evolved a perfect community system.' Clearly, she meant it.

'Oh yes? They eat their male partners, you mean?'

'That's just a natural process. They'd die anyway. But socially, they're much more complex. In their web communities they coexist with lots of different kinds of spider. See, that sort there. And those. And they never leave their system, once it's established. You never get Golden Orbs indoors, for instance. They're not predators. They don't go around on a search and kill, they're sort of gregarious.'

He could see the light glaze of sweat on her forehead too. The upper lip.

Boyd shrugged. In the slight pause he wondered had she noticed just how provocative that skimpy outfit was? He looked at his shoes. Ergot from the paspalum seeds had stuck to his trouser-legs. The women who claimed him always shared this tone: play in their anger, anger in their play.

'You came to look at the flat, I guess?'

Boyd saw then that there was a sign in the front window (once his grandmother's forbidden bedroom): FLAT FOR RENT. ENQUIRE WITHIN.

Marie

'*Wunderbar! Wundervoll!* Most wonderful of softnesses. Here. And here.' In the shower Helena Maria Adriana stroked her soapy fingers down and around the swoop of each buttock, arching her magnificent back. Delicately she parted the crease for her ablutions but then her hands returned to the buttocks themselves, as if unable to resist their fascination.

'Smooth. *Die glatte oberfläche.* Smooth and still hardly a dimple, hardly a small wrinkle. Most wonderful softness.' Her hands, gently soaped and obedient, strayed round to the front, and then coiled around her gourd-like gleaming belly. She was beaming. Higher: the large rounded breasts rolled out under her massage. 'Softness, and yet firmness still.'

Helena Maria Adriana took a very long time in the shower.

At last, with a swoop of steam, she opened the glass door of the recess, and put one delicately pink foot onto the deep pile carpet. A carpeted bathroom: she still tingled with delight at it. She revelled in the luxury.

One wall was a maze of mirrored tiles. They revealed the body, yet displaced it in ways that both flattered and teased. Before Helena Maria Adriana had time to enjoy the sight of her pale white and pink flesh, the mirror surface sheeted over like ouzo when someone adds water.

But the giant towel was its own comfort.

'Marie,' she called out, her face still nuzzling. 'Marie, little *Pfennig*, can you hear me?' She did not wait for a reply. 'Marie, you will bring me a second towel. This one will not dab the half.'

She sighed as if she had an audience. 'Not the one half of me.'

Helena Maria Adriana once was the lover of a German Major. She was fifteen at the time.

'It is a joy to have a generous body, but it is not to be taken lightly. It is not enough to have two towels merely. Marie, bring me three.'

When she was seventeen she was eating grilled rats and nettle soup. There was a knocking at the door.

'Bring me three, my own *Pfennig*. Three of the new ones, the thick new ones new this week.'

Tiny pellets of mud, the size of rice seeds, could be digested with cut cress and fennel. They quelled the hunger pangs.

'These new towels are so thick your five fingers sink into them without trace and when you place them down again it is like foam, no wrinkle.'

The German Major had been succeeded by three American Corporals, who held her down.

'Three of my crimson new towels dear Marie, in my camphorwood box at the foot of the bed.'

Helena Maria Adriana had been raped by the German officer with her mother dead in the next room. The young Americans seemed almost to need encouragement, once they had demonstrated their own assertiveness to their fellows.

She breathed out, still dabbing. She rubbed a place on the glass and pouted. With her fingernail she cleaned the space between teeth. Her reddish blond hair lay in matted coils about her face, but it was still beautiful, still untinted. What use in this world to be born with neat features or good hair if you treated yourself like the coalmerchant's widow? The young American soldiers apologized later, and she had been patient. There was no other way and that way led to unexpected indulgences. You are so happy, you are always so happy, one of the Corporals gasped. He had said he adored her. Not happy, made rich, she had replied. Happiness is far too foolish a thing; richness has comfort and many forms. She had let him explore her warm, translucently white breasts. That was where she differed from her sister, poor Arabella. She, Helena Maria Adriana, she had seen it all before it could possibly happen. What use? Arabella burned up with anger inside before her red body was burned up.

She caught herself in the mirror: patches again. It was true, wasn't it true? There was the proof of what she had learned. Why should she not rejoice to admire. Her face, still round and quite without lines, none that were visible. Such red lips! Even her daughter did not believe it was still her natural colour. When she was very young, she had been rose-tinted marzipan like some sweet in the window of Dehmels. Even here, in this climate of Melbourne, she had always taken care of her skin. Some things must be held like medallions. The bathroom was over-brimming with unguents and canisters of her lotions.

'I still do not have my three extra bath towels, Marie. I am shivering.'

Oh, delicious gooseflesh. She threw down the one sodden wrapping and stood naked. In the misty blur of the mirror segments she was a creature out of the sea, a Rhinemaiden. *Ach*, didn't she know what was the gold that the Rhinemaidens were hoarding! It was not metal.

The burnished she-gold of her own pubic hair was not vicious and wiry (like poor Arabella's), it was soft, springy, a down where the gods might find comfort. Helena Maria Adriana stroked and explored. Even the gods. It was true, every man she had, did he not feel a god when she admitted him? It was not coquetry, the body is not merchandise. Aaaaach, yes, she whispered. Secret cold, secret flame. She had endured. She harboured the secret still.

'*Mütterlein*? *Maman*? Mum? Here are your towels, may I come in?'

'*Mädchen, Mädchen*! There is a hundred miles you have been! Here I am shivering, all of me, for your towels waiting.'

Her daughter so skinny. Anorexic, was she? What did that man do to her? Scrawny as a mere boy, this child of hers.

'Marie, Marie, what will I do, what will I do? Thank you, treasure. Come closer, let me look at you.'

But her daughter winced from the large naked woman's wet embrace. She had seen her mother fondling herself; and still beaming. When would it ever end?

'No, *Mütterlein*. I am going out and I don't want this linen suit spattered. The towels were not in the camphorwood box, that's why I was so long. They were . . .'

'*Danke, danke.* They are here, thank you, darling.' Helena Maria Adriana could not restrain her irony. She knew Marie at these moments thought of her as a caricature; so much for *her* perceptions. 'In the camphorwood, in the wardrobe, under the bed, it is all the same where I might store them, just so long as my clever daughter tracks them down, hunts them out, delivers them up with their softness and pile and their splendour intact. Aaaaaah, sweetnesses; ah treasures.'

Exultation cost nothing. It cost everything.

'How much did they cost, your new Manchester?'

'What is that? Cost it is? You talk of price, already. What is price for a specific comfort?' Delicately she was dabbing each shoulder. The wonderful breasts were accommodated. Helena Maria Adriana curved around to admire the sweep of her back (again) in the mirrors: but her back was broken into segments.

She said aloud, 'Is my back still not beautiful?'

Marie was again the awkward schoolgirl witness. Narrow shouldered; tight.

'No; comfort me. You are not in such a hurry. I never see you. Perhaps I should thank Boyd for this, scooted now he is. What is it he sees in a scarecrow, and you are, that part of it is a puzzle.'

'*Maman.* You did promise not to do this.'

'Yes, yes, but a promise is filigree when my daughter is not telling me her unhappiness. You think I do not see your unhappiness? Well, you must wait for me just these few moments. On that stool, dear *Pfennig*, sit until I am ready. Are you ashamed to see your own mother naked?'

'Mother, we've had all this before. Endlessly.'

'You are relentless, you are the one. Can't you see, I am doing this for you? I tell you this, what other women my age have their bodies so lovely, so caressed, so well owned? All for you. How else can I teach you what you must know? You must learn your body is a full used expression. You think sex, life, happiness, all these things are tied in with the pimples of youth and the first headaches? This is gold.' She slapped her round, firm belly. 'Gold.'

'You're just a sensual old hedonist . . .'

'I am a magnificent hedonist. I believe in the sacred.'

'You're a middle-aged woman at menopause, secretly panicking with lust at the body's tricks.' Marie pulled her arms across her blouse. Scratch of nail on linen. 'Like all the textbooks.'

'You know nothing!' her mother hissed, picking up her lace panties. She reached out one arm to gain balance while she pulled them up her legs. Her small feet still looked delicate.

Unwillingly Marie was drawn to her mother's body. She noticed that under the upper arm the flesh exposed the first real sag.

'You know nothing, you want to know nothing. You are sunk in your books and your teaching of book lessons. You have lost a good husband because you have no respect for your own body and I suspect you have no interest in his. I have seen you, these years, the way you collect objects and tokens and substitutes. All you need is a bed, one with wild squeaking springs and brass knobs that rattle. That might wake you up, both of you. You are all on the surface, both of you, for all your clever jobs and your actions. On the surface.' Helena Maria Adriana caught the glint of a real knife in her own voice. The thin, pared body of her daughter winced, as it always did.

'*Maman*, shut up. If this is all you want to bore me with, yet again, then I really am going.'

'*Ach, nein*! No, Marie!' Her mother stopped fastening her bra. She exuded sprays of powder as she strode across. She did not have to reach out to touch her daughter. She dropped her voice significantly. 'Marie, Marie, you must know my concern.' As the voice softened in its old familiar confidentiality Marie tightened. 'But this is what we have been both repeating. You will never learn. Well, but I must tell you secrets. Perhaps you will learn from my secrets. Perhaps you will learn someday from my secrets. I have this week a new lover. Do you hear? Yes, it is true, I have a new man, a lover.'

Silence.

'It follows.'

'He is rough, very hairy, small – but not all small – and he falls asleep immediately. Yes, he snores. He is wonderful. I look at him sleeping, I cannot take my eyes off him, off his body. I am so – what is the word for it? – so fulfilled, deep down in; wonderful.'

'Good for you. You let him sleep in, in the mornings, too? Then you bring him in breakfast.'

'But of course.'

'And he leaves crumbs on the sheets, and bits of smeared butter.'

'Nothing. You understand nothing.'

'And he goes off whistling after another fuck.' Marie made the word as short and impatient as possible. 'And forgets you.'

'You know nothing.'

'Don't keep saying that. I'm not a child. I'm not sexually inexperienced, and I refuse to go through each contortion of the bedroom with you, something's got to be my own, something you don't get at and finger, something private.'

'You always end up saying that, Marie. I shrug. I who would give you everything, and since girlhood gave you privacy.'

'You gave me only the boastfulness of your big body. Always. Trying to stifle me.'

'Marie, you are cruel.' In her floral silk afternoon dress now, Helena Maria Adriana looked as if she intended a stroll through the Gräben. She aged twenty years.

'Do you know I did read something yesterday,' Marie proceeded relentless, changing the subject. This was her one opportunity. 'It was terrific. And I thought of you, Mother, when I read it. It's from a book about Proust: "He was to discover that in this life all our desires are fulfilled, on the condition that they do not bring the happiness we expected of them." How's that? You have to agree. Don't you have to agree?'

Click and tear of long fingernails against linen.

'Proust was a homosexual. That explains everything.'

Marie was looking down. 'I am sorry. It was me, us, I was thinking of. Me and Boyd. Oh, *Mütterlein*, it's true, it is true, isn't it? I can't think of anything we did not want that we did not have, or get in the end, Boyd and me. I know why Boyd's made that trip up to Brisbane.'

'Still chasing desires?' Her mother was ice.

'It's not me, us, he's running from. It's just knowledge. *Mütterlein, Mütterlein*, what do you do when you realize that, the very condition of desire is that it must end up as such real bitterness.'

Nothing she could say. Her daughter, thin, hunched, angry and disconsolate. So lacking in finesse, lacking in any sense of true style. Directing every piece of knowledge against her own self, and against Boyd also.

Although she had just achieved her careful coiffure, Helena Maria Adriana reached out impulsively and rubbed herself into her daughter, scooped her up (so unwilling), hugged her for a long time. Oh, the small, tight ridge of her backbone; the little, thin buttocks. Helena Maria Adriana held her daughter close, thrust her own vast breasts with their endless warm secrets so that her daughter could rest, cling, be comforted. Helena Maria Adriana, sobbing, gave herself to her daughter. Gasping, at last Marie disengaged herself.

'You keep doing it,' she whispered. 'You will not change. You keep doing it.'

That night Joszef came in covered with grease from the garage. They spent hours in the bathroom together. She swathed him with all her new towels and laughed keenly when the first was instantly smeared with grease marks.

'*Ach*! Dirty man; you still have the stuff in your hair!' She threw out the towel. On the white pile, too, there were stains.

'Not to mind that, not to worry.' She scrubbed him down like a boy. She could not keep her hands off his tight, fine drum of a body. She had brought in a large cheval-glass, so as to admire her back without interruptions and so that she might admire their two bodies together.

Cora

Early morning. She moved her thighs and encountered the dead weight of Don's body.

Almost before she knew it her right hand had moved gently around his thin hips. So smooth, the secret places of boys. Wonderingly, she was cupping him into her hands: limp, gentle, softer than any part of her own body. She was smiling.

Don stirred. Like some creature with its own motives, his genitals crawled and came in under her touch. His slackness already was achieving a different shape, assertive. She withdrew her hand.

Don stirred, rolled over.

'Keep sleeping,' she murmured, and pulled the sheet over his shoulder again.

But it was too late. Don's own hand had begun to encounter her. Cora rolled back. As he discovered the nipple and the firm handful of her breast she gave an involuntary gasp. Her entire body instantly wired into that nerve. She grabbed Don tightly, stifling her panting in his bony shoulder.

'Jeezus, Cora, you're terrific.'

Later, as she puddled around in her happy-coat getting them coffee, Don came out yawning and naked, thin as a stalk. Vulnerable. Cora smiled at him and tried, once again, to hide her sudden urge to reach out and protect him. He did not like that. He relished his manhood, not understanding the great currency of the boy still active within him. Why did they all want to be adult and crass? Why did they urge themselves on with heavy, bull movements: insensitive and urgent, inconsiderate? She thought of her own father.

No.

When he came out of the bathroom he came up behind her and gave Cora a tickle.

'Oooooh yes,' she murmured.

'You were meant to jump.' He sounded petulant. Then he sprawled, naked, on a chair, exposing himself innocently.

'I always jumped like a struck rabbit if my father tickled me,' he added. 'What about yours?' Then he clapped a hand over his mouth, as if stricken. 'Sorry, Cora; forget that.'

'Don't be silly,' she was feeling warm, still, and generous. 'Don't be silly, it's not taboo. My father, most of the time, held off from any form of physical contact. As long as he could. So perhaps that's why, when he did, well, make contact, it was always over-reaction.'

Don had got up. He returned to his room, not to her sleep-out. She could hear him dressing.

It would be another warm day. Don and Olof, the other co-tenant in their flat, had gone off into town to meet up with some friends. They were going to picket the Bellevue Hotel and Cora had at first promised to come along too; it was a cause she could reach a quick anger over. The flat, though, was still complete muddle and, if nothing was done soon, they would settle right into it and never get anywhere. The Bellevue: the ruthless way it had been half-demolished overnight, at the private behest of someone high in Parliament. What was that line in Joni Mitchell's *Big Yellow Taxi*? – 'You don't know what you've got till it's gone.' Did those politicians realize that? Half demolished. They probably were still chuckling into their expense-account Veuve Clicquot at how smart they had been. No, better she use her anger and energy in tidying out the house.

She was half-way through the business of clearing the front room when she heard the taxi stop. Looking through dusty lace curtains (the landlord suggested they were the originals and perhaps he was right), Cora saw the burly, well-dressed stranger look around, pause, take off his coat (thank God) and open the gate. Just the last thing she needed this morning, another salesman or agent or Mormon or Jehovah's Witness. Cora snapped down the dusting cloth. She caught her eye in the hallstand mirror, a rickety old one that had come with the place.

She had to grin at herself, then. Yes. That was better.

And then, as she opened the door, there he was ripping right into the big Golden Orb cobweb as if he owned the entire allotment. As she slapped back the door she could hear the hallstand rattle.

Boyd

The girl strode, businesslike, to the front porch.

'Who owns the place?' Boyd accepted her lead.

'Not me,' she squinted back at him. 'All the work should be put into this joint.' She slid her hand down one of the wrought iron bars. Long, purposeful fingers, short nails. 'You're not thinking of buying it, any chance? If you are, do us a favour, let me know. We've only been here this last couple of weeks. Had to wait long enough for that.'

'I'm not here to buy it. Just arrived from Melbourne.'

'Melbourne. Adds up.'

'Who is the owner? Personal reasons.' Tight.

'Guess it's Mr Apollo.'

'Mr *who*?' Clean-bowled! Back to base one.

'We pay rent to Mr Apollo. Conias Apollo, Real Estate Agent. Down Milton Road.'

'Apollo the agent?'

Boyd stepped into the cage-like porch, suddenly reminded again of Handley Shakespeare. The time Handley taught him how to make the tiny fly cages. You got the cork from a bottle stopper; then with your fingernail you dug into the pith to perhaps three-quarters of an inch, to hollow out the little cell. Then you stuck it through with bars made of pins. Handley would sit gazing at his captives for hours as they buzzed and protested. Often he would let them out. Sometimes not. He liked the sheeny blue-arsed ones best; you got them at the horse manure from the baker's van. There had been a horse-and-cart baker those first years.

The door to the untenanted flat was cheap plywood. It breached his grandmother's front bedroom at a place where, inside, she kept her vast crystal-knobbed wardrobe.

Whatever remained, by the very nature of things, would be distorted. He should back out of it right now.

On the other hand, twenty years, if it had to be exorcism, then he must make it complete. He must roll in it, the buzzing fly back in its manure heap.

'You have a key?'

'Certainly.' She pushed back the original front door. Glimpse of the hall, of cardboard cartons, old rolled carpet, three large car tyres. She came back. 'Your side's only small. Enough for a single.'

She had an unnerving, almost mordant look – in middle age she would be intolerably right in everything. Unimaginable. At what age do we declare ourselves?

'What's your name?' Even as he asked, he knew. He had to stumble on. 'My name is Boyd Kennedy.'

He reached out his hand. Mistake again.

'Boyd Kennedy. Yes, I'll remember that.' Not entirely mocking. 'You can call me Cora. That's enough trademark and copyright for anyone. You agree, Boyd Kennedy?'

She shoved the key into the Yale lock.

'Boyd Kennedy,' she thrust the door inwards, 'go in singing.'

Some things tightened Boyd instantly. Advantage made vindictive. 'Treat them like hell until Easter,' his father had advised him, first year of tutoring, 'then you can afford to be gentle.' Marie mocked his methods.

Stiffly, Boyd brushed past this girl.

'Oh, and Boyd Kennedy. Your briefcase. Never know, Boyd Kennedy, who might be round this neighbourhood. Dole bludgers and dropouts here, not your sort. You've come to the original dole bludger territory, Boyd Kennedy. The Prime Minister talks about us. Perhaps you talk about us too, Boyd Kennedy. That three-piece suit – wool is it? – it looks uncomfortable, this climate. Yes, I would think you're feeling pretty prickly and sweaty right this minute, Boyd Kennedy.'

She leaned against the doorway. – Boyd chose to ignore her. But he went back for his briefcase.

Firm, perhaps, not really vindictive. Spoiled daughter of someone in the professions, slumming it for a bit, playing the party game of tattered clothes and tattered lifestyles. When she tired of the lentils and mung beans there would always be a full fridge at home. These kids got more boring, more predictable each year.

The main bedroom.

Nothing.

He could dredge no association from this grubby area with its two maroon-and-grey plastic Ezyrest chairs, the stained Axminster (surely his grandmother had better carpet than that?). What, then? The large, dark wardrobe, the huge bed, a room crowded with prizes, all of them forbidden. He bumped into a wire smoker's stand, something retrieved no doubt from the dump. The coffee table (presumably that was what it was): an old TV turned on its side, and with innards removed. A grey glare of glass.

No association. No associations.

Beyond, through another jerry-built plywood door he moved into – of course – his own room. The original door into the hallway was still there, but sealed off with mouldings. Even that had been left unpainted.

His room.

He did recognize the linoleum, blackened almost beyond pattern now. And the bed against the window. Boyd moved over. Yes, the same bed, his.

He could recall clambering up to its soft springiness. He felt it now. A large innerspring mattress emphasized its unfashionable height. And the half-moon frame for the tropical mosquito-net was no longer there.

The nights of clambering onto the mattress, reaching up to pull down the waterfall of cotton gauze from the net's little web, then of getting it tucked in, from the inside. So that mozzies could not penetrate. Some always did, but the white mosquito netting had been sacred as an aura. It had been caves and oceans and rainstorms and private sails, it had been an unmapped continent for explorers. It had been something you woke up to find, midnight, surrounding you like a warm set of arms and sweet breast, a place of cool fantasy. Boyd had slept deeply in that white hospice. Only in his later years, when he was thirteen and fourteen, had he realized how much hotter the bed was with that shroud of netting around him. He had tossed nights, then, aware of the jeer of mosquitoes, and preoccupied only with finding the one place they could get in. Sleepless nights those.

And the curtains. Unbelievable, still the old lace curtains. One touch would destroy them.

Another ripped doorway, this time into the small kitchen. Kitchenette, no doubt the agent's inventory put it. Had been the larder. Boyd glanced briefly through, not really registering stove, motel-unit refrigerator, minute sink that must contravene every local authority hygiene regulation. Small thrift-shop dresser. Off to one side, showerroom and toilet. Once this had been the end of the old hallway. A balcony out the back: new.

Boyd hesitated, then walked out. The past can extract tribute enough.

At first glance, nothing was changed. The two huge mango-trees close to the western fence; the custard-apple tree. At the bottom of the little gully, where there had been the fowl-run, now were only overgrown remains – wire fences choked and sagging with choko, catsclaw creeper, morning glory, some antignon vine overriding the lot. And the two yellow-box-trees – possums had nested there.

A rotary clothes hoist: that was new. A patent from the later 1950s. Its frame was tilted and rusty, bespeaking long employment, or many swinging kids. There was the old outhouse, the jakes as his grandmother always called it, in some echo of her boarding school jargon. It was still there, under the weeping-fig, though it must have been long superseded by indoor plumbing. Not in his grandmother's time. Boyd had almost forgotten the outhouse and its attendant rituals. The candle-lit trek, before bed, up the worn brick path, always getting pyjama bottoms damp. The need to be on guard for spiders. The spiders that spun their webs between bushes, freshly each night, and then gathered them up again in the morning. Some of them large ones. And the huntsman-spiders that could be lurking behind the lavvy door. Grandmother had insisted they were quite harmless; she said she had grown fond of them and they kept the flies and mozzies down. She had described them, when they scuttled away, as lifting their skirts like little old ladies. Somehow that had made them less scary. Handley one day showing him how to make them spin their thread by catching them, putting them into a matchbox with only the abdomen projecting; then slowly squeezing the lid shut. The strange uncoil, not of excrement, but of fine gossamer web — silk.

The time the blue-tongued lizard was in there. Grandmother had come hooting. Old Mr Shakespeare striding over with his blue kelpie. The excitement and the horrible way the dog had ripped at the lizard, suddenly making it become red meat and exposed soft innards. Then placing it proudly at old Mr Shakespeare's feet. That wasn't the thing he had remembered about Grandmother's. Still, it was there.

Boyd looked over towards the two mango-trees, moist with a new burst of leafage, that dark inside-colour. The not-quite-moist colour and feel of the inside of a woman's vagina. Marie would laugh at him for that. Perhaps he should write to her. They had shared so much. That must not be undervalued.

All the second week at Hayman Island — Marie's skin finally protected by lotions and glowing and brown with only small blister scars on her shoulders. The absolute delight of waking to find gentle exploring hands beside you. They had touched, reached, rolled together endlessly. And then showered, bitten into fresh toast, gone into the circular pattern of enjoyment. Marie learned to brush over his shoulders and explore him, also. They did not believe Melbourne, when they returned. 'This must be Manchester. Someone swapped things while we were away,' Marie had moaned, rain-swept and shivering. They soon knew they were back with it all, right enough. It was simply, Marie said later, that they hadn't realized earlier

Melbourne *was* Manchester, translated.

'I've got it. You've been here before, haven't you?' The girl – Cora – had followed him.

'The way you ripped up that web, first off. That really got me. What sort of stranger would do that, just strolling up the path? Did you live here then? How long back?'

He was not going to be caught. 'I did not live here. But you're right.' Boyd had nothing to be ashamed for. 'I know this place. It belonged to my grandmother.'

Cora grunted. Then she relaxed. Her whole body loosened.

'Bit of a shock, this?' She might have been much older.

'Twenty years. Got to expect shocks.' Boyd had his own protections. 'Yes . . . it was only this backyard, the gully. Not really altered. Shock of seeing it all still here. Thought it would be bulldozed. Almost hoped it might.'

'Probably will be, soon enough. This whole area is being torn down. You a developer? You look like one.'

'Fat lot you know. About me, about anyone.' Boyd slapped his palm onto the rail. But, turning to face her, he was again disarmed. 'This place has the whole key. If I were to think of this place it would be as a restoration. This house really was pretty grand in its way – before they did this to it.' He pointed. 'If you think I'm into subdivisions and home units, you've certainly got the wrong message.' It was as if his apartment in Carlton no longer existed. He went on more vehemently. 'What value a home unit, plaster that cracks in eight months, tiles that fall off like an insult, leaking aluminium windows . . . ' There was a pause. How could she know one tenth of what he was feeling?

'You jump to conclusions.' But his tone was well controlled again now.

She shuffled. 'Yeah. Mostly right. Hey Boyd Kennedy, why don't you drop the Kennedy stuff? Boyd's big enough. Even Boy, if you like. Hey! You like that, don't you?'

She laughed. White even teeth. Her breasts nudged and caught on.

How could he fail to respond to this sense of enjoyment?

She handed him the key. 'The rent's $20 a week, but the agent wants bond money. Best we go down, see Apollo together. I get a spotter's fee for this.'

When he had first touched Marie, she flinched. He had persisted. Finally she let go violently. He had believed in his inheritance, then.

INTERLUDE

The Bellevue Hotel

'When you are old you will remember this place.' His grandmother smiled over the cut crystal. 'You will take your family here and point out to them that in this very dining-room you were taken by *your* grandmother. And I am sure it will always be the same. Some things are part of us, they define us. The Bellevue Hotel will be nurtured and maintained as a treasure. Fortunately,' she dipped her heavy silver spoon into the soup, 'with the Queensland Club over the road, and the Parliament on this other corner, it is in a position to be well protected. One cannot imagine cheap speculators setting their eyes on *this* little corner of Brisbane.'

Boyd nodded. He was thirteen.

'I was saying to Arthur last week – Mr Fadden, dear – that if there's one thing the Conservatives care about, it's the past. Although this is not the Brisbane I grew up in. Oh dear, no.'

'I thought you grew up in London, Grandmother?'

'The accident of birth and life gives us one growing up; but at a certain stage, dear boy, we decide upon our own birthplace, our spiritual birthplace. It may be just the same place. It may not – you have the choice. For you, who knows, it may be Brisbane. You cannot understand what it represented for me, a busy young thing fresh from Girton. This was my first stop, really, and it was early September. Magical.'

'Why did you come?' Boyd knew, but his grandmother always enjoyed going over her life story.

'Well, I certainly did not intend to go back to London. How I loathed it, all that stuffiness, and the fogs that always clogged my whole head up every time I went down. I was a wild young thing, also, I can tell you. I had them all frightened of me, very early on. No holding me down, my father used to say. And there wasn't.'

'But you were going to be a teacher in New Zealand.'

'The ship berthed at the docks not all that far from here. I was to stay a few days, and your grandfather met me. He had come down from the country especially. They still had the property at Jimna then. His family and ours had corresponded for two generations. They stayed with us in London when they came home. We were distant cousins. September: it was an extraordinary season, every tree seemed a garden, wherever you walked, overhead it was flowers. I was drenched with perfume. And at nights! Magical, magical. And it still is, quite magical. Ah, my dear, do not take it for granted, none of it.'

'No, Grandma.'

'Grandmother, please, Boyd. You know I prefer that. He was a confident, silly young man. He was very passionate. They say these Australian boys are insensitive and clumsy, don't you believe them. Your grandfather was a gentleman. And in those days that meant a very great deal. It did not mean clumsy. It did mean a capacity to be immensely serious. Immensely passionate, no half measures, no half measures in anything he did.'

Boyd was fiddling with his mashed potatoes now. The food was eating-out food, all right but you were conscious of everyone looking, especially the waiters. Waiting for you to spill peas.

'How long before you got married?'

'But you always ask me that, Boyd. You have an absolute fetish about dates, wasn't it only last week you were grilling me about your own parents? What the mind doesn't count, the heart need not fret over. If you think it reason to fret, and why should you? You came out into the world a fine bouncy boy, that's what matters. But as you know, your grandfather and I were engaged almost immediately – well, quickly enough to astonish his parents – and we married just as soon as the proper messages were exchanged and the blessings given. The War had just started, you know. We would have married without parental blessings, of course, but your grandfather was eager not to antagonize his new family. I was the one who said, "Let them rot in hell, or in London, which is just the same." The feeling of liberation. No, how can I expect you to understand that, you who have grown up in this country and taken it all for granted.'

'I like his photograph.' Grandfather had died young, in the Great War.

'Yes, Boyd, you do, I know that. I can see you in him. Him in you. I think that is why I like to bring you here. We spent so much of our young life together in this hotel.' She looked round and an attentive waiter was at her side. She was their oldest customer. 'The house in Toowong; that was a part of my life I had to create for myself. After he'd gone. Though we picked out most of the furniture together – with the help of Mr Rosenstengel.'

The dining-room was not crowded. Four or five other couples were at lunch, and a family group was being just a little boisterous in the far corner. At their window table Boyd could stare out through the shade of the curved iron overhang to the white elegance of the Queensland Club opposite. Very tall palm-trees; a huge, swooping fig. And yet under it all, a sort of torpor. A lull by mid-afternoon when nothing seemed possible.

'Thank you for bringing me.'

'Dear Boyd, I am trying to educate you. Goodness knows, your parents do, too, I suppose, in their own gauche way, which I'll not go into. But there are casual graces, too, to consider. And if you do not learn the special little corners of your own city – I am speaking now of Brisbane, not Melbourne – then you are so much the shallower. Look at the architecture of this place, for instance.'

Boyd had seen it many times. He rather liked the old verandahs, one topping the other, outside. But in the very next room, on his left, there were the Bars, Public and Private. The smell, even midday, was like stale sodden dustbins, how could people drink there?

'Aren't the rooms a bit small?'

'That is their period. Victorian: they liked a sort of cosiness, it was not until the Edwardian period that the craze came for space and vast distances. This remains intimate. But look at the plasterwork. Well . . . ' She turned around and shrugged at him, quite energetically. 'Perhaps I am sentimental and this is all very ordinary. I adore it. And verandahs are by no means ordinary, not anywhere, not in any city. I had an old Cambridge friend here this year, an English poet, and he was enchanted. Swore he'd carry it back, brick by brick, if we didn't appreciate it. I assured him it was one of the prizes of the city. And it is.'

Boyd knew this was true. He'd shown his photos of the Bellevue to his school friends and they knew where it was, hadn't it been in the newsreels?

'I think it is very beautiful,' he said supportively. 'I wonder, could we go up to the top verandah?'

'But of course. Why ever not? Excellent idea.' His grandmother lifted her napkin. 'This very minute. Waiter, hold our dessert for ten minutes. We,' she whispered, a conspirator, 'we are going on an expedition.'

Everyone watched as they went out. Boyd was long used to that. Nobody could ignore his grandmother.

He stumbled into the corridor.

'Watch the ledges,' she sang, halfway to the stairwell, which was somehow smaller than he'd remembered.

The rooms upstairs were all closed, but they strode out to the verandah on the first level. The ironwork, with its swoops and big fronds, was pretty dusty, and the floorboards were weathered and looked splintered. The precinct around them was a wall of green, opening across to the Botanical Gardens, whose high, iron fence seemed helpless to hold in the tangle of bamboo, acalepha and rampant Honolulu lily-vine that threatened the spaces left beneath massive hoop pines, and the perpetual jacarandas.

From the top floor it was strange. They overlooked so much. Even the Queensland Club seemed to slide away downhill from them, and the Gardens became less clustered. Brought back to size.

His grandmother caught his expression. 'Do you know, Boyd,' she said quietly, 'if you love anything too much, you are in great danger. I was in great danger. This was our room.' She nodded at the closed French doors behind them.

'The best way to hold on to something is to pretend to ignore it. Because if you do love too much, be it man or woman or even something like this – a pile of bricks and mortar, or that garden – if you love it too hard you will lose it. That is true as I stand here. It is the nature of things: you will lose it.'

What was she saying? Had she lost Grandfather, then? Not by war, but by loving too much? This was all embarrassment. Yet Boyd knew she was asking something, wanting to involve him entirely.

'If this place makes you sad, Grandmother, why do you keep coming back? You don't have to bring me . . . '

'You will see. You will discover. And do you know why you will lose it?' She tidied her hat, as if in front of yet another mirror. 'Let me tell you why, up here where we are above all these other – ' she paused, 'this rabble. If you love anything too much, it means that the other, the recipient of your love, becomes exonerated forever from having to love you enough; from having to love you at all. Indeed, each of us knows it instinctively: the more you become an object of love, the more you resist it. You hold back. You can barter. You can make terrible demands. You could not believe the tyranny of the beloved. It is like this city . . . '

She turned away, and walked, as always, briskly along the shaky verandah. The floorboards really were weather-worn, as if endlessly fondled by soapy water or the cyclones of interminable Februaries.

'If you set your heart on anything, you must be prepared to see it taken from you. If follows almost by axiom. No, I am not joking. It is as if you yourself were part of the destructive force that generates it all.'

It was hot here, under the tin awning. Hot and oppressive, as if he were under a steam shower. His shirt stuck to his shoulders. His new serge trousers clung to his calves. He could see that his grandmother, also, was perspiring.

'Only last week, as I took my usual walk down to the post office, I said to myself: if there is one thing I live for, it is that wonderful silver-wattle on the corner. When I see it, my heart opens, I am awakened to wonder. To live with such a simple thing; that is a living delight, that is enough explanation for anything.' Her voice had become, as it sometimes was at night when she was talkative, more vibrant and resonant. Boyd was sure people across the street – students and a few chauffeurs – must have heard her. 'That wattle was chopped out. The very next day. Gone.'

'Perhaps it had borers?'

'Gone. That is not the first time. Do not trust even possessions. Do not trust anyone. Most of all, do not trust your feelings, they will destroy you, Boyd. I can see you are mine, you are like me. We both have the same tragic power. Well, all I can teach you, I shall. But, gird yourself. You must find ways of coping with this truth, otherwise it will destroy you. It is not that you will love. You will love. It is not that you will love too much. You will love too much, you do already. It is that you must never, never whisper, even to yourself, that this is so. You must not let the objects of your love be aware of their power. Once you do, you are destroyed.'

She came back. He could see her face was a tumble of sweat and she did not even attempt to mop it. 'Destroyed – or worse; made to suffer, to endure the silence of a pain you cannot share.'

They went downstairs, Boyd leading, *not* the gentleman. His grandmother went to the powder-room for a very long time while the boy fiddled with the already dried-out piece of bread that some waiter had negligently left – perhaps to indicate that the table was occupied.

She looked radiant.

'Grandma,' he said as she settled herself. She did not reprove the locution, 'Grandma, I know what you mean, but surely, if what you say is true, surely the Bellevue must be threatened?'

She looked around.

'If I thought so, I would truly despair. But there are some things, Boyd, even my ego cannot destroy, try as I might.' She laughed then, and he wondered if he should remember her words or forget them.

His mother called her an evil old woman, possessive, destructive. He had heard his mother say it, at home, before he came up this time for his Christmas holiday.

His grandmother spoke to so few people, but when she did, intolerable streams of claim and demand netted them.

In the heat of the verandah roof upstairs, it was as if he were under the armpit of some beautiful flawed idol. Love, she had said. What was that? How could he know?

Going home in the bus to her Toowong house he comforted himself with the cool, clinical image of the mirror-glass vase in her hallway. It did not even occur to him that his cool, protective withdrawal on the bus journey was part of the tyranny. He took for granted his grandmother's love. All these things are instinctive.

Hayman Island

Yes, it had been a long flight, an interminable series of flights and they were crazy to believe the tourist brochures.

They were crazy. Boyd repeated it, grinning, and Marie caught the joke and said 'Oh Boyd really . . . ' but he had squeezed her arm in the silly public seat and had buzzed the hostess button yet again ('Oh Boyd, really . . . ') even though he could see the poor girls were already gathering up the last things before the plane landed.

'We're on honeymoon get us . . . '

'Sorry, sir, see the Fasten Safety Belts sign, that means no more liquor.'

'Liquor! Who needs liquor? This is my liquor!' Boyd pointed marvellously to his new wife. 'I want . . . I want guava juice, mango juice, papaya. Fruit of the tropics. I thought this was supposed to be a tropical holiday voyage, all connections covered, everything tailored to get us into the Hayman Holiday Mood.'

'Not when Fasten Safety Belts sign goes on. Sorry, sir. And good honeymoon.'

'Bitch!'

'Shhhh.'

Boyd's fury was so great he could have pulled out his safety belt by the roots, would have throttled the hostess. Marie looked uncomfortable.

'Don't take it out on her.' She relaxed herself, patted him then. 'Let the girl go, she has little jobs to get done.'

The man sitting next to them eased himself out of a feigned slumber. 'Gawd, you two.'

'Hey. Hey,' Boyd grinned. 'Come on, we've got the key. It's allowed. It's permitted.'

It was a pretty, small cabin. They walked in. The baggage would follow. Tropic. A heavy closeness in the enclosed room. Cane furniture.

'Very hot inside still, as if the place hasn't been used for a fortnight.' Boyd strode to the windows, which were screened for insects.

'Pretty good-oh.'

Marie smiled, the old smile at last. 'What was that?'

'Pretty good-oh. It's an old way of saying okay. My grandmother used it sometimes. Pretty good-oh.'

He could tell that inside the now crumpled going-away suit she had allowed her shoulders, her body some relaxation. She kept her smile: did she realize how dazzling it was?

'Hey, pretty, hey pretty good-oh, let's try the bed?' Her body, caught within the sudden circle of his arms, became like some trapped bird. He felt protective. Dear, dearest Marie.

After a few moments she broke free. She laughed nervously, stepped to the wardrobe and pulled open the door, as if looking for something.

A double-breasted navy-blue suit hung on a wire coathanger. The wrench of the door had set it into a slight motion. Empty, yet curiously inhabited.

Boyd was behind Marie now, he had followed with his encompassing arms, longing, not daring, to trap and enfold her again. In silence they stared at the suit. It became motionless. Marie, feeling him close, instinctively pulled away, but then thrust herself into the shelter of his body. She turned to face him and whispered Boyd Boyd until they were both free of the strange sensation of their discovery.

They did not have to discuss it. Later, decisively, Boyd had wrenched it from its metal hanger and thrown it out the door. Someone would find it. Someone would take it away, or claim it, or do something with it. Later, they would invent jokes about it, turn it into a benign ghost.

Its presence had not been benign. It had been all the ancestors.

MONDAY AFTERNOON

Boyd

One of the first acts of definition in a new town, another country, is the slow, appraising walk down the church-aisles of the strange supermarket. It is the way to note cultural distinctions, to gear to the ambience, become acclimatized. Supermarket culture has overtaken language, it rides roughshod, from Budapest to Brisbane, over old street boundaries and leaps to the acquisitive heart. It cuts corners. It is everywhere.

Is it possible for someone alive in the latter part of the twentieth century to be ignorant of supermarkets?

Boyd Kennedy has never been inside one; not to his memory.

For Boyd this is, indeed, a First Day. He does not even have to justify himself to himself for such extraordinary ignorance. The women in his life appropriated that territory. Even when he was nineteen years old his mother still bought all his clothing. He was an industrious student, *things* did not interest. He had not really caught up with our century; he had not yet been taken up.

How had he become unmanageable? He had not changed. Why did Marie look with betrayed eyes at him when it was she, surely, who had betrayed that first child-marriage and its contentment? There had been no children.

The sliced-off little flat was gloomy. Still, he had gone down to the estate agents, he had signed forms, written out his cheque, been handed receipts for bond and for the first week's rental. He had even enquired the going price of the property. Not for sale; future potential. He had been asked to pay for the cost of the agent's phone-call south to verify his bank account credit. Even this had not upset him.

The time Marie grabbed up the scissors, yelling at his indifference. It had not been indifference, he had quieted her, put her to bed. He had gone back to his Law Reports, shaking.

Back inside the flat: undeniable hollowness. And yet, also, the knowledge of something cast off. Could it be the loosening grip of his grandmother's possessiveness? Or escape from the reproachful claims of his wife? And yet he loved this place, surely? He felt full of appetite. He felt decisive.

The flat was empty of food. In this new, generous mood Boyd recognized the need for self-provisioning. He would seek out the Toowong supermarket.

It was this heightened sensibility: everything seemed new-rinsed, all things bright for him. How easy it all was.

Pushing his trolley before him like a talisman (chrome, mirror-like) he started with instant coffee: Nescafé espresso.

The first choice took some minutes. He did have to learn the labels, weigh up the alternatives. After that: easy. With a recklessness Marie would have disbelieved, Boyd heaped into his pile sweet mustard pickles, French mustard, an intriguing anchovy sauce (which he would never taste), bottles of mineral water, grape juice, irresistible glacé pears, the largest packet of macadamia nuts, a huge plastic cushion of muesli, canned peaches, beetroot, carrots, baby potatoes, mango, four varieties of soup, bottled honey, vanilla essence (Why? His mother always had vanilla essence). A kilo pack of sugar: he hadn't realized there was a difference between raw, castor, refined. He could not conceive of cane or beet or the yellow first-processed stage, in thick sheets, sold in third world countries.

Then he discovered the cold section.

When he checked out and paid the cashier ('Thank you for shopping at Woolworth's; have a nice day'), Boyd refused to be abashed at his booty. He felt great.

'Take these with you? Or delivery?'

'Just one sec. I'll get a taxi.' And he even remembered — after twenty years — just where the taxi rank was, near the post office and the big old leopard-tree. Nothing fazed him.

The small delights of unpacking. At home this had never been his duty. His mother had a housekeeper twice a week. For his grandmother, just occasionally, he had run to the corner store with her list in his hand. His grandmother always instructed the shop assistant, on that list, to give Boyd sixpence worth of sweets. She had an Account. The time of the chewing-gum was the only crisis. Boyd had never lost, dropped or spilled anything.

If Marie were with him, would they have shared this? Who would have been possessive? Some lessons must be learned solo.

The flat was becoming his own. Each item placed on the shelving defined him. He understood the possessiveness of women, ruling their kitchens.

Boyd had forgotten some items: he needed cutlery, for instance, and bedlinen, towelling. It was four p.m. Already? He was grinning as he knocked on the flat next door to ask bus timetables.

It was not the girl, Cora. A lanky young man, long hair in rats' tails. Barefoot, soiled denim. The chest smooth and underdeveloped. But the face somehow friendly, open, not surly like some, thought Boyd.

'Hi there. I'm the new neighbour, just in. Wondered did you know about bus services . . . '

'Sure. I'll get Cora.' And the youth ambled back through the refuse in the old hallway. Boyd noticed the seat of his pants was frayed open. There was no underwear.

Boyd chafed for the modern generation.

A beer in the Public Bar of the Regatta Hotel. Normally, Boyd was no beer drinker (vintage wine with the meal; latterly, more cask claret after), but he was drawn by the Brisbane 'feel' of the place, this old, three-tiered wedding-cake of a building with its cast iron and improbable timber. It reminded him of the Bellevue, back in the city. Grandmother's afternoon treats. The ceilings here were higher, more airy; and the ironwork was clearly one of the standard mass-produced patterns. Boyd remembered the lacework of the old Bellevue Hotel as being all tendrils and air. Irreplaceable. The rooms themselves had been darker, smaller.

Taking his pot of beer onto the verandah, Boyd grinned again to himself. Grandmother could not abide beer drinkers. That's right; it was brandy she tippled. And on those Bellevue excursions, her brandy-lime and soda. At home, the crystal decanters. Scotch for the gentlemen: did she have gentlemen callers? Boyd had not witnessed any, apart from – once – the Archbishop. And he was a relative.

Oh, perhaps others.

But the beer tasted excellent. Tart, yet seductive. He thought of the girl, Cora. Yes, he could imagine her drinking beer, butch to impress the others. She could afford roughshod gestures. Why did some girls retain that? Boyd thought of Dagmar, Marie's friend, with her new-cropped hair disturbingly mannish, though she had been the softest of debutantes – and on, right through university. Some people change, some people know themselves.

Cora's authority. Perhaps it was disturbing: what did that other lad, in the flat, think of it? How did he cope? What did he do with it? Boyd put down his glass, surprised it was empty so soon. Pervy old man. Good thing some thoughts were invisible. Not like the teenage years, every nerve strung with trapwires to his pants. Such embarrassment. He could sit here, now, quietly idolizing that young bit of girlflesh with not a trace of guilt or self-consciousness. It did not impinge on his relationship with Marie. Whatever that might be, or was at. It was all knots new loosening, unravelling.

Boyd looked around him. This was, clearly, a sporting man's pub: white shorts, football jerseys. A group in from tennis. Mainly students, by the look of them. The University just upriver. Few old regulars, one in a fireman's dark green overalls, one clothed in the uniform of a dentist (strange, dentists drinking – why not?). The old barfly.

A group scraped the metal chairs beside him, sprawled around, grabbed more chairs from Boyd's table with perfunctory apology. Boyd waved them access, benignly. This group had reached the bellicose state, or was close to it. The good looking one nearest him had control. Some local victory.

Boyd stood for another ten-ouncer. He asked the fair one near him to keep an eye on his table. 'Dead cert.' Male camaraderie. When he returned, the smaller olive-skinned one had grown loud, inarticulate but emphatic. He was trying to prove to the fair one some pride of union, some trace-element they shared together. The others indulged him, but not viciously. It was that moment between sympathy and embarrassment.

The dark youth put his arm on the other's thigh, proving his point. Held it there. Began stroking. Boyd looked away. The exhortations became louder, slurred, desperate. 'Look, I love you, mate, understand that. Mates understand that. Why's it got to be serious?' And he turned to the others, aggressive, daring them to call him a poofter.

One of the group caught Boyd's eye. As his friends carried off the drunk youngster to some less awkward diversion, he came to Boyd's table.

'You didn't see none of that. Just you forget it, see. Jim's up to his eyeballs in piss, won't remember a thing in the morning. None of us will. Get me?'

The varnished light. The great native fig-trees across the road from the Regatta, riverbank trees, drenching themselves in the late sunlight. Unreal colour – like Kodachrome. Boyd laughed. There. There etched into the moment as if the moment were compressed. Registering the moment, declaring it perfect, transformation. Boyd walked out lyrical.

Past the old motor bodyworks, under the rail-bridge (sounds from childhood) and, in this slant sunwash, by the playing field and the parkland off Sylvan Road, a forest of more weeping-figs, Port Jackson figs, rain-forest natives planted in avenues.

In the still air the first flying-foxes swooped to their eating places in the large figs. Boyd remembered that sight. The coloured-glass sliding windows on the back sun-room that opened out over the gully. Those same fruitbats, the reddish flying-foxes. Brisbane. Endlessly, stressing recurrence, stitching the suburb into its cycles, its tropical silences made up of such small, individual noises.

He walked slowly uphill. Inside his flat he turned on his lights. The naked bulbs made him blink. Yes, that too: he remembered the suddenness of darkness up here, swift as an axe-chop, a fist brutally smashing into a mirror.

Sleep was not easy. The bed he lay on was not his old holiday rest. That was a boy who had lain there.

His feet pushed out the end, between rails of silky oak. No modern bed had rails at the end, why had they made them like that? Then he remembered: to keep the mosquito nets high, away from the sleeping face. To give air and ventilation in the white cavern.

There were mosquitoes. But it wasn't that. It was the first turn-off from activity. Boyd had never felt so purposeful, settling in.

Later, compelled by his provisions to attempt his own cooking, the aloneness of the place seeped slowly up. What was Marie doing, this moment? Perhaps he should phone her? It was not as if he intended betrayal.

He got up, dressed again, and tried to work on his paper for the conference.

Next door, through paper-thin walls ... The old walls: had it always been like that? Had his grandmother then heard him, in the next room, that last year, when he had begun compulsively masturbating? The flush, after twenty years. Some guilt, it seemed, might be perpetual. Not for himself, for his grandmother. How could he explain to her? Those strong urges, his first real compulsions. Why should guilt sneak out of his childhood? Who was his grandmother?

She.

The noises next door. It seemed there were three people. The first was Cora. He had learned her voice, her particular intonation, quickly. Then the tall boy: Don was his name. There was another, deeper voiced, slow cadenced. The hirsute young man with the motorcycle who swaggered in just on darkness. What was their relationship? The three of them in there, close in there together. Boyd tried to prevent himself imagining a vast bed – a round waterbed like the one seen in his only porno movie (called *Bel Ami*, supposedly after Maupassant). The three writhing bodies, Cora's blond pubic mound, the sheen. The two boys struggling for position, rivals.

The night, damn it, was unaccountably hot. By the front window he stood and groped for a cigarette. After a while he opened the door of his flat, onto the caged porch. The other front door, Cora's, was wide open.

A candle flicker somewhere, soft television glow, volume turned to nothing. An unmistakable smell of marijuana. He could have expected as much.

It must be the boys. Boys? Why did he think of them in that way? They were almost certainly men. Young animals, in full prime.

Envious.

A sloppy dog ambled out of the other flat, nuzzling him and claiming friendly caresses. Boyd leaned down. It was part spaniel, part terrier, but with enough of the softer animal to make the pelt pleasurable. It could take this treatment endlessly.

After a while Boyd stretched up. The dog followed into his side, certainly familiar with the entire territory.

'Hey, not in here, Fido. I don't want your fleas. There's your world; this one's my property.'

Boyd decided to ignore it. It would take the hint eventually. He must take a shower. He could not get over this sauna atmosphere, so late into autumn.

Flicking his new towel, Boyd slipped out of his prickly wool trousers, dragged at jockettes. Remembered he had forgotten soap, even in his toilet case.

Nothing for it. Wrapping the towel around himself he knocked at the neighbour door, now shut. The old brass knocker had been long ago stolen. Adjust to the Queensland hedonism, was the way he thought it, standing there, his skin unused to exposure, his blur of shoulder hair reddish, dark, above freckles.

It was the dark one came out, lurching a little, but grinning when he saw Boyd.

'Ah there. Look, it's just a tiny thing. I've got no soap and I wanted a shower . . .'

'You want ours? Look, half a tic. Hold it.' The youth disappeared. That gruff voice.

Cora came out. She held out an unopened tablet of Pear's soap. 'Settling in then? Keep this. My father's a chemist. Tell me what lines you might want.'

Boyd took the soap. As he did so his towel slipped. Grabbing it up he blushed with embarrassment.

Cora's smile was deceptive. It was as if she did not even notice the physical world.

'Well, if you do need free shaving cream, razors, contraceptives, don't bother laying out dough. Dad provides everything.' She did grin then, tight over fine cheekbones. 'Daddy damn well better.'

The eyes, now, doing him over. Beaming in somewhere. It was not Boyd.

'Some father.'

'Would you do the same? Boy? Boyd? Tell me. If you had a daughter – me – what would you come up with?' Then she made an upthrust gesture, clenched fist and forearm. Phallic thrust. Pure obscenity.

Boyd felt startlingly naked.

'Excuse me. I'm stoned. Have a nice shower. And I see you've got Kali. Have fun together.'

Later, as Boyd sat, naked, on the one kitchen chair drying his toes ('Be careful for tinea in Queensland, Boyd') the dog, Kali, sidled up. Began licking. Snuffled and poked straight for the genital area, was insatiable.

Boyd was shocked. Who had trained this thing? It was a salaciousness he might not have imagined.

Later, he put the dog out.

Holding Out

Under his grandmother's house was a secret place. It was also a refuge. Boyd had crawled to the tightest, most narrow part, where the hillslope almost touched her wooden floorboards, under the kitchen.

It was a house on stumps, but down at the opposite corner it was high enough for the so called 'garage', a cased-in room of fibro with cool cement floor. Grandmother stored her old papers and magazines there, and other wonders. At some time in every Christmas holiday Boyd would slouch through, and be trapped. Hours later he would emerge, blinking into the hard sunlight, dazed by the images, words and messages of some twenty, thirty years back. Time coiled into a circle, like the little millipedes on the floor. Everything there, Boyd felt, was waiting, just for him, so that it could be reinvented.

Today he had retreated to the dark end, the top end, the under-the-house end where house and sunless dirt almost intersected. The unreachable end.

Smell of creosote. The dirt under him was a sort of dried-out dusted-off dirt, dirt that had not seen light, dirt that had forgotten rain and storms. A few trails left by snails in an obscure script. A forgotten corner, a niche. That was what Boyd was seeking. He was clutching the glass-mirror vase.

He did not know what he was going to do with it. Perhaps he would smash it, yes why not? Perhaps he would not. It was too strange and glittery to be wasted that way. Perhaps he would hide it and smuggle it home with him, to Melbourne.

Serve her right.

He knew his parents would not allow him to keep it, would send it straight back to Brisbane. And besides, vases were not the sort of thing a thirteen year old cared about.

Right?

He had to show her, he had to get even. He had to take something, and something that mattered, not any old thing like the kitchen sharp knife or her money purse (he knew that did not matter) or just scrawl dirty words in the bathroom. He had considered smashing all the medicines in the medicine chest and then smashing the mirror there. That was too appalling. That was desecration. He did not really want that.

What did he want, then?

He wanted . . . was it revenge? Was it just to get back at her? Why? She had been as generous today as she always was, even more so: lunch at the Bellevue, that long intimate conversation. Never before had Boyd felt the privilege of sharing secret things, secret knowledge and feelings. On the bus, going home, he had felt great, powerful.

Even though Grandmother had said rather terrible things, like that if you loved someone too much, you would lose them. Of course she had been trying to tell him about Grandpa. She must have missed Grandpa terribly. They hardly knew each other before he went off to that War and was killed. Boyd was old enough to know how she felt, losing him. He even could see how that made her angry – at fate, at the War, at everyone.

His father said she was a very stern mother. His father went to boarding school at eight. She could not stand to have him around: he had said that, Dad.

Boyd was her darling.

He had been so happy this afternoon. He had asked his grandmother what jobs? He had cleaned out the whole area behind the backyard jakes for her, he had dug up the soil in the rosebed.

When he came upstairs, sweaty, yes, and his feet were of course pretty dirty from the rosebed, he had still been bursting and smiling, wanting to keep up that sense of her sharing things with him, secrets, anything.

She was not in the kitchen.

'Grandma. Grandmother. Done that job. Anything else you would like me to do for you?'

He had loved her so much. 'I could prune the roses too, if you'd let me...'

Her neck was powdered, he could see. She was straining over, bending, with a filmy grey dress, one he had never seen. She was dressed as if for something special. Standing behind the big settee, leaning over.

She was funny, awkward like that, what was she...?

'You little bugger! Get to hell out of here!' She started up, straightened. He could see the fire in her eyes. Like skinny claws her hands clenched, unclenched, then suddenly seemed to find their grip on her amber necklace. With a wrench she ripped it from her throat and hurled it at him. Beads scattered. It was way off beam. He, stunned, did not even flinch. But she was already upon him. She gripped his shoulders violently. The contact opened doors. He had never experienced hatred.

'Grandmother, but I was just...'

'And your feet, just look at your feet, your feet; can't you see what a mess you are making with your feet! My carpet, boy. Filthy animal! Filthy!'

She had backed off, hand to her cheek, then abruptly to her dress, tugging it, twitching it into place.

'Go and wash, right away. Don't come in. How dare you walk into my living-room like that, without knocking. And filthy. Worse than the filthy next-door dog. Off with you. Off.'

The last bit was almost a joke. But Boyd had seen, he had heard. He was shattered.

Shuffling him out, becoming increasingly theatrical, his grandmother swooped her arms around like a chook, or as if she were trying to hide from him something or someone behind her, there on the couch. Boyd could not forgive her.

He had gone, of course, and when he scrupulously washed his toes, his ankles, his legs and all of himself (damn her) he made sure to make a big noise before entering, and went straight to his room.

He had never heard his grandmother swear before. Never. He had never seen that white fury. Anger, crabbiness, yes all the time, she was always a tetchy woman, especially with others, though until now Boyd himself had evaded most onslaughts. He was the favourite.

Even, at lunchtime today, he had felt he was the real beloved. *You little bugger.* Funny, he would have laughed if anyone else had said it, even his mother though she never swore.

His grandmother had meant it.

After too long, moping on his bed, he came out. Nobody around; she had left a note on the dining-room table. It was for him.

Boyd darling (huh!) *really quite special, will be back perhaps by suppertime but you are a big boy now and after today's special lunch get yourself bread and butter* (he would eat nothing, nothing of hers: nothing) *and I did appreciate your gardening, forgive your tired, short-tempered old grandmother.*

Nothing he could do about that. It was not a matter of forgiveness or not forgiveness. It was fact.

It had happened.

That was when he caught sight of the glass-mirror vase. That was when he had come down here. *You little bugger.*

No, the vase was not the thing. It was not something she had ever really made a fuss about, perhaps she would be glad to see it gone, something she kept there as a sort of duty because it was given to her (his mother was always moaning about being obliged to keep things on show that she personally detested). Confess it: it was Boyd's own special favourite. He wanted to keep it, not destroy it.

It would hurt nobody, but him.

He clambered out again, and restored the vase to its hallside table. She had not come back. It was growing dark now, quite suddenly as always in the Queensland summer.

He turned on the hall light. Her bedroom was shut. He knew it was forbidden, he had only been inside that room once or twice. Her 'sanctum'.

Even to try the knob, then push open was a sort of victory. He was not quite brave enough to turn on her light, but it was not really dark yet and the hall light gave good illumination. He took a few paces.

The room seemed somehow more cramped than he could remember. The huge double bed, the massive mirrored wardrobe with its crystal knobs, and her chest of drawers: they all claimed the space, and were reflected in the big cheval-glass that he did remember.

What caught his eye almost immediately was the framed photograph of his grandfather, the man who sailed off for the Trenches. It was a scrolled silver frame, almost as large again as the actual photograph. He picked it up. Strange, for the first time he realized this was just a kid, someone who was about as old as Handley Shakespeare's big brother. He stared at the photograph. Sepia, tinted. Touched up, too, you could tell, so it seemed hardly real. Were his cheeks really that delicate flush? His eyes that glint? Younger than Handley's brother Ted. Almost as young as himself. Almost . . .

He put it carefully back where he found it. Grandmother would know if it was half an inch out of place.

Almost himself.

But that was not the image: the image said something quite different. This was not just some young person, early twenties perhaps, dressed in what was clearly a new and unfamiliar uniform, trying to look serious and important.

Behind the tinting and the regulation pose from some fussy studio in Alexandria, it was a face whose eyes nurtured hatred, and a curse.

How could she live with that photograph? She said he was twenty-four when he left.

Did she hate herself so entirely?

Marie

The waiter gave her his grin. Marie had decided, martini. On the rocks. And with a twist, please.

She ate the sliver of lemon-peel. There were no olive stones to keep count on you. This was the third. Or was it the fourth? The taste of lemon skin was tart, almost impossible but it could be gone through with. The slimy gin taste, after, renewed itself.

Marie enjoyed watching the waiter go through his functions. Only Marie had ordered martini. Dagmar asked for a daiquiri but changed her mind. The waiter was a young man, a student earning extra, part-time. He handled the shaker with a flourish, and filtered the concoction into her glass as if he were born to the trade. Marie did not want to tell him that the button on his white shirt, just above the cummerbund, was undone, revealing every now and then a very smooth, pale skin. At some point in the evening, she knew, if she remained pinned to this spot, she would tell him and he would blush and fumble, and wonder at her bright eyes upon him, and all his charming confidence would be humbled.

Marie felt her smile to be hooked up with very sharp safety-pins. Her spine was the long, thin tautness of the South American Alps. The thought amused her: all that volcanic instability.

Dagmar arrived back with a look of collusion and secrets, as if she had just overheard wonders in a lavatory cubicle. She clutched Marie's shoulder and leant over to whisper. In her mother's living-room she always managed to look a slightly surprised visitor. Her frantic pink organdie flared like Hollywood in this room of Bavarian moss colours and heavy frilled curtains. All the mirrors seemed intent on reflecting only old gilt and imitation rococo borders. The mirrors were black.

Dagmar, in this room, would play Marie her corniest Elvis discs, very loud. She would scatter the tapestry divan with *Vogue* or *Cleo*. On the bookcases all along one wall was the complete set of *National*

Geographic. Dagmar's father had subscribed from the beginning, in Vienna. Their apartment had been requisitioned first by a Commandant in the Medical Corps who had been a contemporary at Linz University, and later, when the Americans arrived, by another old acquaintance, a younger man from Princeton who had worked under Dr Schafft in the Thirties. Dagmar could not understand her father's decision to uproot and come to Australia. She had been born here. Her father, on arrival, found his high qualifications were not recognized. He was over fifty when she was born. He then spent ten years rebuilding his life. He had married late and Dagmar was the only child of that marriage.

Mrs Schafft still looked almost as if she could be Dagmar's sister, but behaved as if Melbourne were some outreach of the Austro-Hungarian Empire. She was a coffee-house queen, as Dagmar insisted, small and *torte*-plumpened. It was only at University that Dagmar liberated herself from two stone excess girth and swore she would speak neither German nor French at table. Her accent broadened into raw Australian. That is, when it did not hinge on its soft American twinge, an inexplicable echo of her father's first conversational encounters with the language through his Princeton colleague. Dr Schafft had died before Marie became Dagmar's most constant companion. His only presence now in the room was that long queue of American journals. Marie had never seen one of them opened. The subscription was still current.

Mrs Schafft was spending a few days at the Windsor. She often did that, to taste again the service. She looked upon Marie as if she were some waif, but would always chatter to her volubly in the soft Viennese dialect. Dagmar would clap her hands to her ears then, and squawk some Rockabilly protest.

The waiter stood behind the bar as if to serve martinis in an overcrammed, private salon decorated with endless rows of yellow *National Geographics* were everyday. Correction, everynight. The older, ivory spines were swamped by the insistence of the later, yellow *Geographics*. Marie caught her own eye (again) in the mirror behind him. Was this already the fourth martini?

The bar had been installed at Dagmar's insistence. Its garish padded and buttoned imitation-leather was an insult in that corner. Heavy fringing had been tacked along the serving area in an attempt at compromise. Dagmar caught to perfection. The outrageous gesture; the final compromise. Marie felt ancient. She was two years older than her friend.

'Marie if you don't stop gobbling little Jimmie Graham with your eyes I'll tell on you!' Her voice sank four tones. 'You've been on this stool *all night*. You couldn't be more conspicuous if you had a python round your neck instead of that . . . ' here Dagmar paused, reconsidered.

'I'm a free agent.' Marie was pleased with her precision. Around her neck were at least a dozen chains, mostly junk Indian silver, but one was an antique piece with links of ivory. They all had been gifts. Boyd. Marie had thrown them on at the last minute, an attempt to give a sort of vivacity to the wilful black she had pulled over herself.

'And besides, Dagmar, you are perfectly nonensical. Nonsensicle. Nonsense. Icle. You are quite ridiculous in your conclusions.' If Marie had been in a different mood she would have flourished the last of her drink and ordered another. Or else she would have stiffened her neck with her too easy hauteur. Her mother, today, had rattled her. Boyd had rattled her. And Dagmar knew perfectly well that the formal air meant nothing; nothing at all, it was an illusion.

No, not illusion – Marie had found it real enough, as reflected in other people's reaction, even Boyd's, those first few times. Boyd: the clear and unmistakable delight that evening when he had first somehow nudged under her defences. Her own sense of waiting, waiting for exactly the one who would not be deceived by her youthful habits of defence, high and mighty as one of her (male) teachers incessantly nicknamed her. Boyd: lured, attracted by that very hauteur for what reason – he said she reminded him of his grandmother once, though that woman could never have been so exposed and defensive as Marie felt in the early years of her mother's scandalous life as an Exotic.

Boyd persisted. He would not be put off by cold formality (he could equal it, but with panache), or by excuses, or by Marie's obnoxious mother – from their first meeting Boyd fell in love with her mother, and she with him. Boyd courted Marie with an instinctive skill and possessiveness that at first humbled, then flattered, and then warmed Marie until she began, for the first time, to realize that her mother was only an annexe to her own life and her mind and her future. Boyd had been so awkward, in the midst of his cleverness and skill. The big, lumping body that wanted to be elegant and svelte. The little habits and twitches.

She should have noted the small pointers, but of course her mother had achieved at least that success with Marie: 'Do not distract yourself with details and fiddles, look at the strengths and size yourself up with them, or against them. Decide. Then act as if you believed in your decision.'

Marie had played her mother's game, even at the very moments when she mocked it. Her mockery was an acknowledgement of its power.

The waiter, now little Jimmie Graham, had moved to the other end of the bar. Dagmar motioned him back.

'Just how many martinis has Marie had tonight?' she demanded.

He looked to Marie for some directive. He looked not unpleased with himself.

'And oooooh look!' Dagmar was in with her finger before Marie could restrain her, 'Lookie, look, I can see Jimmie's navel!' Her hand was right in. 'And smooth as a baby!'

She withdrew it, as if she had wanted something dark, hairy, swarthy and tight-muscled. 'Softie,' she whispered.

'Dagmar, be careful. What have you been drinking?'

'Service is extra.' Jimmie crooned and Marie realized he was, indeed, an old smoothie.

'I want to drink champagne out of that navel,' Dagmar hissed back. 'And there better be no fluff.'

'For that I can't serve you myself. Without spilling.' He was surely not more than eighteen? 'Another martini?' He turned to Marie, conspiratorial.

Dagmar was always tangling herself up in situations she did not really want to pursue, and then out of pride or stubbornness, she would pursue them relentlessly. She looked to Marie to get her out.

'Dagmar, our waiter is waiting for a reply,' Marie murmured, and hated herself.

'Oh well, make it two martinis, dearest.' Dagmar leaned confidentially forward, as if her own small breasts might make up for the glittering eyes. And in her most crooning tone added, 'Are you hairless all over?'

'Are you?' He was as polite. His fingers splashed in the gin, the ice, the hypnotic shaking and the theatrical gestures. Marie could not take her eyes from the still unbuttoned area above the cummerbund, now widened by Dagmar's rampage.

'Olive or lemon?'

Marie hated herself. Her mouth was sour. Her mind was surely sour.

Marie did not want another drink. She did not want to drink, ever. Dagmar needed protecting against herself. This boy was altogether too cocky. At sixteen years of age what was he doing serving alcoholic spirits?

The glasses clinked. Dagmar put her hand on Marie's long thigh, each finger was crammed with rings, even the thumb. Most of the rings were antique, with dulled jewels and ornate designs that had become worn or gritty. Already the hands of mid-European ostentation. Dagmar's dress screamed back at them. Dagmar's eyes burned into Marie, large black centres of pain. Why did everyone turn to her, why were there always claimants, dependents?

Boyd: claiming her even before she had learned her own space or her own capacities.

Her mother: possessing her even when she had dispossessed herself of every single embarrassment.

If she had known her father, he would be in there making claims, staking out some part of Marie's body, the backbone perhaps, the tight, high cheeks, the genetic betrayals into rigidity and aloofness that Marie had spent her life trying to break out of. Was that her father's genes? How would she know, and did it matter? She had, at last, learned to refuse to accept such pure genetic conspiracies, to take responsibility for herself.

Dagmar was giggling.

Jimmy the bartender put her in her place. Suddenly Marie recognized the extent of his disdain. Why did men get away with such things? He had the body of a fourteen year old. He got away with it. She felt protective, defensive. For Dagmar's sake. Dagmar's hand weighed down through the firm black dress and was eloquent.

'Shall I button that up for you?' Marie offered, turning back to the mirror. 'Or do you prefer to keep it like that as a conversation piece?'

Black mirrors, and he had such small eyes, little blue sparkles. Sometimes, Dagmar's eyes were her entire face. She hated his insolent politeness. Knowing little boys.

'Some parties I have been required to serve drinks naked. Others I wore only the cummerbund.' He would gaze lovingly at himself in mirrors, those times, he would be amazed at his own appearance. Five years' time and he would be anxious for the first sagging, the tell-tale dimple, Marie thought.

'It depends on the host, and the fee,' their waiter explained, sensing the circle of female current around him.

'And you do that sort of thing?' Dagmar gave a shiver of incredulity. Her hand leapt from Marie's safe contact and appeared about to strike. 'What is your price, little prince?'

But he was tidying things. There were no other drinkers. There was no one else in the room. The party was in Marie's honour.

'It seems,' she had said, 'that I am on my own.' This was their 'on our own' party.

Marie suddenly reached out to Dagmar, clutching her. The waiter eyed them both speculatively. He was smiling in that fixed, knowing way.

'Dagmar, you know what it is about Boyd that I find most difficult to handle? It's his helpfulness.'

'Forget Boyd,' Dagmar clutched Marie in turn.

'No, it's Boyd's helpfulness. The way he wants to keep rushing in before I have a chance to get things done my own way. When I make a cup of coffee in the morning, I can sense him itching to grab the percolator from me and fill it himself.'

'That's not helpfulness, that's possessiveness.'

'That, too, but it's the helping part that galls. I can feel his impatience rising. Then when I light the gas. Dagmar, you can feel his muscles tighten. He wants to knock me out of the way and flash his little efficiency: snap, the match is lit; snap, the gas is on; snap snap and the water is practically boiling already.'

'Revolting!'

'If I make myself toast for breakfast, there he is, rushing to the fridge for the butter, asking me, "marmalade? honey?" before I have a chance to think. He'd have it spread and in my mouth, if I let him.'

'Mmmm, sounds wonderful,' murmured Jimmy the barman. 'Do you lick the crumbs from his fingers, darling?'

'Shut up you!' hissed Dagmar.

'Of course I exaggerate. But you know the feeling, Dagmar. Being watched, being looked over. It's a form of criticism, always telling me how inefficient I am, how nervous and fiddly and useless I am, while at the same time asking that I thank him for his thoughtfulness, for his consideration, for his damned endless helpfulness. My mother thinks Boyd is just heaven.'

'He should have married her, then.'

'He didn't need to,' Marie said dryly. 'As it is, he got two for the price of one, didn't he? Dagmar, Dagmar, you know what he's done to me, don't you? I'm addicted. Withdrawal symptoms. I *need* that big bear-like helpfulness around me, I feel so lost without it. If he came back tomorrow I would let him make the toast himself, I would let him manage me, I would let him.'

'Marie, martini lady. You know you would not. You! I've seen you manage that man as if he was just a teddy bear. Don't give me the blanket-and-thumb story. I'll... I'll tell on you, I'll tell your mother. Imagine what she would say to that story!' Dagmar suddenly leaned forward and embraced her friend, partly to protect her from toppling from her bar stool. 'And if you cry, Marie, I'll throttle you with my own pantyhose. Don't do that to me. Don't. Please, Marie, please.'

But Marie was in control again. She pulled back her lips into the smile, mopping her eyes.

'Boyd has gone to Brisbane and I hope he enjoys it. I hope he takes in its culture and its opportunities.'

'What culture? What opportunities? You mean the bikini girls at the Gold Coast?'

'Oh, come on, Dagmar, the Art Gallery's okay. It has a terrific Picasso, one of the Blue Period masterpieces.'

'In Brisbane? You're telling me I'd find a Rubens or a Titian up there next.'

'*La Belle Hollandaise* it's called. I've seen reproductions; I think Boyd showed me . . . '

'You don't think of Queensland and Picasso together. Queensland and Beenleigh rum perhaps.'

'Did I ever tell you the story about it, the Picasso?' Marie could see that the waiter was captured. Boyd's big laugh when he told her the anecdote. 'When the Gallery up there did get their Picasso they tried right away to sell it. Cash it in. Said they could build a whole up-to-the-minute new gallery for the sale price.'

'And what would they stick in their new gallery once they got it?' Jimmie put in scornfully. 'Or are they loaded with treasures?'

'Well, a group of students stole the painting, and leaked out the news to the press. Didn't give it back until they extracted promises from the Trustees, in writing: no sale. But of course they lost the donor entirely. A Major Rubin. He had left them his whole collection in his will. He changed that pretty quick smart. He owned one of the best collections in the country; it all went off to Sotheby's when he died. Not long after.'

'Serve them right.' Jimmie the barman wiped the counter again.

'And that's the place you tell me your Boyd has his heart set on!

That's the place he longs to return to, to identify with. Marie, you let him drown in it.'

'You know I can't.' But Marie was not to be drawn.

'Jimmy waiter,' she said, her voice brightly articulate, 'Jimmy with the peekaboo navel, tell us more about the naked waiter performance. Do you do it on top of the bar, or a table? Or is it merely a circulating library thing? Are people allowed to finger the pages?'

The waiter had finished tidying. He polished a clean glass.

'The naked waiter act is not usually done in mixed company,' he pointed out, gently. 'And the fee is a matter for mutual negotiations. The performance is strictly commercial.'

'What do you do at the University? What are you studying?' put in Marie before Dagmar could make another transgression.

'Combined Law/Commerce. Your husband is my lecturer.'

Marie held the lemon-rind on her tongue a moment. She reached over, and for an instant was undecided whether to button or unbutton.

'Little mother!' Dagmar leapt up too.

The young man knew he would have to explain more patiently. He was used to that. These two women were really into some weird thing together and he wondered if they had been sniffing coke. He felt disappointed in his lecturer, but only for a moment. He was used to all sorts of behaviour. He lived in a tiny cottage at Footscray with a widowed mother who was amazed that he went to university and thought that all men went out where and when they wanted to. He had already four thousand dollars in a building society, in the name of Alfred Lord Douglas. He rather liked that invention.

In the darkened mirror Marie's face stared through her, the face of someone unsatisfied, restless. How had this all happened, she wondered, idly twisting her cocktail stick. Dagmar and the boy were in glass boxes, deep frozen in the black mirror. It was the peaked face of someone with no past, she decided. Ridiculous! Her own past had been so crowded. Ten years with Boyd! Like yesterday. Her mother; yesterday and today. She did not know that woman in the glass, it was a woman shaped by fear and evasion. How could that be? Marie had prided herself on her decisiveness. She had kept current. Dr Steiner praised her for her honesty and strength. Dagmar worshipped her way of managing people, events, everything. The face in the mirror was a lie. Boyd's care and consideration was a lie. The lying boy behind the bar. Dagmar was inventing Marie in terms of her own need, as perhaps she herself had once invented Boyd – and herself.

Dagmar did not have to invent extravagance, she summoned it. Strange, thought Marie, how like her mother Dagmar was. That surely could not be the reason Dagmar appealed to her? No, Dagmar was enthusiastic, without guile. Helena Maria Adriana's entire power stemmed from artifice and duplicity. Marie had run to Boyd. Enthusiasm, Boyd's enthusiasm and his directness. Not only his possessiveness and his impatience. Suddenly the thought of their own living-room, the armchair and the safe corner filled her with longing and emptiness.

At three a.m. Marie insisted on leaving. As she unlocked the door to the apartment, she knew there was nobody in the entire world to whom she could confide anything.

TUESDAY

Boyd

Boyd lay in his old bed. The first sounds that woke him were the bird noises. A kukukukukuku, like cold water being tipped out of a narrow-throated bottle. It was the brown swamp pheasant, the coucal. Twenty years.

The little metallic ticking of a grey thrush. The first magpies gargling shadow out of their throats, round tubes of it, flute noises. The currawongs, noisier but still virtuosi: what was the phrase Marie claimed to hear in their refrain: *Ain't she afraid, ain't she afraid*. Yes, that was it. He could hear the phrase now, too, in the call of the currawong outside.

Somewhere down in the gully the ratchet rattle of kookaburras. Drone of traffic too. The grey wallabies would be nibbling dew grasses and stalks in the outlying paddocks. Once Boyd's grandmother took him, sleep-clogged from bed, to watch a quiet wallaby down in her gully. It was eating her lettuce. She had not seen one so close in before; it was a drought year. Boyd recalled other noises: chip-chip as his grandmother worked in her garden. She was often up at dawn, weeding and edging. It was the best time of day, she said. At noon she would never venture outside. She had long kips after lunch.

There was the sound of a mattock, outside. The same sharp thwack of metal into earth. Again. Boyd roused himself.

After he had dressed – the new shirt had an unwashed stiffness and he almost caught himself on yet another hidden pin – he made coffee and took it out to his back balcony.

The air was still fragrant: that made-new flavour, discovering again, for the first time, the savour of frangipani. Boyd breathed deeply. It seemed he had never, for so long, felt his five senses so responsive.

Cora was in the backyard, she had dug up the old garden, almost the entire vegetable patch. Her hair was plaited again, this time pinned up, Scandinavian style (or was it Swiss, Bavarian?) in rows at the crown. She looked thoroughly exotic, thoroughly at home. Perhaps Marie's mother had once had such a blonde, springtime look, in her unimaginable girlhood.

The tight jeans hardly pretended to cover her smooth shapely arse. When she stood up they caught into the crease, exposing two mooncurves of her buttocks.

'You're at it early,' Boyd called out cheerfully. 'Make you a coffee?'

'Sounds fair enough.' She wiped with her forearm. Even in this brisk air she was sweating. She must have been at it for hours.

Boyd came down with two mugs.

'Did you know that was my grandmother's vegetable garden? Exactly in that spot. You've revived it.'

'What was she like, your grandmother?'

'What was she like – to look at, you mean? Or as a person?'

Cora turned to him. 'Please yourself. Name your own preferences, she's your grandmother.'

'She was an old woman when I knew her – the last six years of her life. She died just after I turned fifteen. I only came up here at holidays: Christmas. I remember her fine white hair, always kept in a bun. And then, the last time up, she'd had it all chopped off, into an Eton Crop she called it, very short. Rather blew my mind, that, as you'd say.'

'You didn't like surprises, things to change?'

'I always thought of her as stable, and that was so unpredictable. I don't think I knew her at all.'

'But she meant a lot?'

'She was very formal, very good manners. Rather English. Which she was. Thin as a bird, and – work this one out – her favourite colour, she told me, was mauve. Wispy, mauve scarves round her throat, the real Grandma touch. She did have a temper.'

'And I bet you loved it.'

'What do you mean? I'm simply telling you that my grandmother told me her neck was once considered her fine point. It was long and beautiful. Age does terrible things to the throat. Think she was very conscious of that.'

'How old are you, Boyd?'

'Me? I'm not the point. This is my grandmother.' He knew his conversation betrayed him somehow. 'She was often sharp, and sometimes I think really upset, you know: dithered. It's just that she had this formal front, kept it hidden most of the time.'

He blurted out further secrets. 'She and my father didn't get on. In fact, I can only remember them once together, the first time I came up when I was about ten. Dad stayed for three days, and then went back to Melbourne. Looking back on it, I think she nagged him all the time. I only remember the formal meals, the three of us sitting up at table. My mother had refused to come up. I think the fight had first started when my parents got married. They had me too soon for comfort — or for prudery. Little fact I worked out around that time. I was very interested in that sort of thing, around that age. Sex, I mean.' Boyd laughed.

They were sitting now on the old green garden seat. 'Perhaps I still am. Some things get you hooked.'

'Go on about your grandmother.'

'She was a small, thin woman with no real friends.' But he relented. 'She kept this house beautifully — with the help of an old migrant lady who came once a week. Yugoslav, I think.'

'Olof's Yugoslav. You met him, last night. Olof's also supposed to be a Muslim. You know, no alcohol. Only hash. Did your grandmother indulge in any little vices?'

'My grandmother used to tipple a little brandy, just before bed.'

'I bet.'

'No no. She was not the sort of person to get sloshed.'

'Sloshed. In a bottle, swishing round stupidly. The word for how you lot like to wipe themselves out – legally. Sloshed. High is a dry high feeling. And no hangovers.'

'Dry out your brain cells though. Rot them right up, smoked oyster braincells . . . '

'About old Grannie . . . '

'She preferred me to call her "Grandmother"; occasionally she allowed "Grandma", but not often.'

'You think of her often?'

'I never think of her at all. It's coming up here, something's sort of reconnected. It's suddenly turned on all the old lights. Things I'd forgotten.'

'Nothing else?' She was swishing the dregs of her coffee in the mug, round and round, round and round. 'What brought you up anyway, if it wasn't – all this?'

'Nothing. Business. One of those periods of crisis when you've got to get away.'

'So you ran away?'

'I never run away. I just needed . . . a bit of peace.'

'So you came up here.'

'I came up here. The decision, if you'd like to know, was just spur of the moment.'

'That your line – spur of the moment?'

'I don't know. Not usually, but perhaps that's my real identity. Hence the crisis.'

'You're too middle-class middle-aged for that.'

'You're cruel.'

'Not at all. Only precise.' She was looking at the new garden bed, laid out straight. Neat rows of new planted lettuce and carrots.

'You'd have liked my grandmother.'

'Well, I like her house. Feel like I own it. If our old friend Apollo doesn't intend junking it, think I'll set to with a bit of paint and a hammer. Have you seen the fireplace?'

'What a question!'

They laughed together. When she did relax, her whole body was involved.

She jumped up. 'Now I must water my seedlings.'

He found himself at windows, at the door, looking for her.

Later in the morning he explored the front yard, tore off a few of the dead branches. In the corner he recognized a plant from former times, something that was now marketed under the name of 'Chinese Happy Plant'. His grandmother who had areas of wonderful imprecision as well as her firm worlds of knowledge had always called it 'Leila' after the friend who gave it to her all those years ago, and for Boyd, 'Leila' it remained.

He was careful to preserve the web cities as he did his clearing. Dozens of spiders, the yard was full of them. Boyd could not remember seeing this sort of web here before. Never.

The webs themselves, when he brought himself to look again closely, were fascinating. Built vertically, they were strengthened either side by that maze of strong supports, all those struts. On some of the connecting threads there were wrapped corpses, a supermarket of juicy suppers. They were like strings of beads, aisles of packaged food supplies. These supporting webs were of a silvery silk, but the spiral itself was golden: not yellow, but the colour of gold paint, the sheen of something Carter and Lord Carnarvon must have been dazzled by in the boy king's tomb in Egypt.

Four or five close set lines of this golden spiral rippled between each pair of colourless scaffolding lines, so that there was a group of golden threads. Then what appeared to be a space. Almost like staves on a sheet of music, though the web was by no means symmetrical. Usually the hub was near the top. Staves of music. Boyd was becoming adjusted to these insects. Did Cora notice this new interest? The dog, Kali, was sleeping out on the sun porch.

'Boyd! Well, voice from the past! What are you doing up here, no don't tell me now, I'm with a client. But you must be up here for . . . well look, Boyd, what about lunch today, hey? No, that's out, I've got a luncheon engagement. Look, tell you what Boyd, you come right over, we'll sort out something. Years; it's been years. Hey, good to hear your voice, mate. Can you make it say 12.30? Today that is. Great. Great. It's been years, when did you get up? No, hold it, save it till lunchtime. What's that? Two or three times a year I get down to the old dump but you know how it is, Boyd. Look, won't hold you up right now, I'm, uh, with a client but see you 12.30 Brisbane Club. You know where that is? 12.30. Right.'

Bruce Patterson had been Boyd's best friend at Camberwell Grammar. At University they had kept up with each other, had egged each other on, had competed in everything. Bruce had been tall, athletic. Big time footballer those years. Boyd, shorter, dense-knit, had seemed Bruce's natural counterbalance, the tall and the short, the taut and the tight. Inseparable. Boyd had been Bruce's best man, was godfather to his son. Boyd had not seen the son, Craig wasn't it, since the christening, just before the Pattersons moved up to Brisbane and Bruce became a junior partner in an uncle's law firm.

They had competed in subjects at University, too. There had been times when it seemed they did not have to talk, the communication was there anyhow. Bruce's marriage had been sudden but, as was his form, impeccably connected. It was only after the wedding that Boyd himself was reminded that he must also consider the passing of time, the need to settle down. His own twenty-fifth birthday, and Bruce not even there for it (he was on an extended European honeymoon). Yes, things came to focus. They always did. Boyd had not exactly missed Bruce, they had not, indeed, made serious attempts at contact after the Pattersons moved to the tropics. Still, here was Boyd in Brisbane and, once out of the hothouse atmosphere of his grandmother's place, the sudden recollection of Bruce Patterson gave Brisbane a whole new sparkle. Good old Bruce, and, my God, how old was his godson now, was it nine, ten? What did one do for godsons? Should he whip in and produce a Presentation Bible?

Lunch at the Brisbane Club side-stepped the problem, though Boyd hoped he might remember to do the dutiful thing, ask for photographs at some stage, say over port and cigars. Bruce had always been partial to old forms and ceremonials, hadn't he? How did Bruce manage in the shirtsleeves and swelter of Brisbane?

One thing was certain, if they were to have lunch at the Brisbane Club it would be air-conditioned. Or did the Club have punkahs and servants in white jackets and turbans? He recalled punkahs swaying above him somewhere in his Brisbane boyhood, could it have been the Bellevue?

Boyd was guided by a uniformed usher (without a turban) into a large, dimly resonant lounge room with armchairs and tables. The bar ran along one side.

He recognized Bruce immediately, the old lanky streak. My God, but wasn't his face tanned these days. Like leather. Beginnings of a paunch beneath that summerweight suit — and the hair style! The short back-and-sides of their boyhood. Boyd had forgotten how Bruce's ears used to stick out. These days even politicians had blow-waves — didn't his wife nag him? Or were there other regulations up here, other conventions among farmers and small businessmen?

Bruce was leaning forward in his armchair, speaking to someone. The other man was certainly well groomed, in a suit of tropical fawn silk. Small and dapper, his neat round face was framed by glossy black hair. Very trim.

Bruce saw him and gave a welcoming shout, waving Boyd on with a large hand. The other man sank back into his chair, cool and observant. The greetings were hearty and protracted. Bruce Patterson threw himself back into his own chair and gave another chortle.

'Isn't this great! Boyd Kennedy, face out of the long gone dead. Boyd, you haven't met Rob. Robert Huntingdon; Rob's been working with me on a case. Rob this is me old mate Boyd Kennedy, the champion marbles player of fourth form.'

'I'd forgotten all that.'

'Not me. This bastard won my best yellow tor. Never forgave him for that.'

'So you were at school together?'

'School, University. We were like that!' Bruce gave a tight click of his fingers, a snap of joyous friction. He laughed. 'But that's all water under the bridge. When he phoned me this morning I was clean bowled. Couldn't get over it. So I had to see the old bugger. And here he is.' Bruce jack-knifed forward in his seat and clamped his hand on Boyd's knee. 'Would've recognized this old feller anywhere. Isn't this great. Well, Boydie, well well well.'

'Twelve years, isn't it?' Boyd sat, still, on the edge of his deep chair. The old Bruce kept flickering into focus, teasing and challenging. It was like looking at an old photograph and realizing how the once smart fashions and the once smart sayings had been frozen. This person, Boyd's old school chum, had a face that was no longer a boy's, a manner clearly full of confidence and know-how. Yet he seemed held in the frame of the old photograph, even his lurching heartiness which had slipped from memory, it had the buzz of old vinyl.

'It's been years. What brings you up? No, what are you having, first? We've started. Gin and tonic? Beer? Rum and Coke?' Robert Huntingdon smiled at his colleague, reached out and drained his glass. 'Make that two.' Then he slumped back in his deep chair.

'Good as done. Me old mate here,' Bruce said, leaning over to give Rob a thump, 'never misses a trick. Not a trick. That's why I've got him as barrister in this case. Absolute tops.'

A waiter took their orders. Robert Huntingdon closed his eyes. His face seemed a mask of perfect relaxation, even to the almost beatific smile. Bruce seemed to delight in manhandling him. Perhaps he had learned very real skills.

'Rob has been doing brilliant things for me on a sub-development case. Very big bikkies. Very big bruisers.'

'Bruce likes to exaggerate. This one's nothing; just takes patience, really. I rather go in for detail.' Rob dragged himself up, leaned forward for his gin and tonic. 'Bruce tells me you're in law yourself. Or in theory. Very good thing. It's like chess in the courtroom, the best barristers are theoreticians really.'

'It's not theory, it's theatre, when Rob takes the floor,' Bruce said admiringly. 'That man is like oil; seeps in everywhere, should have seen him yesterday arvo.'

'You know Bruce from way back, Boyd. Boyd is it? Then you'd know, Boyd, how he moves on the offensive. We sort of make a good team.' As he sipped his gin Robert caught Boyd's eye. Was there the barest trace of a wink?

'I've never been tempted out of the University. Though my current area of specialist research is computer technology and the law.'

'White collar crime. Boring, boring,' Bruce asserted.

'White collar crime; law of copyright; international treaties and licensing. It's really fascinating stuff, and it is a field that is opening up like wildfire. The Rights area alone has raised major theoretical discussions.'

'Perhaps we should have a chat sometime,' Rob now seemed wide awake. A drop, two drops of condensed water from his glass had spilled onto his jacket. Had he noticed? 'There are a few angles on micro-chip copyright I've been looking through lately . . . '

'Don't let him suck you for anything, Boyd. Butter wouldn't melt and all that, but you better be warned. Charge like a wounded bull. Nothing comes free. And besides,' Bruce jerked himself up, forcing the others to join him, 'it's about time we moved to the dining-room. I've booked a table.'

When they sat for their meal, Robert Huntingdon pulled his chair closer to Boyd. 'Bruce has a lot invested in this particular case, so he's a bit edgy at the moment. That's so, old boy?' he added, loudly.

Bruce was examining the menu. He appeared to have forgotten Boyd and the first flurry of solicitous enquiries. Rob moved the edges of his smile gently.

'But Bruce and I understand one another. Bruce has made himself more Brisbane than the natives. Wouldn't you agree?' Boyd resisted the collusion.

'Back in Melbourne I would have said Bruce might have become more tweed than the jacket. It was strange to see, up here, how exactly the same origins, as it were, take on a different colouration.'

Bruce looked over his menu. 'Your colouration, old chap,' he intoned, 'remains Varsity-dun and bricked up.'

Had Boyd offended? Not to worry; Bruce after these years hardly impinged.

'What I mean is,' Bruce continued, 'the old Boyd, that same one who swiped my best marbles back in fourth form, ended up in his schooldays hoarding keys – keys, can you imagine it? I remember your collection. Jeez, I thought he was the cleverest out of the lot of us!'

'Keys?'

'Yes, keys. No one was safe; that collection of keys in Boyd's pocket. He had the key to the lot of us. That's what we thought at the time. He could open up everything.'

'Oh, you had a skeleton key, something like that?'

'No,' Boyd laughed, half remembering. 'I just collected the things. I think it was more for the shapes of them, the decoration. Though I admit there was that time when I found out the *Health & Efficiency* magazine in Bruce's locker.'

'See! I started my career from that bastard's example. Though it wasn't till Brisbane that I found the real key. I call it colouration. Effective colouration.'

'As in do as the Romans do.' Rob placed a discreet finger on Boyd's wrist. 'Or if you look unobtrusively behind you, as in Pashim Khan at the next table but one.'

Bruce almost exploded. 'There's a feller I was a fool not to take on. Who would have dreamed he'd come out of it, brilliant colours.'

They all were turned now, as if to consult with the hovering waiter. At the further table the large dark man in a suit to rival Robert Huntingdon's was rising to greet some business associate who had joined him. A smile of eager welcome broke across his face. It was a smile of enormous sweetness that transformed him even as they witnessed. Boyd could imagine that person as a thin boy, a youth, almost embarrassingly beautiful, the vulnerable and pampered son of some Pakistani family, surrounded by adoring sisters and aunts, his father's most proud possession. Now, the smile still had that disturbing quality of charm though clearly it was superimposed with a more cautious social awareness.

'A fool not to take that case on.' Bruce turned to the waiter, ordered for the three of them without bothering to consult. 'Horrie will make up my usual platter and if Fruit Of The Sea isn't good enough for you, gentlemen, consider yourselves excluded.' He laughed again. 'You saw, of course, the last twelve charges dismissed. The whole bloody lot of them.'

'The whole bloody lot is not twelve charges,' Rob explained. 'It's fifty-seven.'

'Charges brought by that man over there; what's his name, Khan you said. Pashim Khan?'

'Good ear, good retentive memory. Boyd you're a loss to the industry.'

'Bruce has a habit of referring to our profession with that jaunty insolence. Goes down well with the indigenes.' Rob pointed again to Pashim Khan. 'That one over there had everything against him. But he had one hell of a good barrister. I can see why Bruce feels pipped now. With him and me on the Khan case, who knows but we might have had a similar victory.'

'And Khan himself? What were these charges he brought, and against what other party or parties?'

'Boyd, even in Melbourne you must have heard the Khan story. It hit world headlines. Police raid on slave labour camp, Commonwealth and State Police involved. Drunks bailed out from the city watchhouse for 10 cents and then used for this forced labour, their pension cheques signed over, oh, the news was full of it.'

'That was ages ago, last year, year before. I've forgotten the story. It all sounded pretty horrible.'

'There you go,' Robert poured out a wine, a white Burgundy. 'I would have thought that you, Boyd, with your theoretical sense, not to mention your adolescent preoccupation with keys, might be able to see beyond headlines.'

Boyd caught the grin between Bruce and his partner. He was invisible, a witness in some chess game. He nodded. Rob continued.

'The beauty of it becomes all too visible, now that the full scenario is over. Screaming headlines, Pakistani villain, unfashionably dark, unfashionably big, uncomfortably foreign: a line-up of poor old derros, pathetic reunions with families, and journalists digging for gossip.'

'What Rob means, Boyd, is that the whole case came down to a mob of old drunks. And I can tell you I see them in the courts all the time. Give Dad a raise he blows the lot on booze and the kids live on Kentucky Fried and Coca-Cola till it's gone, then next week the power gets cut off because no one paid the bill. Some of the ones you see, well you don't light a match within a hundred yards or the metho will ignite.'

'The newspapers had a field day,' Rob interrupted. 'Well, Boyd, just think of it. Khan is a non-Christian, a Muslim. Every time, in Iran, Ayatollah Khomeini incites murder and mayhem there are fundamentalist Christians in Brisbane reach for their whip. Just imagine Pashim Khan's own kids, going to school, say, through that gauntlet. Well, Boyd, you've got to admit there are big emotional issues at play there. Newspapers, Police, Religion. It was some line-up.'

'Fifty-seven charges. Not one stuck. That's the real story.' Bruce picked up an oyster shell, slurped. 'Taking them out of the snakepit, all those drunks, drying them out, sobering them, giving them work to do, providing board and accomodation, some bread and nourishment. Yes, giving them some self-respect if you like. There was a strong case to be made by the defence.'

'Eighteen months later, it all meant nothing. Not a thing. Not a charge has stuck.'

'I tell you what, Boyd,' Bruce looked over to Pashim Khan again, admiringly, 'just try to think of the situation. Someone would have to hose some of those wrecks down, physically, scrape the dried shit off, de-louse them, burn their clothes. It would not be too much to require in exchange an assignment of dole money, pension money, those pathetic hand-outs of cash that they'd spend on metho anyway . . . '

Boyd looked at Robert, then at Bruce. In ten years, twenty years, where would Bruce be? He saw a widow re-ordering fabrics in a comfortable high-rise, a petulant son stamping out of the room, frantic with boredom, doped to the hilt on cash.

No, it was so easy to criticize others.

Bruce reached for the wine bottle.

'A case like that was a golden opportunity.'

The Theatre Party

Little Boyd had never been out at night before. Not that he could remember. His grandmother was 'dressed to kill' as she put it. She wore a strange and hypnotic gown that swished in a lean swoop to her ankles, where the black high-heeled sandals looked astounding on someone Boyd thought of – always – as very old indeed. The dress itself was like the Gibson Girls watercolours (originals) she had in the guest-room. It was jangly in red and orange and purple. It was inspired by Bakst, she said, as if that meant anything to a twelve year old boy. It had no waist. Around the alarmingly low neckline (back and front) was a sort of ruffle. She brought out her silver fox fur.

The event was a performance at His Majesty's Theatre of *Rio Rita*, with Gladys Moncrieff – 'our Glad', as his grandmother insisted. She had known her, briefly, many years ago, she told Boyd, and was half inclined to call backstage 'just to say hello'. Only if the performance warranted it; that was understood.

Boyd listened to his grandmother's talk and understood the tingle of excitement. Would it be like the pictures, he asked?

'This is real theatre, darling. This is *there*. It is happening. Before your eyes – it is not a play of shadows.'

'Shadows?' Boyd had never thought of the cinema as being shadows.

The human passions and effects were real enough. An entire audience could shudder or laugh or even call out loud, especially in the matinees at Camberwell, where he had gone before joining the Wolf Cubs.

'You will see, Boyd. It is very exciting.'

So Boyd had watched his grandmother prepare for the event. First of all she had allowed him to see her gown, and had even, flirtatiously, sprinkled him with some of her precious perfume. He yelled furiously, which delighted her. She had shown him the long dangling earrings she intended to wear.

Why was it an occasion?

'You will see, my darling, this is the first real theatre we have had for so long – since before the War. You will not have heard of the amateur things, or the Theatre Royal with that terrible Roy Rene . . . '

Boyd was prepared to be excited, too.

It was exciting enough as they approached the foyer. Crowds of people, even though it was a sweltering night. He could see why his grandmother had decided on the gown that looked like a singlet, down to her feet. At the last moment she had abandoned the fur. He was surprised, at first, that she had powdered her back and neck. But also he was a little startled to see how not-old she was. No sagging or wrinkling, to speak of. At least, not in the exposed parts, like the shoulderblades. Around the elbows perhaps, and though he tried not to look, a certain limpness in the front, a sort of flakiness in the skin. Her neck was not as scrawny as she always said it was. How old was his grandmother? She looked ageless, younger than last year.

Someone came up to her as soon as they crossed into the lit vestibule. Boyd was concerned only with his good black shoes and at the way the heat made his grey trousers prickle already, even before they sat down for long. Later, he knew, it would get scratchy up around the crotch. Would he be able to do something about that and still not be noticed? His grandmother had eyes like serpents. No. He would have to be 'setting an example': her favourite words.

'My dear, you look like something Lady Ottoline Morrell would have envied. How audacious to startle Brisbane. Mmmmm. You wicked trollop. Oh, sorry, but of course the boy child.'

The big man lunged on one toe as if to cuff Boyd. 'And how are we today?' he bawled, as if Boyd were across the street, or the stage apron. 'And so big. Mmmm. Growing, eh? Growing?'

'Rick, don't be shameful. Boyd, this is an old friend of mine and I won't introduce you. I have to look after his moral welfare, Rick, so you will forgive the froideur . . . oh look, Boyd, there is the girl selling programmes. Do be a gallant officer and join in the queue for one.'

She fumbled in her silver-chain purse for a note. Even Boyd could see that her friend Rick was supposed to step in then, and offer to pay.

The theatre was crowded. They had seats in the front row of the dress circle. Boyd could see Rick downstairs, in his plum silk shirt and linen suit, heavy as a buffalo but strangely delicate. His grandmother told Boyd that Rick used to act once, before he got oversized. Now he was a famous radio announcer.

There was an orchestra. The sound of their tuning up was enough to hold Boyd's attention. A buzz of anticipation just in that. People were talking, shuffling programmes, detailing the way other people were dressed, calling across aisles to each other. It was all real, and unlike the pictures, yes, unlike anything. Lights dimmed. A reluctant hush, as if everyone wanted to listen but the very event was too much, it was hard now to concentrate. The conductor, in black tails and white shirt, tapped again.

Wait.

Sound: a cutting, thin splurt. After a few moments the players seemed less startled by their own noises and it all settled down to the rollocking beat and the tunes Boyd could tell people were expecting. He knew none of them, so it all sounded funny and flat and thin, scratchy: each tune ended too soon, each phrase cut off, or else slid on in a way that was not expected. Jazzy, his grandmother said, as if that explained the way it was.

The curtain opened.

After the first moments of surprise – the chorus looked so old, the costumes were not as good as even the worst movies – Boyd leaned to see what was happening. Everyone looked so small; he had to concentrate.

Gladys Moncrieff did not come on for ages and, when she did, she was old, almost as old as his grandmother. Boyd did not like her voice, it also was an old woman singing. But there was something; the audience all around told him there had to be something. They loved her, even when she had to strain for the high notes.

Later, when his grandmother asked him how he liked it he said the best bit was when two of the comics came onstage revving motorbikes. You could not explain about the music, how it had crawled in and taken him over, in the end.

Summer night outside. They had to walk to the bus stop, past the Town Hall. His grandmother had talked of going to see Gladys backstage, but in the event they went straight from the theatre. She had also talked, to Rick, during one of the intermissions, of going to Littleboys Coffee Lounge but that, also, seemed to have been forgotten.

Was Boyd to blame?

His grandmother complained at the evening chill and wished she had brought the fox fur.

She kept looking around, on the footpath, after. They had swept off together, at her command, towards Albert Street, after waiting until nearly everyone else had departed.

'We must not miss the bus.'

As they rounded the corner a disruption stopped them. A group of youths were in the middle of the road. It was a fight.

Four young men, all dressed in white, had cornered some others, and were pushing them into the middle of the street. One of the white ones grabbed an opponent and started putting a neckhold onto him. They stumbled between cars. A few people shouted but quite quickly Boyd saw that some were backing off. It was the intensity of the violence, not its actual action. It was, indeed, only the two; but just as the others in the opposing groups were dragged into their vortex, so onlookers were pushed away.

They were right in the middle of Albert Street now and a car coming uphill stopped. A horn tooted but the combatants took no notice. The one with the headhold used his other hand to punch, punch, punch his opponent. The victim tried desperately to kick and retaliate. His supporters crowded in, but not close enough. The white-clad others loomed as a sort of threat but did not engage except to make occasional strange leaps in the air, kicking wide their heavily booted feet, like a sideways mule-kick. The couple broke. There was a further scuffle but the group had shoved back to the footpath and then into the entrance of a milliner's shop. The big one in white cornered his opponent there and solemnly beat him to the ground. Boyd's grandmother stiffened and tried to move on, but Boyd had been held, mesmerized.

'Not a policeman in sight, and on Saturday night. This is scandalous,' she muttered. Other people edged away, as if they did not wish to be caught as witnesses.

'And those boys are all Grammar lads,' she concluded. She dragged Boyd on, but he looked back in time to see the victor move off, surrounded by his adoring gang, the other boy crouched almost to the ground, raising himself and holding his battered head. His supporters, one of them a girl, slowly edged in, then helped him to his feet. People made way for them.

'All of them from families that should know better. Animals.'

'How do you know, Grandma?'

'Do *not* call me that name, it's detestable, it makes me seem eighty!' But she relented. 'I recognize two of them,' she said tersely. 'And just might tell their parents.'

Boyd looked back again. The street was almost empty. Nothing had happened.

'That big one was a real bully . . . ' Boyd began.

'He'll be head of a retail empire before he's thirty,' she said briefly.

In the balmy night air a familiar restlessness of fruitbats rippled the shadows of the weeping-fig near their bus stop. The statue of George V over in the square looked stiff and noble and police-like.

'What did you think of the musical comedy?' his grandmother

asked, to change the subject. 'Did you enjoy it, Boyd?'

'The pictures have a lot more action,' Boyd began. Then, 'But the people all around us; yes, that was different.'

'Why so?'

'Well . . . well . . . I suppose because they believed those people on the stage were the people they were pretending to be. And then, then they did some of the funny bits and were pretending to be pretending, well, that was a different thing too. Like you could have both sides. The real people and the characters.'

'That's very perceptive, Boyd. I am glad I invested in you for this performance.' His grandmother caught sight of her image in the glass of the bus window as it pulled up to their stop. Boyd did not know what to say. He was thinking, still, of the boys fighting. The violence. The raw energy. The unthinking immediacy of it. It was wrong of his grandmother to spoil it all by telling him these people had names, and families, and good connections. He wanted something without past, without future. That could never be.

Boyd

Foolish, to be caught by surprise.

Foolish, and without credibility. The ironwork ripped off. The verandahs and their flooring: a warehouse, a demolition site. Hideous.

Boyd stopped so suddenly the person behind bumped into him. Muttered apologies.

'Yair. Bit of wreck ain't it. Shoulda pulled the whole lot down while they was at it. Never've guessed that was all that it was, underneath. Not with all them fancy old landings. Never guessed.'

'But that was a great old building . . . '

'Oh, yair, yair, they all say that. Fair enough, too, in its way. Look at it now but. Just goes to show.'

'Goes to show what vandalism is.' Boyd, too vehement. 'Official vandalism at that.'

'You can call it that. They certainly took the icing offa the cake. Didn't they but. Thought that was a pretty smart move, meself. Not that I wanta take sides mind youse. Couldn't care less, I didn't get caught up in all the screaming and newspaper headlines about the old pub. Never drank there meself, I usually drop in at the Carlton . . . '

'But how could they rip off the exterior? The Bellevue was the centre of public debate, people trying to save it. The National Trust had it named as a prime heritage site, architects and town planners . . . '

'That was the beauty of it. One Friday night, quiet as lambs, in they went and ripped the whole business down, all them verandahs and landings. Got 'em all hid under the Storey Bridge is what they say. After that: what odds all the talk and the National Heritage and all that. Overnight they did it. Chop. Bloody brilliant. Shut up the lot of 'em. Chop.'

'Ruined the building.'

'In this business the best man wins. The first one in. Wham. Overnight it was. Bloody marvellous. I'll vote for that sort of no-nonsense any day.'

Boyd lingered in the shadow of the gaunt shell. Monstrous not to tear it all down. Now it was merely a trophy of battle, defaced. A way for the Government to mock its opponents. Very well you can have her now she's been publicly stripped and exposed. After the ritual rape, she's yours. If you still want her.

A tall, spruce-looking man in cream linen strode out of the Parliamentary grounds opposite. Boyd stared at him with fury.

Sweat streamed down his back, it broke out on his forehead. Ridiculous to get involved in weak provincial politics and redneck scandals. Nothing to do with him. What was the joke line: when you come to Queensland put your clock back one hour and your mind forty years?

Boyd forced himself to scrutinize the building. Could it be salvaged? What would a really competent architect say? Were those verandahs merely cosmetic?

The noon air hugged him till he was breathless. Harsh sunlight scraped every brick. A small, temporary awning was erected over the main entrance. Until recently the hotel had been used to house out-of-town Parliamentarians.

It was a shell.

Marie

Marie woke with a start. A suffocating dream; someone had pushed her nose inexorably into a shallow basin of water. It was all calm, without drama or fuss. She had been in the bathroom – a bathroom – leaning over the handbasin, wringing out her hair. Whoever it was had been beside her: a hairdresser? her mother? Boyd?

No, none of them, certainly not Boyd and never her mother. The presence was too calm for those two, they would have spread instant turbulence. Someone in hospital robes, white, faceless, softly incurious.

The feeling as her face was submerged. She tried to breathe. Snorts and gulps, struggles. A white flash of instant panic: she found herself threshing the sheets and duna, gasping, coughing. Had she somehow half suffocated in the pillows? The panic had been real. Even as she rushed to her own bathroom Marie's throat felt bruised.

Her small cosmetics case from last night was out of place. Marie picked it up thoughtfully. What time did she come in? She had slept perfectly, until the breathless panic of her dream.

No, the apartment did not seem empty without Boyd. Could she admit it was because his presence still followed her?

What had he said yesterday, over breakfast? He must have said something. Did he try to, but she was already absorbed in her own events? It had been the morning of those first wretched assignments and she was desperate to be off, there were still four undone that she had promised for first lesson. Or did he notice the way she stared into her coffee because she did not really want another post-mortem on the night before?

That time, years ago, when her mother took her to the Exhibition Grounds. Hay and barns and animal odours out of some impossibly remote past to do with old estates and Europe. She dragged Marie, protesting, into the smelly stalls and among the coarse jacketed men and the big untidy boys. Amidst all this nostril-burning heartiness they came to a stall where an orange cow had given birth the night before. The calf was still wobbly but it butted against its mother's side and searched out the teat and was greedy. Helena Maria Adriana was rapturous. The more her mother laughed and pointed and slapped and fondled her the more Marie cringed. The big men.

'Marie! Marie! *Wunderbar*! *Wunderbar*!'

The one who owned the cow kept them company all that afternoon. He would perhaps have been a kind, generous man, probably the ideal stepfather, Marie suddenly realized. She had been spiteful.

'*Ach*, the young!'

'Yes, the young,' he had agreed.

Her cheeks stung. Her throat was still aching. Marie found toothpaste. This morning, at least, she had no overdue last minute assignments.

Not fair. Others escaped without guilt. What was it that made her always other? Always trapped into dependence, debt?

In the refrigerator she found the half eaten yoghurt Boyd had told her to save till he came home, it was so good. She took it and spooned greedily as if she half hoped for his taste on the spoon. The taste: a bitterness she associated with mornings and her mother's presence.

That moment of choking: had it been real?

Boyd

Following the edge of the large, shallow pond he came by a creaking clump of old bamboo to a quiet backwater of the Botanical Gardens. Boyd squatted.

Waterhen with shoe-horn red beaks dabbled, the black swan came gliding over, eager for scraps, the lazy red of its webbed feet motoring diligently under. Boyd looked deeper into the water, thick with algae and muck. There, very close, a huge eel hovered motionless. It must be several metres long.

Marie had once called his eel dream simply an inner fear of sexual urges that threatened to overwhelm him. Boyd had been indignant: he had all that under control. Hadn't he always been considerate? Efficient? There had only been that one gulping, reckless jabbing when he blindly thrust into her time after time, a whole night of uncontrolled explosions, detonations deep inside his every nerve. Hadn't she gasped, choked, gripped him passionately? and after it, after it all, hadn't she . . . ?

Boyd's limbs seemed bound with thick awkward muscles. The eel was thicker than his forearm. He pushed out through shrub thicket, tramping across composted topsoil.

He knew the way to the lotus pond. Twenty years. The grounds looked thinned out, the sun too insistent, and so many stunted trees: he remembered giants, massive bulk, towers of fig avenues. Boys on hire bikes shot by him: they should be in school.

At the lotus pond a notice still warned of the pool's dangerous depth. The floppy torn leaves drooped, tattered elephants' ears in old circuses, torn to shreds by the keeper's hook. It must be end of season. The great nozzle pods stuck up. One was broken: no petals.

Nothing.

Boyd's shoes clapped out loud challenges to the gravel as he marched back towards the entrance. Nothing.

Once there had been the frightening derros, dirty old men his grandmother used to warn him of. And younger ones: there had been something – what? Nothing to speak of. It all looked so much smaller, tawdry. For years he had been haunted by a dream in which he, himself, in some terrible future became one of their company. Sherry-stained trousers, newspaper vest, stubble and grey skin, a nose pulped by metho, mouth sensitive as a hose nozzle, a smell as the day warmed up like some disturbed edge of the mangroves, and with eyes ruptured of precision or any feeling. His grandmother's warnings had chilled him. It was as if she had some sense of his potential for destruction, the fall that he might teeter on as precariously as the edge of that lotus pond. Single men, untended, abandoned, reverting to seed and less than seed, stubble or stalk-rot. Some of them younger than he was, now. Some much younger, waiting to become what they knew they must become. And openly, welcoming it. Not to be salvaged or saved.

Control had become everything. Those plants themselves lived upon rot and decay. Their bare, black pods were like horrific sea creatures: octopus, anglerfish.

Boyd felt the good prickle of wool right along his legs, comforting the hairs of his sturdy limbs. The faint smell of his deodorant mingled with fresh sweat from his armpits. He was in control. He had never wanted for anything.

He bought an avocado. In Brisbane, Boyd tasted his first avocado. His grandmother one evening had a visitor. A doctor somebody – yes, Dr Summerskill, someone from the University. A year later Dr Summerskill had suicided, some scandal. The man had not impressed him much. His grandmother had been vivacious: the two had spent a lot of the time laughing, bantering. And her new Eton crop, the strange, glittering pretensions of the meal; she seemed to be flirting. Boyd had felt snubbed. She tried to make amends by offering the new fruit, Dr Summerskill's gift, home grown. She attempted to explain its flavour: 'If you put lots of salt and pepper with it, it tastes like tomato with lots of salt and pepper.' After his grandmother's death neither of Boyd's parents willingly mentioned her. At twenty-five Boyd received the shares in his own name.

Christmas with his grandmother was a walk in early morning light. There was always a storm the evening before, to rinse things out, as she said. Their ritual then involved the polite nod to faces in the church grounds under inevitable weeping-figs: brush of cool air from their shade, presaging another hot day and perhaps more afternoon thunder. Minah birds in the trees, competing with each other, chattering. The soft ground littered with the scurf of the tiny, dry-feeling fruit. And the church itself, hushed, distant yet comforting. A womb. Children bright-eyed and laundered, some clutching presents; their parents beefing the very hymns that had hissed out from radio and department stores for weeks. Suddenly even 'Hark, the Herald Angels' (which always went too high) became a thing roseate as the stained glass window. The little organ trundled along note-perfect. Outside, the sounds of the birds feasting; occasional creak of roof iron; the rumble of early morning traffic bouncing away from the wall boards and becoming absorbed by the dense, green canopy of weeping-fig shelter. Inside the scurry and whisper of a late arriving family; rustle of hymn books; the minister's drone.

Later, when she was dead, Boyd found himself unwilling to enter a church. He remembered, walking out from the Christmas service, how she laid her white gloved hand on his arm and her pleasure in introducing her big, young grandson to other parishioners, as if his face were as clear as an altarboy's.

He scooped out more avocado. A small, tight cell stuck in his tongue-hollow. Boyd spat it out. Tight energy ball where some insect had bitten, injecting its poisonous fluid.

Grandmother's New Year party had been a failure. Apart from Handley Shakespeare there were only heavy, elderly people, damp armpits and clothing stretched to discomfort. All of them talking over his head, at each other. It was the first year Boyd had become aware of how much the body sweated. His grandmother's among them. He had hated Dr Summerskill. He had hated the way she was so attentive, always laughing and mocking.

Boyd put down the shell of his avocado. Noises and laughter. The girl, Cora. Flick-sound of water.

Cora was standing, soaked, under one of the big mango-trees. Her clothing clung to her, licking each part. The hose was turned on her body. It made her dance and was what caused the laughter. Don, deep in the shade of the tree, was directing the nozzle. Cora tried to splash back at him, but that was ineffectual, and made them both laugh in continuous bursts. She slipped off her wet singlet – the breasts had unexpectedly dark, wide nipples. They bounced firmly and as if in slow motion. The fingers of her hair as she tossed it made playful darts to grasp the exposed places.

She threw the garment at Don. Direct strike. Then she bent down, unzipped her tight denim, to step up, wholly naked now, under the hosewater. Again, she hit target. Now she revelled in it, and ordered his motions, lifting an armpit, then the other; cupping out her legs. Laughing, she directed his aim. Don dropped the hose.

'Now my turn.'

Cora danced to the twisting hose, picked it up and proceeded to drench Don. The pale texture of her skin, luminous under the mango-leaf shadow. A creature fully co-ordinated. Boyd moistened his lips, unaware of the action.

Under Cora's attack Don quickly stripped. His thin body plantlike, a beanpod, awkwardly beautiful. Anything young must look beautiful. Boyd was aware of his own forehead just thinning, the slight paunch, thick shoulders. Don's skin was smooth as Cora's, but lines and strokes, vertical. Although taller by a good six inches, he looked hardly a third her size, unformed, tentative, just getting the hang of his own body. His genitals, wizened by spray and cool shadow, moved with the same bulky awkwardness of his large wrists and knees. The dog, Kali, jumped round the edges, bright eyed. The couple played in the water, their bodies a game of sunlight and shadow.

Under the second mango-tree was the other one, Olof. Leaning against the trunk, also watching.

After a few more moments Olof stepped out of the deep shadow and to the garden tap, with its ancient giant clam drip-tray. A few firm turns with his strong, dark-haired wrist and the hose went limp. The others stopped playing.

Olof looked up to Boyd. Nodded.

Cora saw him and waved. 'Come and cool off.' Olof took his own clothes off, insolently.

'You got a hard-on up there?'

Don picked up the hose then and drenched Olof, aiming at his mouth.

Impossible proximity. Boyd walked out in late afternoon light. He discovered the Planetarium in the foothills of Mount Coot-tha nearby. He bought a ticket and lined up with school groups in uniform and the dozen pensioners.

The chairs were spaced apart. They could swivel. Raised on a central dais, the complex projecting unit tilted in the centre, a Science Fiction altar.

The door closed. Curtains were drawn. The soft lit dome slowly began to dim. On the point of near darkness the first simulated stars began to glimmer.

Suddenly a woman beside Boyd lurched to her feet, jolting into him with shopping bags and purse.

'I've got vertigo, vertigo. I can't stand this darkness! Vertigo!' She bumped into seats, caught in her own spinning motion. A dark figure rose, guided her to the exit. As the door opened, light knifed in.

Sound of the curtain being pulled tight. A dark more intense this time.

A voice infinitely cool, soothing, rational, explained the enduring wonder generated by the simple act of watching the night sky: *Time is something elusive which lies at the very centre of our lives . . . sometimes we get the merest hint of its shadow in the works of scientists and poets . . . one of mankind's earliest perceptions was the passing of time . . . the sun across the heavens . . . would the sun never return?* Space/time. The way light reaches us a fraction later from far-off things. Stars. Star clusters. Nebulae of definite shape – spiral, elliptical. Boyd wriggled to watch the clear points as directed by small arrows. The great spiral galaxy in Andromeda that takes two million light years to reach Earth. Comfort of numbers. The Virgo supercluster. And the voice explaining calmly: all clusters moving away faster and faster, the universe expanding.

Suddenly, complete dark.

Then a concentration of unfocused light, large above him as a blurred tablecloth, all colours, too close to the eyes. *At the beginning of time all galaxies were in the same spot . . . this was perhaps 15,000 million years ago . . . in the beginning energy dominated . . . cooled . . . a small portion became mass . . . clouds condensed by gravity . . . within proto-galaxies shining to convert mass into energy . . . planets now containing oxygen, carbon, hydrogen, all that was necessary for life . . .* and the wonderful Einstein, 'the most incomprehensible thing about the Universe is that it is comprehensible'. Boyd was absorbed into the voice. *But light can be bent by gravity. When stars shine their own gravity causes them to be reddened . . .* The arrow pointed to Sirius, the Great Dog and its faint companion star, dim and small ('the size of earth') that weighs infinitely more than our planet, tugged by a gravity we could not understand – dim stars that suck in all light, that bending curve, tugging energy, plughole suction, black holes of force. Boyd tried to feel under his tongue for the irritation of avocado.

On their honeymoon, in that clearest tropic night sky, Marie would lie on the warm sand gazing up. She reproached Boyd for his restlessness and regretted that neither had been educated to name the stars. 'There's the Southern Cross. And that's Orion,' Boyd had offered. The rest, a blank. Boyd, always indoors first, turning on the safe light. Inside, air that seemed endlessly used. They had thought they might learn the constellations together. Instead, Marie had bought a cheap pack of Tarot cards, and they tried to spook themselves with fortune telling.

Marie

Dagmar had been right, make it everyone.

Some of the early arrivals gravitated naturally to the kitchen, where they draped themselves around and against the fridge. Boyd's note remained with perhaps cruel obviousness so that everyone's first word was a sort of initiation test. Would they pretend not to read it and say nothing? Did they reach out small antennae of sympathy and support for Marie? If they did, she was not having any of it.

Dagmar had been the first. 'Well, you must get rid of this!' she had exclaimed as soon as she came in to help with things. She scattered the fruit-magnets to all corners as she wrenched the note off. But Marie had insisted it be returned to its place, a sort of icon. She was in a mood to be prickly, protective of Boyd against any bad-mouthing. Dagmar announced a moratorium on the name. This was, after all, to be Marie's night.

In the kitchen some guests cushioned plump jeans against the sink; some tried not to slide the kitchen table. Marie became the acknowledged centre of conversation.

Later arrivals moved to the living area. The corner chair was, by a sort of tacit agreement, reserved for Marie. Her nest of belongings and possessions made even the most obtuse male, sniffing out comfort and position, hesitate to claim it. But most of the guests were young, younger. They sat with springy limbs on the floor, muscles flexible as grass.

School had been trying. Marie wanted to call off the whole damned thing, she did not want to have private matters publicized. Nothing is private in this life, Dagmar promised, and it's the best thing possible to have your friends around when you need them, company gets you out of yourself. After last night. After this morning.

Marie wore her soft cashmere pullover with the roll-neck and her black velvet trousers. Dagmar protested: put on something to startle!

But Marie insisted. Dagmar herself could get away with murder, even her Magyar outfit, though it emphasized her shortness. She made up for that with animation. As the night went on her voice grew faster, slipping through a whole range of accents. Dagmar was a tonic.

The trouble, Marie realized, with impromptu parties like this is that one is never really prepared, there is no focus.

The focus was present, but undeclared. Marie and Dagmar had spent the time after school in making a frantic round of phone calls. One would make coffee or list down more names while the other dialled. Then there was the problem of snacks, drinks. They began to ask some to bring cheesecake. It would be haphazard, Dagmar declared, but no hassle. Hazardous, Marie agreed, but what the hell. Something of their over-bright infection must have been communicated. People arrived at the flat with an already eager anticipation. It would succeed.

The group from the Dance Mime Theatre turned up first. Marie had not met any of them, but Hughie slipped in and embraced Dagmar and then gave Marie a peck on each cheek. Hughie, it turned out, was born at Charters Towers, Queensland. The four girl dancers seemed subdued, bantam hens around Hughie's vivacious gesturing, as he instantly took in the rooms, opted against the living space and installed himself on a kitchen stool in charge of orange juice. It was as if he needed his consort to protect him from outsiders. They were exhausted from the rehearsals, he confided, but any request from Dagmar, or her mother, well that was almost a royal command and look at her, how magnificent, wasn't her new cropped hair magnificent.

One of the bantams offered to try on Dagmar's embroidered jerkin, and was instantly translated into a Lehar operetta princess. Dagmar laughed and offered the garment to Hughie. He leapt, in one sudden motion, onto the kitchen table and began what must have been a spirited czardas, humming and miming a cembalom accompaniment. With wild abandon he jumped off again and landed on his knees at Marie's feet, rattling all the glassware in the kitchen cabinets.

'You twit!' But she laughed, too, and accepted it.

Others began to arrive. Tall Don from the Life Energy Centre, with his curious pop eyes and stoop. He brought carrot juice. With him was a young girl Marie had not met before who said her name was Moss. Like Don, she had a slow smile that stayed for long periods, as if each experience in life were to be savoured for a time and then replaced by something. Their eyes skimmed over the dancers as they sought out their right place. It was not the kitchen. Because of other guests Marie almost forgot them until she discovered them later in the spare bedroom.

'Marie! Mmmmmmm my peppermint baby!' Geoff from school, big, beery Geoff with his wife Karen, more doll-like than ever but with precise appraisal of everything, everyone. Marie liked Karen. Geoff finished his bearhug and turned round looking for another victim. Dagmar offered a cheek, still the operetta queen. Geoff, despite his seventeen-stone rumble, caught her pat, instantly:

'Moussie, who were you with last night ta-ta-boom ta-ta-boom . . . '
He patted her rump after she made a pirouette and then turned upon the four dancers who cringed behind the imitation-Swedish table.

'And who are these delicious confections!' he bellowed and advanced.

'Maul me and I'll bite your nipple off!'

Hughie came to the rescue. 'It's been a tough rehearsal . . . '

Geoff bellowed his approval and recovered, as usual, with an alacrity surprising in one so huge. Deep inside, Marie often thought, must be a very thin, sprightly, little fellow, a featherweight boxer on his toes.

'All those nipples underfoot. I get the picture. Ladies, your servant. M'sieu'.' Geoff reached out both arms to Hughie's narrow shoulders, held him in place, and then planted two mushy kisses.

'Your servant,' Hughie replied in kind, then offered orange juice, perhaps with a glint. The four dancers seemed a tighter knot. Geoff led the way into the living-room.

'So the old man's gone walkabout?' he swept Marie along with him.

'Half his luck. Queensland. The Gold Coast.'

'No. Brisbane.'

'I'd check that out.' But catching his wife's eye, Geoff gave a wink. 'If it were me, the Gold Coast any time. For the all-over tan, you understand.' And he slapped his huge girth. 'Though I don't see Boyd very much as the outdoor type meself.' It was the thought of Geoff, brazen in bikinis, exposing his drum-tight belly that made Marie smile. She offered pretzels. She saw to it everyone had a drink. She avoided mirrors.

Dagmar, after one or two sorties to test out the other rooms, ended up prettily perched on the kitchen table. The dance group had discovered old friends. The two librarians, Peter and Ian, followed and joined them.

'Marie. Just settle in one place. Join in the conversations. People can help themselves.'

Someone had broken a glass in the hallway. Marie was there, mopping up.

Someone had enthused about the *Mondkuchen* Marie's mother used to make. Marie was there, with samples.

After a while, though, she threw herself into the corner chair. Its circle of her possessions seemed to isolate her, hemming her in. She had never identified Boyd with her mother, hammering in some inescapable past. This whole room was his witness.

She leaned forward to hear the others. The room was no longer Marie's nor Boyd's. It had become the rampaging ground for big Geoff and a group of teachers. Staff-room talk could be heard at any recess during workhours. Marie heaved herself out with the intention of refilling her glass, which had emptied too quickly.

Around the dining-room table was a younger group. Marie recognized them as some of Boyd's students. One – Rosie – was reading the Tarot. The faces were absorbed, serious, utterly believing. Marie went over. She should tell Dagmar who was a sucker for things like this.

Rosie had just finished shuffling her cards. She placed them in front of a small, thin-haired girl who was cracking her knuckles edgily under the table. Marie recognized her as the daughter of a prominent Senator. He had recently re-married. The daughter, Deb, was having her third try at a First Year Pass course in English under some form of special dispensation from the Registrar.

'Take thirteen cards,' instructed Rosie in a flat voice.

'Are you supposed to do that?' Marie could not help herself. 'Let someone else touch your own Tarot pack, I mean?'

Rose looked up sternly.

'Someone once told me the magic was lost if anyone touched your pack,' Marie tried to explain. Six pairs of eyes around the table reproached her. 'But I guess each person has their own way of doing it.'

How could they believe in this crap?

'This is my way,' Rosie insisted. 'It works for me. If you want to do it differently, that's okay by me. I'll even let you use my pack.' Rosie had eyes glazed in what could be absorption. Her hair was an untidy wreck of strings and strands. She looked the part, Marie conceded. And then hated herself.

'The essence of a Tarot reading,' Rosie explained, though not looking at Marie, 'is probably guided by the laws of chance. But I also happen to believe in certain fields of positive and negative attraction. Now Deb can take the cards from anywhere in the pack she likes. Or,' she did turn to Marie now, 'she could shuffle the pack herself and then deal from the top. My reading is based on these intuitions, I can only do it this way.'

'Look, I'm not criticizing. Sorry. Perhaps I'm a bit edgy anyway. It's only that someone else once . . . '

'It's a matter of yourself. What you yourself believe. What you yourself *will*. After all it's probably a matter of will as much as anything. Unconscious will. We use that all the time.' Rosie motioned again to Deb, as if to continue, though the silence was entirely respectful and she knew it. 'Strictly speaking, there is no such thing as an accident. We are heading in a direction all the time, probably from birth, and everything we do contributes to that. To that acceleration.

to that direction. We are always being surprised by events only because we refuse to admit the influences at work.'

'Oh, what tosh!' Marie, impatient, made to rise. But Deb caught her with a thin, knobby hand.

'Don't say that. It isn't tosh. It can help you. You weren't here when Rosie read Craig's Tarot.' Craig, beside her, nodded. His fair hair flopped over his eyes. His own future looked utterly predictable, down to the seat on the Stock Exchange. 'The cards had it all. Eerie. About my nineteenth birthday party and what a bummer it was and how there had been that fight. And how I was going to meet someone who would change my life, and . . . ' Deb gripped his arm.

'Forget the oldies, Rosie. They don't *want* to know if they have ballsed themselves up, or if they are going to keep on ballsing themselves up.' Then she whispered: 'Can you imagine my father having his Tarot read? He couldn't see a light shining out of his own arse. He's too busy licking it himself.' The tight vehemence and oafishness of her remarks, Marie thought, already made Deb vulnerable to any influence, benign or malignant.

'Here are my thirteen cards, Rosie. Do I turn them up?'

Despite herself, Marie watched. The pack was a new one, with pictures in a slightly decadent, Art Nouveau style. Marie refrained from stating a preference for the old Marseilles figures, crude and worn as they were. Of the thirteen cards most were only numerals of the Minor Arcana, the equivalent of common playing cards but the four suits more blatantly reformed into cups, swords, staves, coins. Three were cards of the Major Arcana, that set of pictorial stepping stones up through scholasticist theories of the seven stages towards heaven. First card was the hanged man.

'That's a very affirmative sign,' began Rosie, lightly touching it with her finger. Marie noted that she was left-handed. Boyd had a thing about left-handers. It was quite irrational.

'Though coming first, the hanged man does indicate an early period of great instability, of being upside-down as it were, forced by external pressures to this position. You note how the man is hanging upside-down, by his feet, not his neck? And that is followed by the seven of cups. You will be emptied to be refilled.'

Deb leaned forward, nodding.

Marie got up again from the circle of believers. Rosie was still staring at the cards, glazed, absent. Deb, who screamed with each tension-racked gesture for reassurance, would get it. Rosie was no fool. You will be emptied to be refilled. Oh, the pompous young.

But when she refilled her glass from the cask in the refrigerator Marie came back to the dining-table. The circle of theatricals in the kitchen had become jarringly self-involved.

'The repast still continuing?' she asked brightly as she returned. Perhaps the gloss of the kitchen camp had rubbed off. Perhaps she was by nature always a bitch. Perhaps she trusted nobody, least of all herself.

Deb looked up at her slowly. 'You're just so closed off. So hemmed in with your own concerns. You don't *want* to understand anything, or anybody. Not even yourself. And yet you're running from yourself all the time. Nobody could blame Boyd for . . . ' But her friend Craig reached out and covered her mouth. Deb burst into tears on his shoulder.

'It was not a very – cheering – reading.' Craig murmured, as if in apology. Deb thrust up her face again.

'But at least I can face up to it. I'm strong. At least I'm strong enough to look hard at my own direction.'

'What sort of cruel mumbo-jumbo are you into?' Marie turned to Rosie, who had been shuffling and reshuffling her cards.

'You came back here because you knew I would have to read yours, too.'

'And then we'll do the I Ching,' Marie taunted. But she knew Rosie was right.

As if she were about to play gin rummy, Marie sat down. She held out her hand for the cards. Rosie gave them one more shuffle and then passed them over.

'Yes. You shuffle. I can feel the energy level from here,' Rosie murmured. Her supporters glared at Marie. It seemed everyone had forgotten whose house this was, whose party, who it was in aid of. The wave of self-pity was almost overwhelming. Boyd's hand on her shoulder, he would have been leaning forward now, in enjoyment throwing himself into the game of it all, half jocular, half credulous. Marie shuffled long and hard. Boyd's hands, fingering her still, impatient to reach out and do the shuffling for her, even this. Her mother, probing, telling her *now*, finish shuffling *now*. Marie snapped down her thirteen cards into a circle clock-face, with the last card in the centre. Without waiting, then, she turned them all up.

Later, after they had all gone: Dagmar whisked away by the late-staying mime group, big Geoff turned into a slow teddy-bear, the students off early and indignant, the Moss and Life Energy People routed, the librarians tipsily flirtatious with anyone safe (then having a tiff as to which one would order the cab, which one's turn to pay), after wives had mopped glasses, husbands finished off dregs, and after Marie had finally removed Boyd's note from the door, she sat down alone in her chair. Boyd would have enjoyed the party. He would have hated it.

These rooms had been inhabited, shared. A tight pain in her neck which had been there all night seemed at last to have gone. A good party can leave its ghosts a very long time. Some rooms can live forever on the memory of a special party or event, her mother had once told her.

Why this sudden reaching out to memory? Souvenirs, keep-sakes... Marie looked around. She began to count every item in her room. The catalogue began with furniture. The dining-room chairs, seen through the half-opened screen doors: they looked suddenly rather sculpted, pieces of a modern art work in the shape of a horse with thin thin legs and high neck and flat disc face. Hadn't Donald Friend had an exhibition of Trojan Horse drawings and sculpture at one time? The Trojan horses in her dining-room were docile now. Just a little mysterious.

Certainly edgy.

The coffee-table. Boyd had given it to her last Christmas and it still had a settling-in look. Deep blue enamelled tiles. Blue of Boyd's eyes.

Her look moved to the other furniture. The Turkish rug, another gift.

Strange how Boyd had impressed himself so completely into this room. If asked, Marie would have said she had chosen it all herself. They had shared. He had learned her tastes, had moulded his own to them: a room so unlike his own parents' house. They had been in this together.

The revolving bookcases. That had been special, she remembered that auction. Little brass buddha. The two cloisonné vases. Murano glass. At a certain point their tastes had been formed, had grown, had merged. The last card in her Tarot reading had been the Queen, upside down in her own element, water. It meant, Marie had corrected Rosie, too great a reliance on mirrors, and she had confessed to that quite easily. Rosie had scooped the pack up and called a halt to the game of fortune telling. 'You will not admit it,' Rosie had hissed, 'you will not admit to yourself what your hand is telling you, or how great is the danger of drowning.' Drowning in what? Myth? Memory? The past with its hocus-pocus? The cards had come up with not a single image that hinted at Boyd. Now, as she thought it over, it was as if there were no burden.

Boyd

On the front porch the three young people sat cross-legged in a rough circle. They were sipping soup. Kali threw itself down with muzzle instantly at rest in the lap of Cora's thin Indian sari. Darkness was sliding over, a dull bruise from the east.

When Boyd looked at Cora he saw the girl naked under the hose and mango shadow.

Don wriggled thin buttocks in white cotton. 'How's it going?'

Boyd heard his own voice mutter a reply, as if it were a stranger's.

'You're unwinding.' Cora was specific. 'Don't rush it; just let it happen. I'll get some more of this lentil soup.' She scambled up. The dog resettled, this time into Don's groin. Don began to push it off but his long fingers, ruffling and fondling, remained tousled in the dog's hair.

Olof was smoking, readymades.

The silence seemed to bank up around them. If it broke, Boyd could be pulled into some vortex beyond his control.

'Hey; seeen this?' Don lurched up to proffer Boyd a crumpled newspaper cutting. 'Best idea for this country in ages.' He flopped back down. 'Well. Read it out.'

'Yair. Read it to us. Gotta hear this again,' endorsed Olof.

It was a letter to the editor of the journal, headlined 'Unfurling a National Non-Flag'.

As a new national flag, how about a neat sheet of transparent plastic? Think of it: around the world, wherever and whenever all flags fly, there would flutter the bold Oz blank. All eyes would pick it out. Tongues would wag. It would grab not only the attention but also the mind. What, the world would ask, does it mean? The Oz non-flag would be our golden opportunity to show the way to the brave new world. Meanwhile, as a symbol it would work on another level.

'I dig that, man, I really dig that.'

'Better than the car sticker: Up Australia.'

They didn't even know what they were playing with. Control, Boyd felt: control, control.

'Watcha do for a living?' Olof proffered his pack. 'Or you on the dole?'

'I'm in law. University, not private practice.'

Don had a face so smooth he might almost not have begun to shave. 'Good bread?'

'You could call it that.' Too tight. Relax. Without Cora the tensions pulled at the space betwen words. 'The real value for me, though, is the time. For my own research. That gives me some independence.'

They shuffled and nodded.

'That's how I could come up here. Finish a paper I'm to deliver at a conference. In May.'

'Conference, eh? The old Expense Account racket.'

'Doesn't have to be, Olof.' Don reached over for a cigarette from the pack on the floor. 'My uncle the barrister; seems he never stops working. Workaholic.'

'Millionaire, too, dead cert.' Olof's voice sounded a full octave deeper than Don's but was not. It had to do with the delivery, a sort of throaty vibrato.

'He's not short for a dollar.' Don, a reed instrument. 'Boyd, hey! What's your conference paper on about?'

Boyd's own voice, carefully modulated (it had pleased his grandmother). 'Nothing you'd find interesting. White Collar Crime and Computers.'

'Hey spot-on. Spot on but. You should hear stories around here. Not the kids doing a bit of break and entry; veggies from Woolworth's . . . '

'Or cigarettes . . . ' Olof grinning.

'The cops here couldn't care less about white collar crime. They've got orders. Not the white collar crims, they're onto us lot.'

Cora returned. Boyd squatted down then, hunkers.

Her body, leaning down to hand him the dish. The careless confidence of it. A sort of arrogance.

'This is nice. Thank you.'

'Cora's a pretty good cook. You better know it.'

Olof was swarthy. As he aged he would be heavy, more surly. Yugoslav: and a Muslim. Difficult to understand, here in Australia, cut off from original territorial claims. Unreal that only hatreds should still generate energy.

'Big earthquakes this week in Yugoslavia, I see. You have relatives there Olof?'

'No relatives. My family's here. Brisbane: Inala. Far as I'm concerned none of *them's* family neither. Not any more.'

'Brisbane seems to have quite an Islamic community. I saw someone in the city today, at the Brisbane Club. Name of Khan . . . '

'Not Pashim Khan?'

'That's right. Pashim Khan. He'd been in the papers . . . '

'Been in the papers? That bugger's notorious! He's the one with the slave camps, kept them prisoners and took their pension cheques, all those old watchhouse derros . . . '

'Yes, I believe it was something like that. Pashim Khan. He looked Pakistani . . . '

'Lots of Pakistanis in the Brisbane Muslim lot. A few Yugoslavs, though most of *them's* Christians. Slovenes. A few families: us. And the Sprecaks. But I'm out of that scene. Ever since Dad kicked me out. That was it. Over. One day I'll get him.' Olof's eyes trapped the light like very sharp metal.

Cora had been silent. 'Fathers are to be squeezed for all they're worth. That's their only value.'

The boys looked down awkwardly. Boyd scratched the thinning part of his forehead. He lifted his spoon for another sip.

'Fathers are less than shit.'

He didn't know the rules.

'Oh, forget I said that!' Cora thwacked her head above her ears. Then she jumped up. 'Come on, if we're going to that thing at the Uni.' She grabbed Don by the arm.

Elbows and ankles, brown skin and a flurry of excuses. Boyd felt dismissed. An ancient, small hurt tightened again. But Don paused to explain. There was a meeting on campus, a group to picket outside Parliament House to protest the threatened Bellevue Hotel.

'Thought that was old news.'

Don held up his hand wisely. 'While it's standing, there's hope.'

'Yeah. And besides,' added Olof, 'someone's got to fight them bastards.'

Boyd eased himself onto the floor. He stretched out his legs.

'At last the penny drops.'

'Meaning?'

'The idea of saving an old National Trust building. You lot: the connections didn't fit. I would have thought you would be against all the business of conservatives clinging to the past.' He could hear his voice expanding, taking over. 'After all, the Bellevue was a home for the real conservatives: my lot if you like. But Olof has put his finger on the pulse of it. You're just interested because it is a fight, a bit of street theatre, basic energy, a game to be mucked around with. You're not really interested in the building . . . '

'Now hold on,' Cora flashed. 'You know bugger all about this, and bugger all about us and what we want or what we stand for or what we are on about. You come here, flashing your Melbourne hoppy-badge as if you knew a damn thing about the Bellevue . . . '

'But have you seriously thought through the issues? Why do you think it's raised a storm? What does the Government have in mind by tearing it down? After all, the National Trust is one of their own constituents, all the farmers and graziers who made it a home from home most of this century . . . '

'You're out of it. Those types stay at the Crest, at Lennons . . . '

'Still, by tearing it down, what's gained? Well?'

Don took up the challenge. 'We all know that they want to put up another glass tower. It's just good real estate.'

'Oh, real estate. The thought uppermost in every picketer's mind. You hadn't considered the hidden agenda?'

That held them. 'What do you mean?'

'Okay, the Government's a coalition, Liberals and Country Party. Sorry; they call themselves National Party now. The Liberals are the Queensland Club, the Brisbane Club. Industry. The City. Ones who should have an itch to save old buildings perhaps, join the National Trust. Not the country members; you're probably right. Too used to ripping down everything that moves. Yet it's the Nationals, the Country Party, who are on the upgrade here, while the Libs are losing their grip. Think of it as a game of power. To catch out their so-called partners, the Liberals, in their own stronghold. Embarrassing eh?

Makes them look weak and sentimental? It's true.' Boyd felt himself warming to his subject as if it did not concern him at all. 'It's true: the midnight decision to rip off the verandahs and cast iron was a tactical masterstroke. No need to bulldoze the whole edifice. The point was made and who wants to fight over the carcase?'

'We do.'

'So you say. But I wonder. Let's follow through the exercise.' This was Boyd the Uni lecturer. 'The Liberal supporters of National Trust and old values are clinging to a box of old bricks, nothing more. While the Nationals, bam-thrust, the Nationals have shown energy, decisiveness, and damned clever tactics. The hidden agenda has been successful. Oh yes, there is supposed to be an Opposition Party too. Sorry; have they said anything on this issue? I haven't heard.'

'You're a cynical bastard. Nothing has value for you.'

Boyd ignored her. 'What I don't understand is why you lot all seem so activated. Okay, so you're agin' the Government. And okay, so it's as good as the circus to crowd round or dish out a demonstration. But have you, any of you, ever been inside the old Bellevue? Does it in itself really mean anything? Enough to get yourself arrested or black-listed or whatever?'

'I went there once,' Don said quietly. 'My uncle – the barrister – held a function there. I was just little. It was all pretty grotty then, really run down.'

'You see.'

'No. Not at all. It was grotty but I was aware pretty sharply that it was also something rather special. You know; I remembered it. And the cast iron verandahs. They were something again. I mean, when they were suddenly not there. Sometimes you have to have it taken away before you realize . . . '

'It was enough for it just to be there. Everyone in Brisbane knew that. It was . . . it was history. It was something the city was, or had been. We all knew that. Even at high school we went on parties just to examine it from the outside . . . '

'Yeah? Yeah, you do that too? We did that,' Olof grinned.

'Someone's got to stand up to them. Make them put it all back. If you lie down and take it passively, you don't know what they'll do next. Another midnight smash up. – Cloudland Ballroom... the old Museum building...'

'What do they want in its place?'

Boyd stood up. 'The Bellevue. That pathetic, old shell...'

'Hey. Hey Boyd baby, you know something? You sound to me like you're pretty familiar with the old Bellevue yourself. That's some head of steam you're building up. You know.'

'Yes. I know the Bellevue. It should be razed to the ground!'

'To hell with you, man. You know nothing.'

'I know enough. I know enough: too much. No, perhaps I am being unfair. When you see something terrible, you can only react two ways; throw yourself into fixing it; or throw yourself into ridding yourself of it.'

'That what you're trying to do with your marriage?'

Boyd moved closer to Cora. 'I think you might apologize for that.'

'Okay,' her grin tightened. 'I think I might too. But you know,' she chose her words carefully, 'you're down to ground zero, right at this moment. And I thought you were... you know, Boyd, I thought you were sort of terrific.'

Don jumped up. He put his arms around her protectively.

'Just ignore the bastard, Cora, just ignore him.'

'You lot. You lot.' Boyd swung his shoulders. 'You think you've got a monopoly on feelings. Damn it all, I'm the one, the only one here with a whole past invested in that dump. It's part of me, part of my own flesh. How do you think I felt when I went down there and saw it?'

They did not answer him.

'How do you think I felt?'

'That's just it,' Cora had regained control now. 'That's just about it.'

Something was amiss. What had altered? Carefully Boyd placed his door key on the little front-room table and then looked around more closely.

Things had been changed in his room. He had not left his suit trousers as crumpled as that, over the back of the other chair, surely? Over the chair, certainly, but as always, neatly folded, and not that chair, the one near the door. Had someone gone through the pockets?

And the wardrobe, in the second room, lolling open. Boyd went through the apartment. He could find nothing missing. But the sense of another presence, scrutinizing his things, looking for something: perturbing.

Outside, in the new darkness, he could hear a motor revving, a TV sound across the road, children squabbling. His old bedroom looked skeletal. And this front-room somehow leeched back to its original bedroom, the forbidden grandmother room he had only once or twice entered. The first time he had wanted to look at himself in the cheval glass. Nobody saw him, but that did not ease the burden of conscience. He had confessed, later. His grandmother had forbidden him baked rice custard for the rest of the holiday.

It was late when he heard the others come back.

'Put the dog out!' Olof ordered. Boyd could almost feel those strong teeth snapping, sculpting out the short vowels.

'No, she can come in.' It was Cora, with her own authority.

The overheard snippet, suddenly loud, unexpected, outside his thin door, seemed to reverse all Boyd's expectations. What really went on, or was going on? Who were those people?

Boyd slammed his head under the pillow.

Inside his ears the pulse throbbed, like tides, like the waters dividing. Why had he never conceived of his grandmother as a person consumed by hate? Why could he not accept that Marie's action over his corner chair was the cold deliberation of hate? Or even his own need to supervise her, help her: could that be anger and something more than anger – not really helpfulness, thoughtfulness, consideration at all?

Boyd called it love, but Marie was right, he was uptight with suppressed angers. This girl mocked him. Boyd the Professional, Boyd the provider. Good husband Boyd, Boyd the warm lover – mocked by obscene pets. Even his own self-pity was a mockery of real feeling. Bruce, cynical go-getting transparent Bruce: he was cold-headed and right. Cora: there was something further; he knew this girl instantly, there was some mysterious act of recognition. And with Marie? Entirely. Perhaps his grandmother. Marie had said: 'You never see me as I really am,' but she was wrong. Marie herself could never see her own full dimension. It is like a mirror when you look in: every muscle strains, or freezes. Marie was wrong. Her act of assault upon Boyd's special corner betrayed only herself. The pulse beat was less insistent. Boyd had turned the evidence. He could sleep.

WEDNESDAY

Boyd

Boyd lay asleep in a pool of sunlight. It was past eight a.m. He had begun to perspire. He had jerked away most of the bedclothes. On his side, he had curled into the foetal position: a sleep too deep for dreams. Slowly the edges blurred, he was being drawn out. Someone was shaking him.

He was being followed, manipulated. His body stretched, his legs unbuckled.

He rolled, then, on to his back. The blood began coursing, he heard the pulse filling his ears, felt the tingling fingers and toe joints.

Boyd spread his arms sharp sideways. He encountered firmness, a body.

With a start he was awake.

There, looking over him, was Olof. He had been shaking Boyd's shoulder, trying to rouse him. Now he stepped back a pace.

'Hey! Boyd, Boyd! Only just waking yuz. You was right down *there*.' A pause. 'That's some proud one.'

Boyd clutched for the covers, anger suffusing him.

'We been talkin' about you,' Olof continued inexorably. 'Decided you're okay, just ignorant. Decided we should all get to know each other.' Boyd caught the glint. 'Decided to give you a treat, Boyd man. Take you up river, up to Lone Pine. You know, the Sanctuary. How about that? No no no not yet, don't answer. You're not awake.' He was grinning like a crunchy white apple, red skinned. 'You come over our side, soon's y'r ready. Have a coffee, some muesli. See yuz.'

A body taut as a spring, a rifle body, dangerous. Olof's voice had been coaxing. Apples; a whole orchard; traps and rifles.

Boyd was sure he had locked his door.

All this threat. All this spying. In the shower Boyd willed himself to accept that, with these kids, once you abandon the notion of privacy, then there's nothing that's private, nothing to worry about. Like the film clips of bush communes, Nimbin, whole families squatting down together out in the open, crap parties, bog sessions, communal shitting. What's so private? Universal function. Sex. Universal function. Sleep. Universal. Morning erections. Public knowledge, why the hassle?

The old fear of vulnerability.

Boyd rubbed himself firmly, slapped the towel over himself. He groomed himself in the mirror.

Their front door was open. This was the first time Boyd had gone through that door since 1959. He paused. The arch into the front parlour. His grandmother in the next room or back in the golden kitchen. His father must have sold the whole place furnished. Through the wider arch Boyd saw the white-cedar dining-suite. The chairs, like ghosts still around the table, head-high. Boyd had played horse-and-carriage at that dining-table, with the four side-chairs as horses.

The fireplace. Boyd walked over. The four plaques, Roman medallions.

'G'day there. See how I cleaned it up?' Cora's voice was cool, candid. 'Someone, would you believe, had it painted all over with silverfros'.'

She grabbed his hand to make him touch the cleaned plaque. Her fingers appealing to the vulnerable in him.

'You've got it looking just as I remember. I always thought it was the most terrific fireplace. We had nothing like that at Canterbury. Just gas: central heating.'

'These grates went out of fashion. It was all boarded up when we moved in. Been working on it.'

'You see,' Boyd went along with her, 'I told you that you'd like my grandmother.' He dusted his fingers. 'She would have approved of this. Of you.'

Of course he meant it. This girl: yes of course his grandmother would. All that energy.

'Thank her for me.'

'No. I'm thanking you. For her.'

'Well. Come into the kitchen. We live there.'

What had Boyd expected? The old corn-yellow seersucker check curtains, his grandmother's array of earthenware canisters, the teacaddy with its much worn kangaroo and koala and emu in relief, the huge open dresser with its line of maroon-and-gold edged crockery, the butcher's chopping-block near the larder door where you could hack at anything and not be scolded; the deal tabletop where if you cut you would certainly be scolded: one must never expect to recover the original kitchen, not ever again.

This room was a transit-station. On the walls were stuck, with crude tacks or anything handy, what seemed the most frequently used implements: a rotary egg-whisk, bottle-opener, a string ball, serving tongs, handmitts and a bag with onions. Among the other trophies were postcards, a 'Legalize Marijuana' banner, pages torn out of *Mad* magazine, the inevitable 'Save Water, shower with a friend' button, and the *Penguin Book of Asian Cooking,* threaded through with string. The dresser remained. It was so heavy it would be almost impossible to shift. Its shelves were littered: assorted unmatched crockery, ULVA glasses, bottles with beans sprouting, cigarette packets, elementary medicinal requirements, a battered copy of *The Prophet*, sticks of incense, a cheap brass duck with a blackened mouldy banana inside, tins of milk powder, Milo, an avocado stone suspended by toothpicks above a dark green carafe and sending down long air shoots. Raffia vegetables in unlikely colours, a floppy black schoolgirls' hat crammed with badges. Boyd took in the muddle of it all. There was a smell of soft decay from a large used ice-cream container. The iron sat on the draining-board alongside two empty beer bottles and a scurf of peelings.

It looked lived in.

Young Don hopped up, eager to serve. Then Olof.

'What's all this? You all look as if you've been plotting.'

'Full of plots, lot of us. You better watch it. We're after you,' Don chortled. 'This is Get To Know Boyd Week. Or, if you like, Boyd Gets To Know Us Week.' Don scraped a chair. 'Well, you looked kinda misplaced. And we all felt you weren't *really* against us. That counts. Besides, it can't be much fun digging up ghosts, especially if the Bellevue happens to be one of them. No,' Don raised a hand, 'no Bellevue post-mortems this morning.'

'So we decided. Where does everyone go that's new to Brisbane?' Olof swivelled his chair round, sat leaning over its back. 'Lone Pine the Sanctuary.' He slapped one broad palm down. 'Besides, I like the animals.'

'Olof's a real sook, get to know him,' Don explained, grabbing Olof's matted hair and shaking it. Sudden white teeth, apple. 'He's nuts about animals. That's his dog, Kali. Sookiest animal in captivity. Now if it was me,' Don added, 'I'd go for a Doberman.'

Cora poured coffee. 'Law of inverse proportion.'

'Watch it!' Don made a mock threatening gesture. 'I'll set my dad on you!'

'Dad the Doberman.'

'Yeh!' Don chuckled. 'Yeh. I like that.' Himself a big, angular puppy.

'How did you lot get together?'

'Ask on. Ask us anything. The answers might be different each time, or each person, but nothing's fixed, not a thing's rigid in nature,' Cora challenged, still smiling.

'I've got something rigid in nature. So has Boyd,' Olof said.

'That sort of thing comes and goes,' Cora laughed in his face. 'Merely proves my contention.'

'Dad got me this flat,' put in Don. 'Saw the place being subdivided and made enquiries. Knew how I wanted to move out, get a place of my own . . .'

'Your own? — the three of you?'

'Well, right from the start Cora and I had it worked out, we would move in together . . . '

'And Olof? Where do you come into this scene of domestic bliss?'

'We ran into Olof at the Royal Exchange,' put in Don briskly. 'You know, the pub. And he'd just had this fight with his dad. So we said, come on in, share with us. You know: pool resources. Olof and me were at State High together. He was the smart one. Then.'

'Meaning?'

'Olof's the only one working.'

'Well. Labouring – part-time. Over in Darra. It pays. Friend of me mum got that for me. Things are tough, it's only casual.'

'So you're the man of the house? Provider?'

'We all dob in.'

'And you others are . . . ' There was a pause.

Don again stepped in. 'I sort of dropped out of Uni,' Don yawned, 'told Dad I wanted a year off, the grindstone syndrome was getting to me.'

'Uhuh? What faculty?' Boyd could hear his own obtuseness. He couldn't help barging in, bull in their chinashop. 'What subjects were you taking?'

'Geology. I'll go back. It's not that I didn't find it interesting, I really did. Just couldn't hack the pressure. The exam business. Dad said fair enough, see a bit of living.'

'Don's old man's pretty understanding,' Cora wiped a spot on the Laminex.

Would Boyd himself be an indulgent father? He did not know. Cora kept on wiping, the same area.

'But Cora's been doing all sorts of jobs, since she dropped out of teaching.'

'Training College, you mean. Yes, I've drifted.' A challenge.

'She was top in her grade, too. More than that. Even the Principal came and tried to get her to go back.'

'That means nothing. I had to get out of the system. Life has to be something more than just routine; I'd like teaching, no hassles. I could do a good job. But things got claustrophobic. Nothing new – you could see all those trainee teachers ending up zombies, once they got out and became brain-washed by a few lumpy inspectors and a common-room of drones there only for the superannuation. That college with its "innovations" was just Playtime. Fooling itself. The whole society fooling itself, setting up structures, systems, laws and courts and appeals and parliament and all the bloody time it was all being manipulated anyway by the people who've really got the power. How they must laugh into their share portfolios! They rip down what they want, when they want. Nobody gives a damn. And bottom of all the shit pile are the teachers, nice little bodies who do as they're told, jump when they're told and often even when they are not told.'

'Well, these people come and go, you know.' Boyd felt very old. 'How do you find living with all this moral indignation, Olof?'

Olof gave a snort. 'Right behind it, mate . . . ' Slowly he turned on his chair to the others. 'See. Told yuz he was just a reactionary bastard.'

'He's just not politicized, Olof. The middle classes never are; get things too easy.'

Boyd felt even older. 'Come off it now. I worked my way through Uni. Slogged it out, no free dole-subsidized holidays.' Boyd's inheritance had been held in trust until he was twenty-five. Boyd had been liberated by nothing.

'Big woops!' said Cora, shrugging.

Olof slammed the table suddenly. 'Shit!' Like a gas-ring ignited. 'Shit, man, one whole generation's been sold down the drain, thrown onto the scrap heap!'

'Well, Olof,' Boyd responded firmly, quick to the alert. 'You don't look scrap-heaped to me.'

Olof and Boyd glaring. Cora stepped in.

'Let's get back to neutral territory, I'm not in the mood for Social Studies. Excursions, that was what we're supposed to be on about. Anyone for the dole-bludger's excursion?'

Marie had often warned Boyd on the way he antagonized their

friends. *Her* friends, he had corrected. And then would regret his flatfooted tongue.

The others had gone up to the front of the boat. After a while Don came back and joined Boyd clutching a newspaper. No grudges. Eagerness.

'Zammo! Picked up this on the seat. Take a gekko.'

The headline read 'Three Options on Bellevue'. The news article outlined possible alternatives the cagey Government might follow: 'Restoration, retention of the façade, or the wrecker's hammer?' Joint Governing parties would decide today.

Boyd remembered a friend, a girl lithe as Marie when he had first met her. She had been burned severely in a fire. Had become a recluse. But that was not the entire story. Later, she had paraded her disfigurement in the briefest bikinis, daring everyone to be shocked, defying their sympathy.

An old woman pacing endlessly around her furniture and fine porcelain, raking the garden at dawn, dressed always like a dowager to go out the front gate.

Don was still engrossed, reading his news. He'd be okay. Go back in a year, finish his degree, settle down, look back with nostalgia in mid-thirties, 'those were the days; didn't think your old man was a wild thing,' he'd say to his daughters. Yes, they would be daughters.

Not from Cora. No, she could just drink all his juices without noticing. Golden Orb Spider. Don would go back home, talk of his wild woman, make his dad proud – then dad would find Don a nice partner, the right social set. Don would move back to, was it Hamilton? In his fifties he'd still look boyish. Always popular. Supportive Junior Partner.

Boyd hated himself, the way he tagged people.

They reached the Lone Pine jetty. Part of the steep riverbank slopes were caught in the sunlight as a sheen of silk, a whole bank of movement so that the light hovered: countless seedheads of the introduced Natal grass. Boyd remembered a whole hillside caught in such sunlight: these grass-seeds, another boyhood sheen of the area, something else his grandmother had pointed out to him. Until she had remarked on its extraordinary game with light Boyd had not noticed the hillside of Natal grass. He had taken a photograph. It was nothing.

The others were already up the slope. Olof bought all their tickets, imperiously scorning Boyd's offer.

Boyd had come with fruit from a midtown stall; an impulse collection: four kiwi fruit, apples, bananas, a pomegranate and, because of its colour, an eggplant.

Cora demanded the kiwi fruit before they had slipped midstream. Olof had a penknife. The skin slipped off almost without pushing. The tiny surprise of its softness. Olof gulped the fruit, skin and all. Now Boyd offered apples. Automatically Olof rubbed his on a thick muscled shirtsleeve. Don took a bite straight off, his quick tongue darted out for the juice dribbling to his chin. Cora took her dark glasses off and gazed deeply at hers, turning it over in the cup of her hands. She put it in her shoulderbag, her tagari, for after. Boyd took his bite, tentatively, aware of a recent tooth filling.

The smaller Sanctuary cages were tawdry. Bird droppings, sulphur-crested cockatoos with muck-stained tailfeathers. Dust. Pink Major Mitchell cockatoos beating against wire, beaks like a leper's stump fingers and as grey, or the animal enclosures: wombats, heavy, torpid sacks immobilized by boredom. His grandmother had taken him, once, to visit an old woman whose pet wombat was asleep in the big armchair. The only problem, the old lady said, was it scratched furniture, like a crotchety old man with his pipe habits or his hobnails. The door was ripped to a pelt, worse than dog scratches. Otherwise, it suited her perfectly. The wombat slept all day; it was affectionate; a conversation piece at afternoon teas; in its own corner, self-absorbed; and a watchdog at night, out in the yard. In the mornings, the most habit-bound alarm clock. Boyd had been encouraged to stroke the wombat. Its claws were, indeed, formidable. *Hubby*, she called it.

Boyd turned to the koala shelters. Koalas: such somnolent captivity, just one stage removed from muff, pouch, purse, knee-rug. Don was already explaining their habits: that stolid diet of gumtips, the eucalyptus oils repelling all vermin (and inducing, in the second stomach, almost perpetual alcoholic fermentation; no wonder they looked stoned!). Their claws – formidable. Wild koalas had painfully surprised captors when cornered. Cuddly, seemingly passive, but with their share of deceptions.

A vast stand of rose-gums, in straight columns, dipped over the rise. An adolescent-looking emu strode up, almost myopic, but intent enough. Boyd ducked, but Cora was unflinching. The lectern-legged bird veered beyond them. She gripped his arm. Boyd squeezed his own arm in. Locking her fingers.

'Remind you of Grandma, that one?'

'Funny you should say that.'

'That elegant neck perhaps? Feather stole round the shoulders?'

'You're bitchy. Her neck was very beautiful.'

'You think the emu's isn't? Or did you flinch from the long hard stare? Emus look right into you.'

'Ah, now that's more *you*.'

'People tell me. Can't see it myself.'

'Course not, you're in the driver's seat.'

They went up to the cluster of wallabies, laughing.

Olof was feeding grey kangaroos with corn from the little plastic packet bought at the entrance. They were quite tame, even the young mother kangaroos, suckling their joeys, stooping down almost to ground level to enable the leggy offspring access to the teats within the sagging fur pouch. Indifferently they allowed them to tumble in and out, all tail, ears and hind legs. Often the only visible sign of a nursing mother was the stalk-like protrusion of bony legs, tail, long claws, like unkempt zipper tags out of the fur covered compartment.

'Get the old buck there. Get that equipment! Back to front. Howja be, huh, balls hanging down front of y'r prick?' Olof grabbed Boyd's shoulder, almost pushed him down to look at the large kangaroo male.

Curiously vulnerable testicles hung in a bulging tight pouch by an exaggeratedly thin string; behind it the penis sheath.

'And y'see how they like jailbait?' Olof pointed to another buck in obvious pursuit of a very young doe. And another.

Cora straightened up. 'Let's look at the albino wallabies. Up here.'

Later, she asked for the pomegranate. Ripping her fingernails into the red woody skin she exposed the clusters of glistening seeds. She scraped in with her teeth, then spat.

'That's all there is to 'em,' she explained, wiping her chin. 'A bit of crunchy pith around each seed. Tastes primitive.'

'No taste much at all.'

'They say it's refreshing, if you're thirsty.'

'My father gave me one, when I was little. I didn't know what to do with it.'

'And he showed you?'

'Showed me all right,' Cora laughed. 'That stage, he showed me everything. That stage, I thought he was God.' She spat out another red mouthful. 'Ugh! It's bitter!'

Marie

'But, Marie dear, you've prepared far too much food, just for three persons!' Mrs Kennedy realized she had gaffed again. 'I mean. You must have been slaving in the kitchen from the moment you got in. Just for us.'

'I wanted to do something. Banging a few saucepans around was good therapy.'

Old Mr Kennedy looked up across the table. His elegant, spare figure with the thatch of perfectly groomed white hair always had an unruffled, unperturbed air. Even now, his look was politely quizzical.

'Non-breakables, yes, they are the best for banging around. Jolly expensive otherwise. My mother used to throw plates. Often,' he smiled beatifically, 'at me.'

'I can't imagine it.'

'Oh, I assure you.' He sliced into his schnitzel. 'Excellent, my dear. Boyd is a very lucky fellow. This meat is excellent.'

'Boyd is a bit of a mixed-up fellow, just at the moment,' put in Boyd's mother, looking out of the corner of her eye at Marie, whose features were politely regulated, her grooming impeccable. 'But he'll get over it. Oh, at fifteen he was moody. Fifteen was the moody time for Boyd. I suppose for most boys.'

'Hmmm. Well thirty-five is a bit young for mid-life crisis, or whatever these medical fellows call it. Why at that age we were . . . you and I were still virtually newly-weds. Boyd was just a little fellow. My thirty-fifth birthday. That would be 1950. Well, Boyd was in kindergarten. A terrible summer. All those terrible fires.'

'No, dear,' gently, 'that was in 1951. 1951 was the summer of the terrible fires. The Robinsons lost their house up at Kallista, do you remember? Oh, it seemed so many of our friends . . . ' Mrs Kennedy turned again to Marie. 'There were some trying periods for all of us. 1951 was the year we thought there might be a little brother or sister . . . '

'You two have not considered, have not reconsidered, a family?' Mr Kennedy lifted his wine-glass and appeared to be examining the vintage. It was bulk claret. 'It is very possible to become self-centred, just the two of you. A family does wonders. As I recall Jack McKinney saying one time, a baby imposes the sort of self-discipline we don't willingly impose on ourselves.'

It was as bad as Marie had expected. Why had she, then, made these arrangements? It was rubbing her nose in the fact of Boyd's absence; Boyd's parents, without him in the room, were almost strangers, had a guard up as if they were not sure which way their son would jump: should they regard Marie still as daughter, or should they be preparing for the new possible claimant? Did Marie consider that seriously?

It was true, she had spent two hours in the kitchen when she got in. She had looked up her mother's favourite recipes. That ridiculous Viennese pastry. The Kennedys were eaters of roast beef and baked vegetables, of jelly, fruit and custard, of plum pudding and cinnamon rice. Geoff Collins had not been at school today, she suddenly remembered. Big, oversize Geoff. What a silly party it was last night. What a silly party the night before. Things could not continue like this, filling a vacuum.

The senior Kennedys had taken her silence to indicate reticence or tact. Perhaps there would be no grandchildren.

Damn, damn him, Boyd Boyd Boyd. At a family dinner-party like this he would make Marie the very centre, almost visibly polishing her for his parents' edification. After the tension of preparations (Boyd making suggestions, helping, interposing), he would relax and be a genial, bantering host: 'Marie, tell Dad about what happened at school today . . . Marie, let us hear again that truly awful student howler . . . '

'Oh my dear, such an *elaborate* dessert. You should not have gone to the trouble. Just the tiniest slice. Otherwise I will dream all night. But it does look delicious. Yes, just that much. Thank you, my dear. You really have been labouring.'

'Mmm, thank you, yes plenty.' Mr Kennedy put out his hand. 'We really are not used to such vast meals these days. We seem just to peck at things. The appetite fades, you know.'

Marie had prepared the pastry for the strudel herself, no out-of-the-packet short-cuts. In an enactment of childhood days she had stretched out the dough to membrane thinness, kneaded and re-stretched it. It had soothed her. Her mother never made things or cooked nowadays. There were now so many Viennese coffee-houses.

As a teenager, Marie had hoarded bottles, cartons, containers. Her mother had encouraged her. There had been a time when it seemed possible. When she desperately sought to emulate Helena Maria Adriana, though she squirmed and became embarrassed, would pretend not to know her at school functions, was quite horrible . . .

Mr and Mrs Kennedy were good people, nice people. Perhaps Marie should reach out more to them, their formal barriers were so transparent, it would be so easy to fill them with gratitude and friendliness. She had never called them family names. She did not know what she wanted.

'Why should Boyd be suddenly so involved with this thing about his grandmother?' she asked, pouring coffee, breaking the silence again.

Mr Kennedy looked almost grateful.

'Oh, they were very thick together. Though I don't know why. Well, as we have so often observed looking around us, there is frequently a closer link across a two-generation span. Perhaps grandchildren don't impose the same strains you have between parent and child. The generation gap. It's most pronounced the closer you are, curiously enough. But then,' he nodded his approval of the coffee, 'but then there might be some genetic link. The eyes and the smile; Boyd might almost be his grandmother in some ways.'

'But not the build and the hirsuteness. That is pure Brougham, my family.'

'The temperament, too, I fear is Kennedy, though it bypassed me. I don't think you would say, my dear, I ever evinced notable moodiness.'

'Oh, not like Boyd. From the very first days. No, dear, you were always so good-natured. Indeed, I could never understand your difficulty with your own mother. It seemed, well, uncharacteristic.'

'I was sent off to boarding school very young. But that was not it, not entirely. You see, when my mother allowed herself all those explosions and rages and emotional indulgences, someone had to suffer. She was all right; half an hour later she could be sunny as a spring morning, but anyone else around her, they suffered. She left them shredded, she could be quite shattering.'

'And you were the only one with her, the only target.' Marie played with her strudel. She had no appetite. She had learned early how to counter her mother's extravagances.

'Well, not entirely. My mother had house guests, some for quite long periods. I have never said it, but I think some of them were more than just house-guests. Looking back on it. Indeed, some very funny goings on. There was that woman she had as a secretary for nearly ten years. We loathed each other. Indeed, I think *she* – that woman – loathed everyone. Except mother. She worshipped her. Very possessive. I think she finally got exhausted by it all. Not my mother, she sailed on blithely. Or stormily. They had some absolutely dreadful storms, the two of them. Kept me awake at nights, quite terrified.'

'Well, that was all before my time,' Mrs Kennedy wiped her mouth, 'and perhaps Marie doesn't want to be troubled by old family history. After all, your mother is not alive any more.' But she paused, too. '*I* recall that rather nice gentleman used to be at your house for weekends at the time we were courting. I thought he was really very sweet . . . '

'Oh, Dom Behan. Yes, a wonderful, dear fellow, almost like a father. I think he was the last great love of her life. Until little Boydie. Certainly had a wonderfully calming effect on the old mater. But of course he was married.'

'Oh. I never knew that. Well. I think I should be scandalized. I really do. And your mother! When I consider the way she tried to come between us two, and us innocent as the dawn . . . '

'Hmmm.'

'Well, we were. Boyd's grandmother,' turning to Marie again, 'could be a veritable battle-axe and she took what I can only assume to be an instant dislike to me.'

'My dear, you were too pretty. She was a very pretty young thing, then, and you still are, if I might say so, my dear.'

'Well, I thought her a proud, cold woman. And as for . . . indulgences. Well indeed, surely she was beyond that?'

'Ah, my dear, it may all have been my overheated imagination. You must remember, all those years I was only in and out of the place. A tenant almost. I seemed a strain to my mother. Though at that stage I knew absolutely nothing about, hm, abnormal relationships. Miss Bennett. And indeed, it may well have been all absolutely innocent. We were innocent people in those days. It is only in this modern generation that all this stuff is talked about, and seen and encouraged. I'm sure people would not even think of it, if it were not put in front of them, every news headline.'

'But Boyd and his grandmother . . . '

'I admit that made me impatient. I had not been well disposed towards my mother in those later years. She was the one person could slam me shut like a door. I did not enjoy it, made me feel always the errant schoolboy, even when I was in my thirtieth year. But Boyd, yes, she idolized him. Perhaps she wanted to make up for all her inattentiveness to her own son. Well, that will do. Tell you this, Boyd himself always came back from his vacation with such spirits and energy.'

'Yes, it could be weeks before the moodiness returned.'

'Not that he was entirely moody. But you know him, my dear, sometimes I wonder that you put up with it. I could almost understand if it had been you who wanted to break out and . . . '

'He's a sterling lad, Olga. Marie must be embarrassed to have us seeming to be belittling our own son . . . '

Impasse. Marie knew it was her move. She would not make it. With great effort she looked up, into the faces of the two old partners.

'I'm still here. Aren't I? I will wait for your son. But that's not to say I'll wait here forever.'

They were hasty with reassurances. Mr Kennedy offered to fly up to Brisbane. Marie pointed out that she could do that herself. She had the address. But indeed until that moment it had not occcured to her as a possibility.

Boyd

Cora had prepared her moussaka, justifying the eggplant. Boyd, relaxed now and familiar at the old kitchen table, protested at the thought of this glossy purple-black fruit being sliced. It must be possible, surely, to bake it whole: aubergine stuffed, perhaps? But the suggestion of heat crinkling, then blistering the smooth surface was more unsatisfying. The plant had a smooth inviting texture like dark skin, the most private places of skin, the inside secret places.

Cora spluttered at the idea.

'Go on!' said Olof. 'What else does it remind you of?' and suggested, himself, the bared penis head of an uncircumcised Yoruba tribesman.

'Circumcision is a tribal initiation ritual,' Boyd pointed out. Cora grabbed up the fruit and pushed her knife in. There was a spongy resistance but then she peeled out its green-tinged cream pith. Slice after slice, into thin layers. The seeds were insignificant.

'You'd wonder how they could grow and develop from something puny as this?' Boyd picked up one seed.

'They're the same family as tomato.'

'And potato. And there's another *solanum* up at the new Botanical Gardens; it has the same blue paper flower, only bigger; star-shaped. They call it a potato tree.' Don enjoyed his authority. He proffered his knowledge-cards like confectionery. 'It's also related to Deadly Nightshade.'

'And, in half an hour, to our own body organism.' Cora flourished her knife.

Later, Olof rolled a joint. 'Marijuana, the thinking man's cigarette.'

Boyd shook his head. Marie sometimes tried one.

'Go on.'

'We don't do this every night. But tonight's something special. Welcome Boyd In Night.'

'He's not game.'

'Come off it, Olof, I've tried those things. Tell the truth, they did nothing. Can't stand any smoking, dries the throat,' Boyd lied.

'Let him be,' Cora said. 'There's no compulsion. No one's put on the outer.'

Don passed the smoke over to Olof. He took a deep pull again. Passed it on, then, to Cora. After her turn she made to return it to Don. Then she paused, turned to Boyd quizzically. He accepted.

Rather a pleasant smell, of its sort. He took a deep downward pull, as he had been instructed, back at College, in Marie's room. His lungs filled with dry heat, the smallest sensation.

He followed the ritual of sharing.

Cora closed her eyes, settled back.

Out in the darkness Boyd examined the luminous dial of his watch, tugging among hairs. After all that smoke, what he felt like was a cool beer. A big one. He would stroll down to the Regatta. The night air parted before him. The stars were not artificially conjured as in the Planetarium. Here they did have distance.

Inside, the others were sprawled and far beyond him. Boyd, conscious of primness, sensed that distance. Who was it – Balzac? – said: Try anything once, that's experience; when it's repeated too often, that's debauchery. Something that way. Boyd couldn't remember.

The offer for Balzac hadn't been pot (in Paris, last century, that would be kindergarten; even here it was playschool): it had been sodomy.

Boyd lurched slightly, across the main road. A large sign behind the bus stop caught his eye, PUNKS LOVE YA!

The Regatta was half empty, people finishing last drinks before closing.

Boyd had never tasted beer so tangy. Quickly he ordered another. He was their last customer.

As he sauntered back, past the Toowong park with its deep forest shadows and the moon-struck lake of the sports oval and the rustle of insatiable fruitbats foraging, Boyd paused, seeing a figure. It was a man swinging slowly, on one of the kid's swings.

The conjunction seemed almost mystical, as if moonlight brought out the ghosts of lost children in the forms of stocky adults, back and forth, back and forth, swing chains of insubstantial moonbeams. Boyd paused, mesmerized. Back and forth, slow motion.

Colour drained into negative.

Then he realized. This was Olof. He was about to call out to him when he noticed beyond: the whole area was inhabited with shadowy figures. In the clear drench of the moonlight, moonshaft, stood the bulky squatness of the Men's Toilets.

Marie

To soak in the tub was the greatest pleasure. Marie had always loved that – she would read a book there, had even corrected assignments in the bath, though that was usually on nights when Boyd was not home: a conference somewhere, maybe, or some lecture series. Boyd did not approve of Marie's self-indulgence in the bath tub. She would top up the water if it got cold. She would doze there, floating and buoyant with the water as full as she dared allow. Perhaps in her love of this entirely sensuous floating-off in a tubful of warm water Marie was, like her mother, seeking equilibrium. Though her mother usually preferred a shower, scalding hot and full pelt so her skin was pummelled and massaged. Still, there had been nights.

There had even been nights, Marie recalled, when as a girl she and her mother shared the bath, floating and cuddling, and her mother stroking her small body – 'like an otter, an otter in the zoo at Schloss Schönbrunn.'

Tonight Marie had filled the bath and was soaking to let the strain of the dinner dissolve. Boyd's mother was someone she understood and did respond to, and his father was a dear, really, someone almost too perfectly like the father she had constructed for herself, not having known her own. Still, there is always a strain, a secret reserve. Her neck. Boyd, as always held the key, even though he could endlessly disrupt her. Strange, this sudden idea of stability. Marie reached for the soap. It smelled of spring anemones.

Boyd, the first time he discovered her lust for a deep, slow bath: when was it? Hayman Island of course, and Marie had indeed dozed off in the tub – it was one of those motel tubs that are too short, she had to poke out her knees in order to soak. Poor old Boyd, thinking she'd drown. Thinking she had drowned; and with Marie having to jack-knife just to fit in. Still, she had dozed off, even there, with her hair floating, and her shoulders cushioned and lapped by the suds. Boyd had been quite distressed. It could still come back.

As Marie adjusted the tap with her toes, to let more warm water in, she was thinking of Hayman.

The morning she woke up first. Boyd's heavy bulk familiar by now, and his slow, steady breathing. Outside, calls of birds sounded too loud, as if amplified. She had lain there, trying to make out some language, some discernible phrases in the repeated birdsong. Currawongs, Boyd told her later. The same phrases repeated endlessly, as if the chorus of birds insisted she get the message, frantic to tell her. The call was in two parts. The first a loud but melodious yodel – 'Ain't she afraid, ain't she afraid?' This was followed by something more relaxed. Were the sounds from different birds? The alternation seemed consistent: 'Tootleloo, tootleloo . . . '

No, it must be something more interesting than that: 'Good for you?' 'Thought you knew?' 'How d'you do.' Once the phrase stuck in her mind it repeated itself every time. 'Tootleloo tootleloo.' Then the other phrase: 'Ain't she afraid? Ain't she afraid?'

In the bath Marie turned over and lay on her stomach. Why should she remember that birdsong? Why that? Boyd's body so close. She had been forced to get up, she couldn't tell why. Dawn, and she had been sweating. At that stage of the honeymoon she had blamed herself for everything. Boyd's tolerance had been stifling, just as was his concern.

'Ain't she afraid?' The birds had seemed in on the quiz. 'Ain't she afraid? Tootleloo tootleloo.'

Marie stepped out of the bath. She did not allow herself the normal indulgence of lying in as the water drained out, to beach her up, flesh tingling at the gradual exposure to air.

THURSDAY

Boyd

Boyd was shaving when the sudden noise of Olof's Yamaha slammed into the air, and kept there, dragging all the other noises into its vortex.

It was a smoggy morning. The edges of things were blurred chemical white. Even the air had that closed-in taste of old garages. Boyd walked down to the corner shop on the main road. He would get the morning paper, sit with it over his coffee. Outside the store, a news billboard: DOWN IT COMES.

He picked up the top from the pile on an old fruitcase. The whole city had been drawn into this.

Brisbane's former Bellevue Hotel will be demolished within a month following a State Government decision yesterday that the building would be the first casualty in a $35 million Parliamentary Precinct Development.

Boyd grunted. No, it did not involve him.

However, in a compromise move to lessen public condemnation of the step, the coalition instructed architects to plan a new building with a Bellevue style facade.

The hotel site would become a sunken garden. Yes, and why not?

Although the month estimate on the Bellevue's demolition was given by the Premier, some Ministers and Members believe it will begin within a week. Some suggest this weekend.

Lessons learned from the previous token demolition of the hotel verandahs. Once bitten.

The coalition Liberal leader, Dr Edwards, was going out of the State, across to Western Australia. Turning his back, perhaps, on the whole deal?

Fuel for the kids in the other flat. Let them sweat.

Their front door was wide open. Bearing the newspaper Boyd poked his head inside, then stepped forward.

'Anyone home?'

Boyd tramped into the kitchen. Signs of mid-week muddle, last night's things still stranded, drying and congealing. Wizened peels of aubergine on the sink edge. Filled ashtrays among coffee-stains, now dry. A knife with two flies. Plates everywhere.

Beyond, off the side, was his grandmother's big glassed-in sun-room. The door was half open. Beyond, more general litter. Boyd poked his head around the door. 'Anyone home?'

Don's thin shanked body, naked, was pumping down vigorously. Cora's hair had streamed everywhere, her head thrashing sideways and again sideways. Urgency. Boyd stepped back.

What do you gain from one quick impression? Like a photographic plate, many details are recorded, some not instantly in register, others as the entire focus. The focus had been clear enough.

Why be angry? It was as if they had intruded onto his privacy, not the other way round. Why did he have to be witness to their fornication? In the abstract, he could sense it, accept it, he was a grown man. The beast with two backs, the first parish pump, the straight fact of fuck, root, hump, screw, ram, roger, rout, rut, coitus, intercourse, 'death'.

But to watch it going on in front of him: no way to evade it. So. It was creature, it was animal, brute pump and thrust. It rubbed him raw.

How would an observer have witnesssd Boyd with Marie? Not bearable. Her faint protests, the tiredness, then 'okay let it happen' and her furious submission. And then, later, the heat and the urgency. Once she clawed his back furiously, pulling out hair. Sometimes she groaned loudly, deep, mouth wide and foreign, the noise of some phantasmic creature. That always embarrassed him, thinking of neighbours.

It had been his own fault.

Boyd put the *Courier Mail* on the table, hurried out. He made himself coffee in his rooms. He must face it: these kids are new, they are different. Social mores alter. They are the seed of the liberated generation, they are the prize in the anti-censorship battles of the Sixties. Herpes, VD.

Queensland, he had read, has the highest illegitimacy rate in the country. Always did have. Generations. Generations of Queenslanders ramming it, tropical fever, out in the daylight, openly, legs open, sweating, grabbing, hair wet on brown, hair tossed over, under mangoes, under beach cotton-trees, in full sunshine among sand dunes, brown buttocked, bronze-breasted, edge of riverbanks right beside the new sub-divisions in full sight of roof tilers and builders' labourers, sub-tropical like soft papaws, papaw-breasted, mango-breasted, rolling in fruit-stains and sweat, taking it, giving it, endlessly ripening.

Words. Print. Statistics. The real thing always happened, whether reported or not. Boyd had fought against hypocrisy, his first legal battle. Here he was, thirty-five, and pretending shock at the universal function. How low could you get? How jealous?

Don came in, old khaki trousers, smooth chest polished like fawn Laminex.

'Thanks for the paper, hey!' He tugged his knuckles. 'Hope we didn't turn you off – turn you on. Heard you calling but like, other matters were pressing.'

'I intruded. Sorry. The front door was open.'

'No worries. Nothing out of the normal. Everything nice and normal.' Don thwacked his buttocks. 'Hey, come and join us for coffee, our side.'

'You did see the news headline?' Boyd consented to follow. Don skipped forward to grab up the newspaper.

'Oho. Wait till Cora . . . oho man, this is dynamite!' He raced into the bedroom sleep-out, thumping the air with her name.

Cora and Don gulped coffee. They would catch up with their friends out at the Uni refectory. Something would happen. And their bet was, quick. *Some suggest this weekend.* Don poked one long forefinger at the paragraph.

They raced off, baggy clothes, streaming hair, shiny faces. Cora had made no sign.

Not true, why not admit it? She was glowing. Fed with raw energy. It was Marie who had never purred contentedly. How could he admit either one had been at fault. More than one way to reach failure, there had to be fair apportionment; even his Law could admit guilt to be the most difficult label to affix clearly.

He paced with the sheaf of Law papers, the great wad of computer print-out. It looked alien.

No. He had to clear his head. No way he could concentrate. Yet somehow it seemed closer, so much had already lifted.

Marie, groaning and protesting.

What else was it in that sleep-out? Like a photograph returned to later for clues, the thing there but not noted. Boyd's mind must have registered something.

Marie striving, groaning, never convulsing, and then bellowing as if tortured.

The tossing ecstatic hair, Cora thwacking her head on that pillow.

He had it. With a shout Boyd pushed back into the other flat – still untidied, still wide open. There, in the most obvious place: the mirror vase.

It stood on the stained dressing-table, unambiguous. He lifted it up. Smaller than he remembered. More tatty. The old thirties glamour might be reviving in art-shops and junk-stalls, but this Australian example had a stiff brazenness he'd forgotten. It looked provincial.

Yet something was there in its mirrors. Boyd turned it around. Old ballrooms. Vestibules opening onto the Ladies' Lounge. Bench to a cloakroom, daiquiri and cherry brandy, maple syrup waffles. Brandy-lime and soda.

It looked public. Why ever had his grandmother possessed it? Did it come late into the house? And why display it with such prominence, in the hallway? Who gave it? Someone must have given it. It must have meant something.

Marie, eyes closed, gripping. Cora, thrashing. Olof swinging in moonshadow. His grandmother aware of them all, with a knowledge that seemed terrible.

Shards of glass, bound into a cylinder of mirrors, none of them face-on to you.

A full morning's work. Boyd had thrown himself back into his study. He had sought out the most tedious lists to schedule, he had carefully arranged his documentation of proven cases, gone into each variable, pinpointed each constant. Like the most scrupulous auditor, the one not content to survey general principles in operation but intent on uncovering each minute discrepancy in Stamp Money, every theft from the Café-Bar, every cent out of balance.

By noon Boyd had twenty-four pages of schedules, neatly listed in an appropriate order of feasibility to underpin his argument. None of these schedules would be read at the conference; they would remain part of the mass of handout material shoved into folders, and the folders shoved into cases for filing, later, later.

Boyd had not contacted his wife – or his family – all week.

Next would be the tabulation of the Judgments.

Marie was, surely, managing brilliantly.

The others, next door, had returned. Boyd focused his attention on the web of computer printout.

Why had she not told him, even the first night? She was no martyr, why should she be?

The sun can flash upon glass, shoot out a sliver of light from it. It can blind you.

Boyd had put back the old vase. It must have been cared for; he had left smears, prints where he'd fingered it.

What is rape?

Why hadn't Marie told him, that first night, how was he to know he was violating her? It had seemed a flash of possession, power, pure illumination. Why did she hoard her injury? Slivers. Why didn't she tell him he was raping her, again and again, that night? Why make it shameful – virginal ignorance: they could have learned together. His whole thrust, self-aware, self-gratifying, possessed, blinded, possessive, had been also pure sharing, joining, aware of each minute part of his new bride – her hot skin, the sunburn, the smell of warm unguents, sand, grain of her backbone, tight springiness of hair, the small firm muscles – it had been intended to reach out, to discover; mere selfishness had been the last thing intended.

Why, damn it, did Cora choose one so young, so boy-like, only half grown, scrawny, undeveloped, someone younger? She was too full of life, she glowed with womanly qualities and vigour, what did she see in that chip of a boy, that thin spider?

Jealousy. Lashing out; still trying to hurt Marie. Boyd could not admit that. These kids were nothing. They were nothing to him. Indeed, this whole city: nothing. Their famous Bellevue: not a thing. Let them rip it out, tonight, tomorrow, like a summer weed, like lettuce plants gone to seed, frilled with tired iron-lace. The last time he had been there with his grandmother was a formal luncheon, damask, heavy silver. During the meal, at the next table a woman took a fit. Epileptic. He was upset, wanted to do something. His grandmother insisted: not their affair, pay no attention. If it gets too out of hand, the Management will look after matters.

What a cold woman, Boyd had thought then, perhaps for the first time. How impassive, how determined to pass responsibility across to 'the Management'. She continued with her crab salad, then called the waiter to bring them the trolley with tarts and trifles and the Black Forest Cake. In her new cropped hairstyle she looked an entire stranger.

Boyd, perhaps he should admit it, had no great feelings for the Bellevue. And his grandmother? No great feelings. Boyd had no great feelings. Except anger. How could he concentrate? Nothing. Nothing.

What was the time? Twelve thirty-seven. He could take a break. He slapped his feet on the floor, pushed himself out.

Marie

Helena Maria Adriana had surprisingly small hands. They were her pride – one of her prides. Small, but in proportion, well balanced. She gripped these hands now, both of them, around the ivory plastic of her telephone, caressing it, stroking with her fingers the cool, smooth surface. The fingers strayed to her other wrist, to the cool, smooth place of the inner arm.

'Marie? Marie I have been thinking and I have decided. It is the time for *Spargelfest*. What do you call it: the festival of the *asperges* the . . . '

'The word here is asparagus, Mother.'

'A terrible word in English, word for some disease.'

'It suffices.'

'You are still fretful, Marie? That signifies suffering, the capacity to suffer, to feel deeply . . . '

'And you are feeling deeply for asparagus, *Maman*?'

'You are sharp.'

'I am happy. There! Does that surprise you? *Mütterlein*, you did hear me: I said happy. Happy.'

'How can this be, Marie? Have you a new lover? Has Boyd returned and you hiding it from me? Tell me. I insist, tell me.'

'Nothing like that. No, I simply woke up this morning feeling refreshed. I felt alive. That's all. Happy: that's it, simply, quite simply. Everything will work out, it will take its course and I don't see that I have to involve myself.'

'This is delusion. It will pass. You must prepare yourself for the next stage. The great misery.'

'Christ, Mother! You're the limit!'

'Pay no heed, ignore me. But wait. Then come to me for comfort, that is as it will be, Marie. I will understand.'

'Look, I'm feeling calm, cool, rational. And I intend not to get rattled. Not any more. If you'd like to know, I had dinner last night with Boyd's parents. And I've decided to fly up to Brisbane. This weekend. *Mütterlein*, it is true. Now I've decided, I feel this great calmness. Almost as if I didn't even need to make the trip now. Just to realize I could do it if I wanted – that's all I needed.'

'Marie, Marie. How am I to tell you? Listen to me. This Saturday morning we will go, you and I. We will visit the Victoria Markets. We will buy for my *Spargelfest*. Then – I have decided this – then I will show you the little secrets I still retain. *Asperges vinaigrette* then there is a way with a very light batter, just dusted; and of course the garlic butter that is my favourite. I remember once, a small restaurant in Wien, the Gütenberg. At the next table a small child, quite tiny. So happy and contented, chewing a piece of lemon-peel. The tartness as well as the sweet. The *Spargelfest*. So clearly I remember all this. I deluded myself then that I was with child, but it was not yet to be.'

'You have told me the lemon-peel story.'

'Yes, of course. It is important. So. This Saturday.'

'I fly up to Brisbane.'

'No. No. No. Nein. Extravagance. That will not win the respect of your husband. Your Boyd will be deep into his own concerns, how can this advantage you? You do it to satisfy only curiosity. To spy on him. To announce your dependence and your distrust.'

'Why do you all plug that line?'

'All? So; the parents. Marie, it is important. Saturday you will come with me. We have so much to tell, so much to share. We will be housewives in the kitchen together and then we – we alone – we will eat of the feast. We will consume the delicate stalks. Do you know I see them like the phallus of some green garden god ...'

'*Danke*, no.'

'Yes. It is the time for long conversations. It is the time for work to be done between us. I have been neglectful. Now it is time to start together again. All week I am thinking this and I know it is true. The ceremony of the cooking and the eating will lead to other truths.'

'Mother. I do yoga. You keep insisting my body is tight, is somehow not part of me. It is. Do you think I have not been learning things all these years? You assume I have to somehow wallow in it . . .'

'And if I said: yes? Yes, and yes again?'

'You would only confirm me, Mother, in my knowledge that you are a peasant sensualist.'

'Ach, *Kinderlein*, you still have your spite and your hurt. I say you must come. We will break the old circle. We will discover the new, richer circle beyond. You will see. Tell me you will come. It is important. Important as life and death.'

'Always so melodramatic.'

'Always truthful. You say you feel calmness today. That truly is magical, it is part of the reason to be together. You will see I do not joke. I want to give you your inheritance . . .'

'If it's of any interest to you, Mother, you have very nicely thrown your pebble into the calm pool of my morning already. You know you have a way of doing this. Always.'

'You will not come?'

'I haven't said that. I've already decided to go to Brisbane and yet . . .'

'You would fly by aeroplane? When? Make it Saturday, Saturday evening. After we make the *Spargelfest*.'

'No. Yes. I don't know. *Mütterlein, Mütterlein*, you leave me as confused as ever. No don't say anything. I must rush off to school anyway. I'm late, you have made me late.'

'I have made you. Yes, but have I made you anything?'

'I don't know. Mother, I don't know. I will decide during the day whether I am to fly up, or when. Nothing has to be decided instantly.'

'You are sure?'

'I'm sure of nothing. You have my word for that.' Marie's laughter caught in the line to her mother and was clipped off.

Helena Maria Adriana caressed her receiver absently for several moments. Then she sighed. Then she sat down at last, and put the very neat hands into her mouth, ramming them in as if they could prevent the sobs coming.

Boyd

'Boyd. Saw you working. Look at this; miraculous. My poor Madonna lily, I forgot it. Nearly a fortnight and I'd left it there in the corner. You've no idea how it wilted. But I've been watering it this last hour. Drop at a time. I've been talking to it. You know, the way plants respond to encouragement. Over an hour. But now! Little thing has forgiven me, perked up completely. Makes me feel *something*. Just so damned clever! Well, it's magical.'

'Some sort of power. Water.'

'Oh, I feel powerful.' She looked up again. 'You look grim. No, don't say; it's this morning. Oldies never handle that. Y'know, it's all just natural. Like learning to breathe deeply. If you've never breathed right down to the base of your abdomen, then you never realize what you're missing. These people, down in the bus, so tight zipped you'd think they only rented the air, or it cost a fortune. Or as if they only rented their bodies, and the Hire Company said, don't play with the knobs. And they believed it. Bad as the Middle Ages, when people thought they might die if they washed. That sort of uptight.'

'My wife does yoga.'

His wife does yoga, calisthenics . . .

'And you? Not a chance.'

'I tried it. Once. Not my scene.' Marie egging him on: relax Boyd learn to relax.

'What about good sex? Same problem?'

'Who said I have problems? Damn it that's all you kids think about, rooting each other like bantams, like those kangaroos out in the paddocks . . .'

'Hey. You are jealous.'

'Wouldn't you like to think so.' He walked towards the gate.

'Where you going? Come on come on don't take it seriously, think of my Madonna lily.'

He paused, shuffled, then turned back. There was a silence. She motioned to him: sit.

'That's something between me and my wife. As you've not met her, I don't think you could be interested.'

'Should I be? Why shouldn't I be?'

'No, you shouldn't.'

He kicked his heel against a rail. 'I don't see why you should be.'

'Well. That's an invitation. Okay, what's her name? Says something doesn't it, that you haven't mentioned her by name? No, let me guess: Beverley? Anne? It couldn't be Raelene?' He grimaced, then told her, and she nodded.

'Her fingerprints are all over you.'

'What do you mean?'

'You don't see it? Well, I can't tell you.'

She caught him up half way to the bus stop. Because he didn't want to seem surly Boyd agreed to let her come. All his life he had been surrounded, nurtured. How could he change things now?

At first impression, from the outside, nothing had ever changed. The fanciful old building, really a late Victorian wonder, so much more worthy of preservation than the old Bellevue: those rose and cream brick horizontals, like Siena. Not rose, a sort of tomato-soup-on-milk colour. As comfortably relaxed as that. And the turrets, with little silver cheese-cover lids. The battlements, pure palm-tree gothic. Boyd thought of spade and shovel and lead soldier armies.

The rosebeds were perpetual. Thin angular branches whitened with tropical disease plasters, a wizened scurf of small leaves, crepe blooms. And the old German tank, *Mephisto*, in its box among the roses.

Sturmpanzerwagen A7V. Captured by 26th Battalion A.I.F. near

Villiers Bretonneux, France, on July 14, 1918. It is the only known surviving example of a World War 1 German tank.

'That's what it says.' He led the way.
'Just scrap metal,' Cora shrugged.
'What? And you into saving the Bellevue?'
'This thing's just a military trophy.'
'And that thing's what sort of trophy?'
'Now it's you naming the terms. Everything's relative. This is a trophy because it has no meaning here. Here? In this rosebed? But the Bellevue; for gawdsake, Boyd, the Bellevue came from that spot, it's part of it, part of our location. You know, it's somehow *us*. You know? Forget it.'
'Now who's grumpy?'
'What are these?' Cora grabbed his arm, tugged Boyd over to two huge Walt-Disney style fibreglass prehistoric monsters. Tyrannosaurus, Triceratops. The size: accurate, micrometer measured. The skin: it looked appropriate, but there were no scratch marks, no battle wounds, no Mephisto war scars.

'Swap you,' Boyd said, nodding back. Cora gave him her smile, then a wink.

'Take your point.'

They went together into the Museum building. Boyd recalled the old stuffed lion; and the tiger. To a ten year old they were impressive. For a fifteen year old they had become familiar as old teddy bears: totems.

More space. Fewer exhibits. Two glassed enclosures of lifesize Aboriginal figures. They were part of Boyd's old Museum. Someone, generations back recreated these models into the precise look, stance, community and environment of the original Moreton Bay tribe. Gunyah, camp artefacts, dingo pups playing in the ashes, men with string loin-covers, lubras slack-breasted but nubile.

No going back.

They walked past dull pelts of marsupials. Birds. Stand on the footprint-mark and you, too, can hear the recorded song of the lyre-bird.

Plaster casts.

Cora stooped to a wall case: Deep Sea Angler. The most ugly creature in creation. Four times the size of a deadly stonefish but that same toadlike skin. Row upon row of needle teeth and the long fishing-line of the snout, lure for deep-sea prey.

'Handsome!' Boyd stooped to read.

CESATIA HOLBOELLI: *This species is found at great depth in the North Atlantic Ocean in the vicinity of Iceland and Greenland. All the large free-swimming specimens are females; the males are dwarfed and permanently attached to the under-surfaces of the female. When hatched, the male instinctively finds a female, becomes attached to her body, and is then parasitic in that all food is obtained from the blood system of the female.*

In a world of darkness, these anglers attract prey by means of the luminous lure at the end of the appendage or 'rod' above the mouth.

'There it is!' Boyd exclaimed. 'Shit, it's a dwarf. Revolting. So that's evolution. Wonder how he does it?'

'Does what?'

'How does he get to mate with her. The female angler-fish.'

'He'd find ways. You think she gets a kick out of him? Leeching, sucking the blood from her?'

Boyd snorted. 'Ever consider the good old partnership proposition? You know. Share and share alike?'

'And did you? Huh, Boydie?'

'Don't call me that.'

'I know what it is, you're pipped because you secretly enjoy the thought that it should be *you* being sucked dry. As for being seen as a leech: why, guess the proposition's never been put to you. Meet a friend of mine, Ms Anglerfish. Men always look with a sort of satisfaction at the shells of the male spider, sucked dry after orgasm.'

'You think men fool themselves with that post-coital sadness? What about women? Ever hear that mediaeval theme of the pelican? Know the one? Where the female pelican pecks her own breast to provide life-giving blood for her offspring? Maternal sacrifice and all that. Once very popular. Rings a bell, huh? Mrs Anglerfish down the street, all those kids to look after, that drone husband, oh how noble, she's the one, she's the one carrying the burden. All that crap. Emotional blackmail! Her blood's probably addictive. Those young birds never got it out of their system. The old man emotionally bombarded till he put a brick wall around himself.' Boyd stopped. A giant manta-ray spread out in effigy ahead. At a distance sex is the most indeterminate part.

Marie tearing her breast feathers, tearing herself with the scissors that time, deflecting her anger, her need. And when he grabbed the scissors, put his arm around her, forced her to grow quieter, he had not for one moment conceived it was done for his sake, there are no rituals of self-sacrifice. He had merely, in his heart, stapled the new label on her.

'You making some sort of confession? Well, I'm not hacking it. I'm not going to be offloaded with emotional crap. Pelicans! You ever *look* at those birds? Never mind. All I'm saying, Boyd, is: you look at me as I am and forget your preconceptions. Too much of that in my family. And I'll look at you as *you* offer yourself. That's where you are. I don't want to know a thing about your Marie. Now we've got to shake on that.' And she did.

She strode on, out to the loggia.

Boyd changed his mind. Upstairs. The tribal artefacts and some old memory of Handley Shakespeare. Whatever happened to Handley? Head Botanist in some institute? Or deflected? That could easily be; suburban husband on the six p.m. train, who gave up his studies and married young, died out, dried out, deadened by habit.

Boyd stared at gaunt figures, each one alien, separate. The assertiveness of their genital members. Why? Eyes. Faces, thin proportions. Pricks. Cunts.

Handley would have evolved beyond that initial excitement to a bland lofty impersonality: senior anthropologist. Senior Customs Clerk.

Boyd returned down the old staircase. He looked for Cora.

'Come out here. Daylight out here. Show you the lungfish. The most sluggish damned thing in captivity: survived the entire evolutionary bit just by passivity.'

There were posters, blown up cut-ins of spider anatomy, with just a few specimens (redback, trapdoor, funnelweb) preserved in blocks of clear plastic. Boyd paused by them on the way to Cora's commands. As she moved back inside away from her discovered lungfish the light caught her blonde hair.

'I always liked these old files and cabinets,' Boyd said as she came into his reach. 'You pulled up the little curtain and there were the pinned insects. Stick insects. Moths. Spiders.'

'Let's see.'

'The little handwritten tags, probably the work of the original collectors last century.'

'Here. Here. Yes, terrific.' But before she could lift up the large, green drape fully, Boyd was reaching over her, taking control.

'Of course, that one! Yes, I remember that one. And this, here over here, here are the giant moths and the spiders. Look, Cora, that beauty! I remember . . . '

'You want to have it all, don't you? You've got to take over.'

'No. Not take over. I wanted to share . . . '

'Right. Then let's do it together. One Two Three. I lift this lid and you lift that.'

'Careful we do it together properly.' He was able to be amused now.

But she was peering already. 'There's another there, like the first case. They must be like the ones we have at home. No look; higher. Well look at them, will you . . . ' Peering and examining the exposed specimens, she was miles ahead, miles away, off on her voyage as if Boyd might be another ghost.

Marie

'Dagmar, I will not do it. I will not. My mother has a way of destroying everything she touches.'

'Marie's magnificent mum? Well, if you're the product of some destruction kick . . . no, it is always the same with mothers. They want to manage you endlessly. Well, I told mine where to get off, years back. Now I've got her where I want her.'

'Where's that? Truly?'

'In the honeymoon suite of the Windsor! Stuffing herself with luxury and escape from me. Bless her little soul.'

'She wants me over Saturday. To do some cooking. I ask you, Dagmar, can you imagine anything more horrible than to be lectured at and reproved by my mother for not getting the batter just perfect so her asparagus will remind her of Vienna. There's nothing more terrible than her soothing, patient tone. Unless it's her soothing impatient tone, when she is just itching to take over the fork or the whisk herself. She's like Boyd in that way. No wonder they get on . . .'

'You really can't get away from him, even from his name. The very best thing for you, Marie, would be to put a ban on his name. Put your own name up front. Coddle yourself for a time.'

'You know I'm flying to Brisbane?'

Dagmar, at the other end of the phone, let out a shriek that seemed to fuse the entire length of the telephone wire. Then she whispered, 'Never. Never, never, never. Marie, you're beyond hope, past help. What am I going to do about you? Leash you to the banisters?'

'I'll make the booking later this afternoon when I go to change my libraries.'

'You intend paying out good money, to chase after that . . . that slob? Marie, you must not. He's not worth it. You must never let him know he has such power over you. Oh, you throw away all the trump cards in your pack. You've got to play it cool. Marie, I'm going to come right over. I'll bring my skipping rope and tie you to the banisters, I swear I will. I'll hold you by force. I'll tickle you, I'll make you helpless and in my power. That bloody Boyd: who does he think he is? What power does he have over you, Marie? What right? No, I'm coming, I will be right over.'

'Dear Dagmar, Boyd is still married to me, he is still my husband . . .'

'He's not your master.'

'Don't be angry. It hurts me to hear you angry, and over Boyd. Dagmar, you know how much I'm concerned about him . . .'

'Concerned! He doesn't deserve it.'

'You always got on with him . . .'

'Because he's married to you. No, I'm coming over, I'll run all the way, it'll calm me down. I'll take you out to my favourite café, I'll stuff you with tortes, I'll fatten you up so he won't want a bar of you then I can have you all to myself. Marie, dear Marie, don't let him climb back just where he dropped off.'

'Let me explain, Dagmar. No, don't let me explain. It's just that I decided that, yes, it was perfectly possible and feasible to fly up to Brisbane and as soon as I realized that, everything seemed to lift. I was somehow back in control. I was able to think coherently again. It's not running after him at all. Perhaps I'll only say hello and pop off again. I'll go and see Boyd's famous Picasso. It'll be worth a trip to Brisbane just for that. You see?'

But Marie did agree to meet Dagmar at the Prater Coffee Lounge, and before she confirmed the booking at the travel agency.

Helena Maria Adriana was there before them.

Marie detached herself from her mother's embrace. She sat upright. Dagmar was delighted and sat conspiratorially close to Helena Maria Adriana. She leaned over and placed her plump hand on the older woman's knee.

'We've got to save this girl from her own rashness,' she whispered. 'All this nonsense about Brisbane and flying.'

Then Dagmar remembered the talk of asparagus.

'Ach, it is ended. That is finished, the *Spargelfest*. I am lost, there is no welcome. Without joy, without love, without willingness; nothing.'

'You've got me onside now. We'll work on her together.'

'*Nein, nein*. It will be the wrong season. In Wien, yes, the markets will bring first of the season. Melbourne: it was foolish. There will be no trace of the *Spargel*.'

'Marie's bullied you out of it then? We'll get to work on her. Of course we will find you some *Spargel*. They fly the stuff over from New Zealand.'

Marie, in profile, had the immobility of the Berlin Nefertiti.

A waitress in black and white lace came over. Helena Maria Adriana ordered sweet coffees without referring to the others. She did, however, command them to make their own choice from the revolving platter.

'You choose,' said Marie tiredly. Dagmar needed no second invitation.

It was not worth the trouble. They had won and it was really not worth the sweat. It was all being arranged without her, Dagmar would arrive with fresh asparagus, her mother would teach them both her little tricks and secrets, they were already planning the whole meal, what was to follow, Dagmar had even slipped back into the despised Viennese almost without noticing. Not worth any hassle.

Marie allowed them to persuade her into a second coffee. She even smiled weakly when Dagmar, too obviously, gazed across again at the cake-stand.

She brushed her grey skirt tight as she stood up.

'You're going? The library stays open another half hour and your mother . . .'

'I'm booking a plane to Brisbane for Friday night. Remember?' The smile might have been a brooch, one with very sharp pins. Marie hated herself.

Boyd

They had gone. A whole crowd were to meet in the city, preparing to picket the Bellevue. The news was that the Building Workers' Union had voted to black any demolition order. Don and Cora had waited for Olof to get in from his job then the three went off together. Boyd was not invited.

In the taxi returning to Toowong he had asked Cora about the mirror vase. She found it, she said, in the back of the dining-room cabinet, stuffed behind cleaning rags. She took a shine to it. When he asked could he keep it overnight she gave him that vaguely disbelieving look.

'Keep it forever, if you want. It's probably yours by right. I just thought it was fun. You know, vulgar, high camp.'

Now the vase stood on his kitchen table. Boyd made himself more coffee; he had never drunk so much instant junk. He had not eaten out at a restaurant, except that lunch with Bruce Patterson. Perhaps he should invite them somewhere. Them.

They had insinuated themselves.

There was a knock. A thin, bearded young man with oversize army shirt proffered a letter, mumbling something about wrong delivery, then was off. He retreated to the crumbling flats across the road. Boyd shrugged, then focused on the handwriting. Marie. Her clear handwriting tugged across white paper like nerve-pain. Sweat broke out like guilt.

No formal salutation. This uncharacteristic brusqueness: what rancour? What accusations? Her ballpoint cut like a scalpel across two thousand miles.

Well, Boyd, you'd be surprised how easy to trace you are. Y'day (Monday), in the bank, Bill Roberts said 'How's the better half of the joint account?' and I only said 'He's shot through.' That snapped him shut. All of a sudden solicitous. I'd watch him.

Then, in his office, it all came tumbling out, think he was caught a bit short. 'Half a mo. Something on Boyd came through just an hour ago.' Turns out a house agent named Apollo phoned through to verify your cheque. See, you're being watched. One phone call to Brisbane and we had you. Hence the address. 'No doubt it's all in the mail,' I told Bill. You writing, I meant. Of course I miss you, damn it.

Now I don't know what to put. It's raining down here. Hope you get a beaut suntan. Hope you're feeding yourself properly. Hope you're managing about washing. How the hell are you managing about washing? If you come back with a caseful of dirty underwear, you can wash the lot yourself. No, course I'll do that. And make you a big roast dinner and put your feet up and get on my knees to look for your slippers, hell Boyd, what else do you want of me?

If you want to know, the bed's cold and lonely and I won't ever complain again of the way your weight makes me slide to the middle even when I want to be right on the edge, as far as possible. Though I do need to do that. Sometimes, I need that. It's stupid, all I can think of is the beds we've been in. Hope yours is comfy – why the hell Brisbane? No, I know why. Your mum told me straight away this address was your grandmother's. Yes, they phoned. We were all worried. If I could reach you by phone I'd be nagging you by the hour. So you were probably better off to do what you did. Hope it's working. Hope whatever it is, you are finding it, or doing it, or learning, or learning to do without, or whatever it is.

No, it's right for it to be without me. I phoned your doctor too. He says he understands and will see you sometime when you are ready. That make you happy? That make you unhappy? He says if it makes you neither, then you're probably just about right to come home.

The beds. Remember that big jangly brass one in Hobart, our second holiday? That's the one I remember. It was the patchwork quilt I lusted after. That was the time I was going to make one for myself, all through the long winter nights. Before I took on the second lot of Grade 8s. Or that narrow bed we both squeezed into at your mother's place, so we had to ruffle up the other one in the morning. We were dumb those days, you should have insisted on a double. We should have taken over their bed, they could have quite happily shared singles for one night. Now it's about our turn. When and if you come back, we've got to sit down and talk. Really talk, I mean, out in the open. A whole new negotiation. Is it crazy if I write about nothing but beds and how lonely I feel in this double one, if I then go and say we should swop it for twin mattresses? Just that bit of separateness. See what you've done, Boyd. I've been doing a lot of thinking too. It can't go back to the way it was before, that I am certain about. I feel as if I am scrawling this against that solid brick wall. Please open a window somewhere, a door, yours might be brick, but mine feels like clear perspex and it's so cold inside.

You bastard, you must know I love you.

But the way it is we keep eating off each other. Come back down as soon as you feel able. Let's share a meal together – fish, fowl, cauliflower, but not fellow.

Yr
Marie

Boyd could feel the way she had slapped the thick pages together, rammed them into her envelope, made a loud rattle in the stationery drawer for postage stamps. He could see how she would stride to the letterbox outside their units. Once it was shoved in, cut apart from her, she would lose urgency. It would be done. No retracting, no way of going back.

He would have reached out, then, wrapped an arm around her, ready to protect, prepared to give her space, make coffee, listen. How long for? How much of anything had he really given her?

The letter clung to his fingers as if the blood drained through them. It was a long time before the pulse seemed his own. It was, perversely, a denial of identity. He was a grab-bag of inheritances, none his own.

He sat down and began his reply. Then he crumpled it. Things had changed. Impossible! He could not fit anything to words yet. Perhaps if he left it until tomorrow?

Marie

She had been at the kitchen table for perhaps half an hour. Her coffee was cold. She was not thinking anything, she was not thinking of anything.

What did Boyd think he was doing? His silence hurt. Was it a calculated insult or merely unthinking selfishness? If he did phone, what would Marie say?

After the first rush of pleasure and reassurance she would be complaining, angry. She had seen that happen with mothers of her pupils. Mrs Fitzwarren the time her Brian sliced himself with the dissecting scalpel. She rushed into the room with bandages and wadding, then burst into a whole storm of abuse, 'You're so thoughtless why don't you consider your mother,' and the poor boy still dazed with shock.

In a little while she would get up, force down some food. She would write another letter.

Poor old Boyd, sitting up there in some gloomy flat, having it out with himself. But he was right. Nobody else could help him.

And herself? There had been Dr Steiner. Yes, of course he was a father surrogate, but it helped. It had helped. Others had helped. She had become conscious of a whole support system, of how many friends she had, of how warm and generous people could be.

In a way Boyd was more dependent. He would find being alone more difficult.

That quarrel this afternoon, with Dagmar. How dictatorial of Dagmar to order her to put Boyd from her mind. How bullying she was about the plane reservation. She just did not understand, she just did not.

Even this coffee cup was one of a set he had given her, two Easters back. And she had given him the percolator. Big laughs over that. Big laughs.

A knock. Marie looked at her watch. Six thirty. Dagmar, wanting to make up. Marie went to the door.

It was big Geoff Collins from school, his tight bulk taking up most of the door space.

'Why Geoff, this is a surprise . . . '

'Come to cheer the wounded sailor.' He broke across her puzzled greeting and pushed his way in. 'Won a meat tray in the Club raffle so I thought, bring it over to poor old Marie, got to get some meat into her,' and he laughed in the narrow hallway so that the regulation height ceilings seemed to be lower than they really were. He slapped a polystyrene slab onto the kitchen table, shoving aside the coffee mug and Marie's book.

'No, you should take that home to Karen. Have you been drinking?'

Out of his baggy coat pocket Geoff produced a half bottle of scotch. 'Won that too. Big day today. Big day tonight. Aw c'mon, Marie, not the sours, not from you. Here I thought you'd be in it for a bit of the old jollity. Now isn't that splendid meat? The royal offering.' He could be like a big schoolboy. 'And besides, Karen has a freezer full of the stuff, she buys up big at the markets. This is for you, love.'

Marie avoided his big beery kiss.

'Geoff, don't be a twit.' She hated herself for the word. So schoolgirl.

'Nice bit of haunch for the lady. Nice bit of raw meat.'

Geoff was definitely tipsy.

'What say I rip the zip, untap the flap, bring it out into the open. Stick it . . . in the fridge.' He bubbled and bumped against the refrigerator door as he picked up the meat tray again and slid his finger in through the gladwrap, wiggling it leerily. He pulled out a large sausage and waggled it towards Marie.

'Geoff you are a big loon, put that down. You're not boasting are you?'

'Marie, my lovely princess, I didn't think you were interested. But you know good old Geoff never boasts. Doesn't have to. Prime beef all the way, and lots of it.'

She had made an error of tactics, but badinage was her best resource.

Geoff ripped his tie half-down. His eyes were focused now, intent.

'Now you just pack up your parcel and tootle on to Karen. Chase her round the kitchen with it. Prove your point with her.'

'Forget Karen. Here I've come to comfort the lost, lorn and lonesome. Don't look so uptight, Marie, for Christ's sake, it's only a bit of fun. A bit of harmless kiss and cuddle.' His large arm reached round to her taut buttocks.

'No, Geoff. Don't do something you'll be sorry for later. You're letting yourself get carried away.'

'Damn right I am. It's you. Don't you see it's you, Marie. You're just one hell of a dish, to put it bluntly. And if you ask me, Boyd can't bloody see when he's on to a good thing. To put it crudely. And okay, I am a bit crude. But affectionate. The little boy inside. And it seems what you really need just now is a bit of real affection, a little bit to boost the morale and the soft warm insides. We could have good fun together. It doesn't have to be serious or rock anyone's boat, nothing like that. Works wonders for the tension. Nature's best remedy. Plenty of foreplay,' he whispered as his arm reached out again. Surprisingly soft hands.

For just a moment Marie allowed contact. Again, a mistake. He was pressing her now against the wall. She tried to break out.

'Geoff, let's be sensible. I'm no slut.'

'What I'm proposing is nothing slut-like at all. It's more a sacred mystery, veils of the temple, let me show you how I can pamper you, baby.'

He was rubbing his big belly against her. Marie could not avoid laughing. 'You have too many wet dreams and fantasies. I'm just an oridinary woman.'

'You tried it with anyone else? Other than hubby? You need liberating, baby. I'll give you the ultimate encounter session. Dream therapy.'

Marie escaped back into the hall. She caught sight of Geoff lifting the phone from the hook, disconnecting it. The deliberation. Predator, scenting out the woman alone. 'That's all they're good for,' he would boast later, down at the pub, in the men's room.

'Why did you do that?'

'Can't stand interruptions. Nice and slowly. Nice and gentle now, sweetie.'

She dodged past him into the living-room, but he shielded the telephone desk with his huge girth.

'Geoff you big, fat tub, how could you possibly think yourself sexy?' She tried to sound mocking.

'You know you're aching for it. You're sending out signals like morse. Have been for days. At the party. Every male in the place panting after you. Perhaps not Peter and Ian. Perhaps even them. Like a pussy in heat. Just on heat to be pampered. I'm your boy. I know how to do it real real, real gentle.' Cat and mouse. Yet there was something hypnotic. When he touched it was soft, explorative. For a moment Marie allowed herself, again, to be touched, fondled.

It was ridiculous.

'Karen,' she whispered, as if it were a charm. It was no charm. 'You're so damned confident. That's what I don't understand. What makes you think you're irresistible? Poor Geoff, poor big enormous Geoff, don't you ever look in the mirror?'

'I look in the faces of others, baby, it's all pretty assuring. Who wants skinny boys when they can get down with the men? Let it just happen.'

'You're smug. You're impossible.'

'Everything's possible. Haven't you realized that yet?' He had exposed one of her breasts. Marie suddenly thought of a baby, needing to suckle. Nursing mothers told her it was immensely sexual, the act of breast feeding.

'You know you've always liked me, admit it. Every nice friendship needs to be taken to the limit. I could go to bed happily with everyone I am fond of.'

Marie gently pushed his mouth from her neck. She tried to maintain her tone of banter.

'What? Even Bob Jamieson? You're friends with Bob.'

'Could be. Never tried it, but there's lots of ways to explore. That's where sex is such a wonderful mixer. You really get to know people.'

'Oh, Geoff, I can't imagine it. You and Bob together; like adolescents down in the showers, masturbating each other. That's really sordid.'

'Well, it doesn't have to be, but Bob's not the subject at this moment. Marie's much more interesting.'

'Does Karen know about all this – this misplaced affection?'

'Karen's some lady. She's some real sexy lady. Say, why don't we make a threesome some time together? Join the trend of the suburbs. All sorts of things you can do together.'

'Geoff, not even when I'm old and bored and forty, or faded and fifty, can I imagine myself joining the frantic suburban panic. Yes, I know it's happening all over. But to me it seems bound entirely to the law of diminishing returns. Sex is not just another bedroom novelty.'

'You're so sure. Come on, you're just aching for it.'

Marie was abrupt. It takes a long time for natural warmth and affection to be tugged from one's perception. So many words and actions can be interpreted subjectively. Yes, she could have fallen for it. She wanted to be a victim. She wanted it.

That was Geoff's expression. The cynicism, unbelievable. Sausage waggler. Impossible. The boor in rut. Blind, barging, stuffed to bursting with self-confidence and swagger.

She was alone with him, and he could certainly overwhelm her, indeed had every intention of doing just that. The telephone. The way he pushed in to the apartment. Taking his fill of her. Then he would swagger out, licking his lips at another conquest.

'I think I'm going to phone Karen. Just tell her what you're up to.'

He did not answer. His body so bulky.

'Geoff. Let me go. I mean it. This goes no further.'

'Baby, there's nothing you can do now, just let it happen.'

'Geoff. Let me go.'

'If you're silly you'll get hurt and we don't want that to happen. Not when it can all be so nice and sexy. Nice and horny.'

There would be no foreplay.

'You're a bloody rapist. I could have you criminally charged.'

'Don't call me that. Just relax, Marie, Christ sake, where's that bed.'

She broke through into the room and as Geoff lurched towards the bed, dragging her down, she managed to twist out. She ran to the hallway.

It would be ridiculous to flee from your own flat. Geoff was still on the bed. Now he began pleading. She saw the whisky bottle and quickly she poured a large glass. Deliberately she took it back to him. He lay there like a very large baby. His erection had subsided.

When Dagmar called round later, Geoff was still sleeping. In repose, he looked vulnerable; angelic. The tiredness seemed unending.

Boyd

The Pattersons lived out at Kenmore on two and a half acres of 'natural' bushland that Bruce Patterson intended to sub-divide 'when the kids have grown up'.

'We'd normally dine out. Gambaro's or Milano's. But you sort of caught us off-foot as it were, Boyd. Couldn't believe it when Sarah reminded me this morning, wasn't it tonight we'd asked you for a meal? I've been kept so busy almost since January. And besides, I knew you'd like most to see the kids. So you could go home, tell the wife shapes and sizes.' Bruce laughed heartily. 'Got some new colour prints last week. Tell you what, you can take one of each of the kids to show, uh, Marie. There's a good one with me in it, down at the boat-ramp. Never really got to know Marie. Golly, it's a long time. Seems generations.'

The swimming pool was enormous, set in a flagged area, landscaped with hardy greenery and pinebark. Behind a discreet screen of abelia were trampoline and swings. Several Peugeot pushbikes sprawled on the lawn. Neighbourhood kids, Bruce explained. They literally lived in each other's pockets here. Whole tribes would descend, raid the fridge then depart. A great place to grow up in.

The living-room was immense. There was a sunken pit in the centre where a concourse of settees made it impossible to do anything other than sprawl. Bruce led the way to the kitchen. 'That's antique red cedar.' He tapped solid wood doors to another bank of cabinets. 'And that's Sarah.'

His wife, a pleasant-looking woman with bouffant hair, earrings and an almost central-European ornamental apron, reached out her hand, apologizing for the mess. There was none visible. Alas, she explained, they would be eating off scraps tonight.

His godson, Craig, was a pale ten year old who became sulky when dragged from television. He stared at Boyd and shuffled those Adidas sneakers. His shoes were luminous, green and blue. After obligatory questions about school, grades and sport, Boyd was relieved to let him return to some undersea diet.

'Craig's really very chirpy and chatty, you know,' Sarah promised. She ruffled her son's hair, an act he resisted. 'But he's had this sniffly cold. It's hung on and on. My God, has it hung on! His nasal cavities must manufacture gallons.'

Boyd remembered he did not really like children.

'What brings you here?' Sarah suddenly demanded, as soon as they were seated in the divan pit.

'I don't know. No, that's not true. I'm preparing a paper for the Legal Conference.'

'But the conference is May. Bruce has promised me a new fur coat for the Conference Dinner. That's if the weather cools off. So I know it's May, fourth to fourteenth.'

'Should be cool in May.'

'Yes.'

'Well, I came up here early to finish this paper. Space to breathe, to concentrate.'

'You not having trouble at home, Boyd? Tiffs with the wife?' Bruce, jovial. Sarah tut-tutted, and looked up.

'Matter of fact I have been looking out my old grandmother's house. Whole string of associations.'

'Oh I see. Sentimental journey.'

'Sort of.'

There were antiques in this room. Over-glossy, perhaps reproductions.

'What suburb?'

'Toowong. Almost to Auchenflower.'

'Good investment there. Got a few old colonials there meself. Rental, but it's the land of course. One of them I might do up, it's sort of pretty, verandahs and old iron, that sort of stuff, very trendy now.'

'Can't stand it!' Sarah put in firmly. 'Smelly old bathrooms and wobbly floors and ingrained grime of a hundred years.' Her weekly help would keep this place immaculate.

The teak dining-room table looked virgin, unused. They had brought out the good silver. Boyd's Bohemian glass goblets were extravagant, fussy in this setting. Marie would have prized them. Dagmar would explode with envy. Things out of one's past.

Over the meal, a microwave oven heat-up out of freezer and the supermarket, Boyd raised the name of Pashim Khan.

Sarah looked tight.

'I found him disturbing. Strangely impressive.'

'You never met him. Face in the crowd.'

'Still; your story. The slave labour bit was sordid enough. Yet there was something, as you pointed out.' Boyd paused. 'We all see the world differently, don't we?'

Sarah put down her fork. 'I don't let Bruce talk shop at home. Mr Khan can stay out there – somewhere – where he is.'

'Sarah's right. Place to relax, place to get away from it all. Oasis.'

'Still,' Boyd insisted, 'I've been trying to remember. Wasn't there some report about broken limbs; resorting to torture? You've got to admit, Bruce, that creates a different perspective.'

'You're so superficial, so smug, Boyd. For instance, you have not even taken into account current fundamentalist Islamic thinking on punishment. And besides, the real point is that all the charges against Khan fell down. That's what counts. That is the only thing to remember.'

'Really, you boys. One would never think you were old friends.' Sarah poured more wine. 'This is the first time we've used this marvellous silver,' she added. 'It's French. Christofle. As soon as I read that the Premier had ordered Christofle silver for our new Parliament House I said to Bruce, that's what we will have. Bruce could make it our anniversary present. We had the old set since the wedding. It was so dated I was ashamed to produce it. And if this new stuff is good enough for the Premier, it will suit us.'

'It was Parliament, not the premier, ordered it,' corrected Bruce. 'But I checked it out. Absolutely invincible investment.'

'You're a fan of Queensland's Premier?' Boyd edged himself forward.

'Oh, I'm right behind him. He certainly knows how to keep all the reds, all the students and protestors in their place. He fronts up to them. Tells them who's boss,' interposed Sarah.

'What about you, Bruce? How do you feel about some of the more – well – restrictive bits of legislation? These constant States of Emergency? What's the legal reaction to all that? You know, there have been some pretty hillbilly things.'

'If you want to look at it legally, I think there's more funny stuff going on in Victoria. Or what about New South Wales under Askin? I'm waiting for someone to lift the lid on *that*.'

'The kids,' Boyd began, but then corrected himself, 'some of the kids I have talked to up here seem to think the Premier's about to tear down the old Bellevue.'

'Not soon enough for me, is what I think of that. Oh, I know there are a lot of people who have a sentimental affection, all that. The old conservatives, National Trust people, some of the old fogeys. But honestly, Boyd, have you looked at that place? It's a wreck. Yes, I know they tore off all the old verandahs and iron-work. It wasn't safe otherwise. Friend of mine told me the whole pub is just sticking together by inertia. Full of dry rot. The bricks turn to dust if you touch 'em, that sort of thing. To restore it would be out of the question. Cost a fortune and you'd end up virtually with a new building, so many things to be replaced. No, the Bellevue's just sentimental claptrap. It's not as if it were any architectural wonder, just another old country pub. Can't turn the whole city into a museum.'

'My memories of it are all sentimental,' Boyd conceded. 'But when I walked down that way, I was shocked.'

'Doesn't it look ugly!' Sarah gulped from her crystal.

'Very ugly. Very wretched. A scene of desolation,' Boyd shook his head. 'It's amazing what effect just tearing off those verandahs has done. Whoever organized that knew he was on to a *fait accompli*. Still, have other architects' opinions been given?'

'I know you'd be all for restoration. Well, I did give it some thought, you know. Some of my friends have been very influential campaigners for the Bellevue. You can imagine: the Brisbane Club. And the Queensland Club, I go there sometimes too, you know.' Making sure Boyd did know. What did it matter?

'You watch,' Bruce promised. 'Six months' time nobody will even remember the Bellevue. Six months at the longest.'

'I wonder. Some things can't be swept away so easily.'

'Take Pashim Khan. Six months, that's all it took for Pashim. When the last batch of charges were finally dismissed, it only made page 8 of the *Courier*. One small par. So much for headlines. You can forget the Bellevue, Boyd. Forget it.'

Bruce offered to drive Boyd back to his flat shortly after the meal. There was a programme on the box he was anxious to watch. He had to get his relaxation.

How could Boyd focus on figures? The heavens were corrupt, pulled into black powers.

If his paper on white collar crime were to have value, it must be expanded infinitely. How many conference delegates were guilty?

Who else in that University? In his own? Which bankers, storekeepers, solicitors, barristers, contractors, parliamentarians? Once you conceived of the idea of this taint, it revealed itself everywhere. Boyd himself, could he honestly present this with immunity? Crime is not always action. All this week, he must admit it, what he was facing was his own self-accusation: guilty.

Boyd took his drafts and his papers down to the dark backyard incinerator. He struck the match. Watched as they scooped up in the air, an incredible distance of flame in so few moments. The leaves of the mangoes scorched and buckled. Those new leaves. With their sheen; dried out in two seconds. The mass crumpled, turned in on itself. Light curving. Boyd waited until the last glows were merely needles in the blackness. He went upstairs then, where he discovered Marie's letter had been scooped up with the other papers. He poured himself whisky.

Boyd could not sleep. He went out to the front room, pulled the tattered curtain. A streetlight pushed in with its brightness. Boyd moved a step, into shadow. Perhaps there had been voices.

Then Boyd grew aware of sounds, down the side of the house, where the crazed concrete path pushed through an avalanche of bushes. Movement. At first he thought it was possums, or the dog Kali.

This was human; sound of harsh breathing. Boyd moved over to the window.

After a while it was Cora he heard, a low throaty whisper, as if she were half listening for Boyd, inside.

'If you'd listen, Olof.' The slight bump of bodies against timber. Nothing. Boyd was straining.

A caught sob. 'Now you've finished. Get to hell out of here.'

'All right, I will. Know what you are? You're a frigid cockteaser. Give yourself graces. Just 'cause your old man fucked you senseless that's no reason you can't give it to me. You and your pansy-boy.'

'Get your things out of this place. You've broken the agreement.'

Boyd wished to sound authoritative. 'Want any help?' There was a scuffle.

'Okay. I'll get out. Whole lot of yuz is screwed. Right to there. Up yourselves to the hilt.'

A door slammed. Slammed again. The bike revved brutally. Olof scorched off with only the things he stood up in. Did that mean he'd be back?

'You okay?'

'Sorry about that. Sorry. Sorry. It was my fault. Yes, if you want to know, I did sort of encourage him. Thought I could handle it, keep him in control. He's just a bloody rapist. Same as my father. Never learn.'

She was, indeed, sobbing. 'You never learn, do you?'

FRIDAY

Marie

Marie sat on a bench in the little park near their unit. The row of huge elms had just begun to turn. A scrawny man came by on a pushbike. He eyed her hopelessly but with lust. She pretended to be reading her book. She licked a finger and turned the page. The man slid his bike to the ground across the path, then pulled himself down and unclipped his trouserlegs. From a hessian shoulderbag he produced a dark brown bottle. He took a gulp. Perhaps he was thirty-five. Perhaps he was twenty-five, or nineteen. He looked used up.

Did it always show so cruelly?

She must avoid this self-pity, it was ridiculous. It was simply not true that every man now read the fact of her aloneness into her stance, her look, her behaviour. It was not true she was dependent, a toy, an annexe – of Boyd or of anyone. Dagmar was right to explode at her.

She tried to brace herself by remembering Jean Cassimatis in the staff common-room weeping and confiding in Marie that she had no bank account of her own, it all went into a joint one with her husband and she had no idea what was rightly her own portion. A week before the separation he had simply signed a cheque and cleared the whole account. She had heard he was in Darwin. She could not even pay the phone bill which turned up just after – he had spent a fortune on STD calls.

Dagmar was right, they were all right.

Boyd's parents: after all these years Mrs Kennedy's surprise to learn her mother-in-law had been someone entirely different. Appearances belie. Or perhaps they don't at all, but if we want to believe the lies then we do.

The young/old man had raised himself and was now pushing his bike away slowly. Two girls, around eight, ran across. Their noise was like gulls, piercing, denying the smoothness and well groomed exteriors no doubt parent-imposed.

A bank clerk walked like a shadow along the footpath under these buildings. He seemed a parody of 'bank clerk', did he recognize that? Down to polished black shoes (almost certainly double knotted) and the dark leather attaché-case: which was smooth, oiled, not like Marie's own case, scratched and furred from struggles with daily work and living and facing up to those students yet again. There was one ink stain that went back to the time when people used ink; that old. Marie could not be parted from her case. It was part of herself and she prized its shabbiness. Somehow, for her, it still had style. It was not true that she was always trying to discard the past. Another one of Boyd's accusations.

Another clerk-like person. The way his head thrust forward; did Australian men never lift their faces and look directly ahead? So many seemed to aim at their own toes, nothing higher. Boyd carried himself well. Part of his boyishness, the husky, young man looking upward.

Boyd was riddled with insecurities: true?

Damn it, she would fly up. He would be astonished and impressed. It would demonstrate her concern. She could fly back after the weekend. She would tell him about Geoff. No, she would not tell him. Damn Boyd! She *needed* him. And yet. Dagmar was right. Last night, finally she had not needed Boyd at all. Sheepish Geoff, when Karen came. The three of them shoving him into the station wagon. Indulgent conspirators. Boys will be boys. Ach!

She stood up and with unhurried but too purposeful steps walked to her apartment block. It was not physical exhaustion. For the first time since Boyd had left, Marie took out their photograph album. She removed the last shot of Boyd, grinning and about to leave the front door. His back was to the camera, that broad shoulder. Head turned back, at Marie's shout. The look, trapped in chemical by her new flash equipment showed surprise (the eye blackened, a white dot of refraction) but also intense eagerness and (what was it?) anticipation that her shout had been a happy, enjoyable one. As if their life together, really, had been sharing and finding and discovering things. No look of caution, nor of being trapped, of expecting complaint or bitterness, from her cry. Marie missed his body. Thought of bed at the moment held only the appeal of pure rest. Her nights had been endlessly restless. She knew, tonight, it would be the sleep of refreshment. Strange, how the mind can so order the body.

Marie went to the kitchen and turned on the front gas jet. She would have a cup of that good camomile tea, not bitter old coffee. The little packet of sachets was at the back of the groceries cupboard somewhere, she had seen it only Tuesday. She reached on her toes but it was not there. There was some lemon-grass tea though; that was even better.

Strange, how even that action seemed to portend well. She really preferred lemon-grass, but had not remembered they still had it. Marie fumbled for matches. The last one in the box broke at the head almost at first touch. Damn. Well, everything couldn't be symbols.

But the phone rang, as if on cue, and Marie dived out to answer it. It was the Kennedy number, Mrs Kennedy sounding quite worried. 'Marie. Thank goodness you're there. We've been trying to contact you all afternoon.'

'Nothing's happened?' Marie's voice tugged with alarm. 'It isn't something the matter with Boyd . . . ?'

'No, no, my dear, we were worried about you. You seemed so strange when we dined with you. So tight. We spoke into the wee hours discussing you, we were so worried. You do see, dear Marie, how important you are to us both. To us all. We were getting quite anxious. And then all day, I could get no answer. I phoned at least six times after I knew you should be home from the college . . . '

'I went for a stroll. They say it's good for you. But I've really made up my mind to fly up this weekend. To Brisbane.'

'Oh my dear. Oh, do you really think that's right? I mean, what if Boyd were not expecting you, and . . . '

'Are you telling me you think he might be doing – something? I don't believe it. Oh Mother, I think that's . . . well, that's shocking, I think. Or hilarious. Or, or something. Are you serious about that?'

'No, no Marie. No, it was a first reaction. It was foolish of me. Something that just flashed through my mind. Well, if you would know, I think it's because you flying up, chasing him up, that seems, well, presumptuous. Even untrusting. It seems as if *you* were taking the initiative.'

'Well, I am.' But Marie was shocked. 'Look, it's to ease my own mind: that more than anything else. And when I say ease my mind, that has nothing to do with what on earth Boyd is doing in Brisbane. He's writing a paper. But he could be leading a wild week up there too, that doesn't bother me. Perhaps I'd even be rather impressed. But I have decided I do have to live with my own pressures, and this is a damned good way of easing those pressures . . . I only have to say, Hello, Boyd, fancy seeing you here, and perhaps just a bit of a natter. I won't break in at midnight with torches and cameras. I'll probably phone him. Only I don't know if he does have the phone. I could stay at a motel in the city, send a telegram, say meet me for cocktails. I am not going to go sleuthing out your son, don't think that.'

'Marie, don't be so hurtful.'

'Oh, I'm sorry. I am sorry. I didn't mean that. Let's forget it. You know Boyd means everything. The last thing I want is to upset his balance, his delicate balance. But I have a feeling he might need me by now just as much as I damn well need him.'

'Ah Marie, you are right, you are really most forgiving. And yes, my dear, you will permit my saying' – oh so timid, Marie's guilt redoubled – 'I think Boyd might really be needing you by this, also. And he is so silly, so pig-headed. He would be the last to say. You know how he can go on. Yes, go up to him, I think that really is a wonderful decision. And Marie dear. Do forgive me.'

'Oh of course. We mustn't get ourselves into knots. Or Boyd will really be right to call us a pair of fussy old sillies.' Marie was an old master at collusive sympathy. She hated herself. Even her hands were shaking. It was silly.

She would have a nice warm bath. That would be soothing, that would be relaxing. She would fill it to the top and use up all the bath salts. She would soak it out of her. She would let it all float around her and through her and into her till she was herself floating effortlessly in water. Marvellous how the amniotic wash of a warm full bath could restore you, take you back to whatever primal source, the earth mother, the sea mother, the star mother, the dream to be everything and nothing, to merge with everything as if it were really possible to be extinguished. But it was terrible getting out. The water suddenly cold and tacky. Your own body blue and roughened and lined like tide ripples on the hands and fingers. We dreamed we were part of the ocean of the world, but we were flat footed, mundane, man with two feet and quivering belly.

Marie smiled, then gave a sigh. She would use one of the new towels that Boyd gave for her birthday. They were enormous, like those of her mother, to be wrapped in one was to be smothered in luxury, with dreams of every sensuous possibility. She did, yes, acknowledge her own mother in herself. She would imagine Boyd here, handing the towel. Grinning. She could imagine herself old as her mother was now, her body just a little softer, fuller and glowing like her mother fresh from the shower. Her mother? Her mother's body had once been raped repeatedly by occupying soldiers. Impossible to believe. Where had she learned such self-sufficiency to let it all slide away from her? Or was she irredeemably superficial? self-indulgent? sensual? Her mother's survival had been commercial and, in its way, ruthless. It was because she valued money that she spent it when she did, fulsomely. But she could be tight. A razorblade in the marzipan. Marie felt a strange warmth, a pride in her mother for that. She would phone her in the morning, she would try to make things up, it would not be impossible.

As she went to get the towel, Marie saw the window was open in the living-room. She shut it and checked the front door. Funny how, when Boyd wasn't there, she felt vulnerable in the bath. She had by now completely forgotten the thought of lemon-grass tea. She did not go back to the kitchen, nor did she smell gas.

Boyd

Marie was not in the bed beside him. Boyd became aware of thick mist, a fog: visibility zero – Marie was out there somewhere and her voice reached him through this muffled texture.

'I can't find you I can't find you anywhere. Boyd? Boyd, have you gone? I seem to be all alone, I can't locate the door or the bed, I just don't seem to touch anything. Is the fog where you are Boyd?'

He wanted to reassure her. Panic does not help. In a fog you just have to feel your way, find a wall and edge along. You will bump into a picture or a wardrobe and soon the door will be at hand, and you will locate yourself.

'Marie, just stay where you are. Whatever you do, don't stumble down the stairs. Use your feet and your hands, they will guide you. Where are you now?'

'I don't know.' Marie's voice sounded closer, just a little. 'I think it's the moonlight; it sort of dazzles this mist, makes it harder to distinguish things.

'I'll get up if you like. Just keep talking in a calm way and I will quickly find you.'

'No, Boyd. That would be foolish. I'm quite capable. It's foolish of me to disturb you. I could hear you sleeping: your breathing, like clockwork. Yes, and you did snore.'

'Come back here then. You'll get cold. Let me warm you up.'

'I can't do that. You know I can't do that. It's something I can't control. I've got to get away from you. I can't share a bed with you

Boyd, you burn, you keep me awake. I have horrible dreams of fires, and suffocation and you rolling over me, pinning me down. You've never felt the panic. It's terrible. In your sleep you keep taking something from me, I can't explain. Don't ask me to. Just try to understand.' It was the old line.

'No don't get angry, Boyd. I can't stand that. You know I feel guilty, I don't want to die. But you're in it somewhere too, Boyd. Is it cold in bed? I'm not cold here, not cold.'

'Marie. The bed is right here. You must be only two or three paces away. Why don't you try? Come over here. I won't even touch you, I promise . . .'

'You never did, Boyd, you never did touch me though we clung to each other desperately. Do you remember . . . ?'

'No, Marie, not past tense. You're ending things.'

'It's you, Boyd. You ended things so long ago. Long before you knew you ended them, you closed off any ways of change or of growing or of learning or knowing.'

'You're a bully, Marie, you always were, in your polite way. You said you had learned to change, you were always saying that; and you haven't changed at all, not since I've known you. You're still rattled by your mother, and you've still not learned to understand what great qualities she has; you still depend on others and yet rebuke them for giving you things; you still . . .'

'And you still speak *at* me, Boyd.'

There was a shift in the air. Not clammy, but movement and downdraughts. And still no visibility.

'Marie. You still there?'

'No, Boyd. You'll laugh at me – but I can't stop these tears. They hurt me, these tears. I'm trying to analyze them, some chemical deficiency I think. It's really very painful. Can the eye dissolve? They say an old torture was to cut off the lids. Is this a chemical mist? It's as if something were eating me away. I'm trying to hold the panic. I can't move. Do you feel this?'

'No, Marie, of course not, you must be dreaming. For goodness sake, forget all this. You've got your wish, I give in. I give you your separate bed. I give you . . .'

'No, Boyd. You don't understand yet. You can't say that. It's simply not for you to give or not give. Just as it's outside my direction also. It's just one of those adjustments that must be. Do you like my lips? Remember you once said, that first week up at Hayman, how red they were you didn't believe they were natural. Just like my mother, but I think she must use make-up by now. Do you think they will be corroded in this mist, Boyd? Can you hear me speaking clearly? I can't tell any more if they are moving I think they have been eaten away, it would be terrible if they were eaten away . . .'

'Marie, Marie, don't panic. God, what can I do? I can't bear to hear someone sobbing. Marie. Marie, come over . . .'

Ain't she afraid ain't she afraid.

Somewhere, deep inside or far outside, Boyd registered that the dawn must be approaching. Birds.

Ain't she afraid ain't she afraid toodleloo toodleloo ain't she afraid?

Currawongs, repeating endlessly their loud yet musical pattern.

Ain't she afraid ain't she afraid toodleloo toodleloo toodleloo toodleloo

Boyd woke in a sweat. The single bed with its sag and its old mattress scooped him in like a captive.

He had a long shower. It misted everything. To train his mind away from that dream Boyd thought of those old derelicts, brought into slavery for 10 cents from the watchhouse. Why should he concern himself with them, with what had happened to them, what was happening, what was to happen? Those who returned, dependent, for more punishment, rather than keep their own freedom. Why was he always returning, in his mind, to the depths of the Botanical Gardens to discover deprivation and stunned, passive derelicts? Nothing had happened there.

Cora last night. That return for more punishments, the need for humiliation. Childhood rape, could that really be correct?

Marie's dream: no, it had faded. Her letter yesterday, burning with humiliation and reproach. They were partners. They were all linked through connective hooks of human pain, need, injury.

Cora, at least, had felt guilt. Consequences. Not so grown up, that girl.

Her father.

Marie claimed guilt too. It was a long time before he had realized. It was years after their marriage that she explained to him the hurt of their first night; rape not seduction. Years after, and then with a sort of contrition. Once spoken, no way to retract. Do all close relationships devolve to guilt? Unsaid catalogues of things done, not done, till the simplest gesture becomes impossible, the most natural becomes a minefield.

On the terrazzo porch outside he discovered Olof. He was slumped, hands over forehead. Boyd noticed the torn leather cycle-jacket; graze across one eye.

'Pranged the bike down the road. Write-off.'

'What about yourself?'

'Just bits and pieces. Fuckin' ruined me good jacket but. Did a slewie, real broadside. Too fast. Where's the others?'

'How should I know? I'm not their keeper. You been inside then? I thought Cora chucked you out.'

'I got nowhere else, man. Spent half the night friggin' round. Burning up the bike. Get it out of me system. Just turning up this street again. I was going to roar the hell out of this street. Up and down. Hell of it. Jeesus I was.' Olof grunted. 'Then the prang.'

'If they're not inside then they must be off to picket the Bellevue.'

'Not there. Think they'd have me back in? If I, if I promised?'

'Who's to tell? They're not my wards.'

'Jeez, me head's splittin'.'

'Here. I might have some aspirin.' Boyd relented.

'Y'haven't got something for this graze too, any chance? S'pose you wouldn't have a cup of coffee? Something stronger? Whisky; haven't got a shot of whisky, hey? Hey, Boyd?'

'Oh come in, goddam it. Let me look at you.'

'Look all you want. Look all over, if you want. Say, how about I move in with *you*?'

'You're incorrigible!'

'You tryin' to flatter me? Fancy a bit yourself, on the side? A bit keen on the sausage as well as the soup, that it, Boydie?'

'Cut that out.'

'I seen you, other night, down the beat. Past the swings . . . '

'What's more to the point, Olof, is I saw *you*. And I had the tact and the decency not to mention it. What you do is your own concern.'

'Everyone's got the right to a bit on the side. You'd be surprised . . . '

'Is that thing between your legs the only motivating force you know, Olof? Indiscriminate rutting, purposeless, without any true sense of yourself . . . ?'

'Mate, I know myself. And I know my levels. Got more energy than you'll ever have. Sure, it's all in my prick. Sure it is. What of it? Likes of you don't even admit to yourself where the power is. Right in the prick, hard-on. Then you get sneaky, squizz out the corner of your eye at it, wanting it, envious of it, the real prick, the real ramrod. Power. No wonder you're all screwed up with women, Boyd, man, you're just envious of those who know where it is. You need some coaching man, need some coaxing. What say I move in over here; what say you and me work up some heat. Forget the ladies a bit. What I could teach you, baby, you'd go out then, and slay the whole lot, every last bitch.'

'You must really hate women, Olof. And you must hate yourself even more.'

'Wrong wrong wrong, buster. It's you's the one screwed up. It's because I love all of me, every part, that I got energy, man. It's just others don't know how to take it, that's where it gets me. Cora last night, tight as a bike-valve, yet underneath really wantin' it bad . . . '

'Look Olof, just clear out. You forget I'm in the law. I'm a legal man. You follow my gist?'

186

'Jeez. Jeez can't even joke round here. That's what I hate, lot of yuz. No humour, got no humour.'

'Swallow this, then out. I've a good mind to ram it down your throat.'

'Rapist.'

'You're the finish!' But Boyd had to smirk.

'Guess I could try over the road; Matt and Stephen . . .'

'So long as you keep clear of Cora.'

'Meaning? You think she's your property? You dig a bit of the ol' Cora for yourself? Say, yeeeeesss. Yes; but that's it.'

'I think you'd best clear off. I find I'm losing my temper.'

'Want a fight then?' Instantly.

'If you think you need that sop to your vanity. God, Olof, the shape you're in. Piss off. Quietly.' Boyd shoved out a note. 'Here. Go see a doctor for those lacerations.'

Olof paused. Then nodded. He accepted it. 'I'll be just over the road. If you want company . . .'

'Scram. What makes you so certain that *you* . . . ?'

'It's easy, mate. Energy. People find me irresistible.' Olof cracked a grin again. 'Give Cora my love, daddy-boy. Tell you this but. You've got nix chance of making her. No one has. Except very close family. Hey! And tell you another thing. That's a damned prick, a ramrod between your own legs there, waiting. You gotta learn to live with that; try it some time. You might enjoy it. See yuz.'

Boyd did not see Cora all day. Don did not appear. Impossible to start any sort of letter to Marie. He screwed up dozens of sheets of paper.

Olof came over late in the afternoon. 'Sorry, mate, 'bout last night and this morning. When I was kicked out like that: just went bonkers. Cracked open a full bottle of Southern Comfort. Wiped me out. This morning. Pretty much wiped me out the full day. Wiped everything out, fact is. Look, tell Cora this. I really am sorry. Like, I didn't know what I was doing. Well, I knew what I was doing but I just couldn't help it. Light the fuse, and bang, I'm a goner. Like dynamite. Yeh. And if I said things, you know, well that was all bulldust. Shake on it? Come on, shake on it, fella!'

It was Boyd who must again be made to feel apologetic.

Besides, the screwed-up letters had already decided it; Boyd knew he had to return to Melbourne. When Cora got back he would go to a phone, make reservations.

Something could be sorted out with Marie. That dream last night. After this sub-tropic hothouse anything between them should seem reasonable. He would not phone Marie, he was not ready. He would surprise her – again. He would. He would . . . he was not quite ready yet. A few last things to tidy up.

Olof was back, eager, ingratiating, an overgrown schoolboy with gravel rashes.

'Stephen says there's the big rally tonight. Outside the Bellevue. Says half the inside's ripped down, done in secret. Spite of the black bans. You better come. You better get there. Whatja say? Huh, Boyd? Better be in this one. With all of us. What y'say?'

Sipping his instant coffee, Boyd shook his head. 'Why should I give a damn? It hasn't touched me.' Then he paused. 'But Cora . . .'

'Forget her, man. Takes more than a bit of a poke to tilt her off-balance. Roots like a wallaby, that one. You believe me.'

Boyd snorted. 'No. Not you. No credibility rating with me any more.'

'None of my business, professor, what your rating game might be.' Olof swaggered off, leather jacket flapping.

Six o'clock.

Six thirty. Dark. The night flicked across suddenly. No gradation: extremes.

Seven.

He was pacing like a husband, a lover, a father, family. Crumpled pages, waste hours. Those incinerated lecture notes. Nothing. Back and forth. They had not returned. Nothing.

Seven fifteen.

Ridiculous. Boyd went to his rooms, gathered up coins, wallet, his ballpoint. They were not his responsibility. Carefully he locked windows and doors.

They came up the street. Noisy; exhausted. They had been down at the Bellevue all day, watching and picketing. It was true: inside people had been hard at it, despite industrial holdups and dangerous conditions. No catch cradles for falling debris or plate glass. The power still on. Half the inside was demolished already. They were saying the real work was about to begin. They had come back to make more placards, grab a bite to eat before the real action.

Boyd mentioned Olof, but abridged his version.

Cora pulled back her hair. She caught him in her sight, eyes scanned him.

'Look, I feel bad. About that. I was wrong to kick him out. Olof's got nowhere. You seen his father?'

'He found somewhere. Your mates Matt and Stephen.'

'That's okay then.' Cora looked relieved. 'Look: you've got to understand. We make our own decisions. And consequences. No protection racket. We make our own punishment, too, if that's how it turns out. So. You think Olof's just some sort of animal? Think I'm different? Or you, for that matter? He's in a situation he can't handle. I goofed it last night; it was me. So it was me takes the consequences. I acted like a fool. Olof's got problems, but so has everyone.'

'A bad investment all round.'

'Not at all. God, you're so superficial. Like your fine tailored grandmother. Behind glass mirrors, letting only small chinks of real feeling surface. Think you can blind everyone else with your prim little dazzle. Here, I'm going over. Think I'd rather have Olof. I know where I am with him.'

'Don't let me stop you. Though for someone who says you "root like a wallaby" I can only say your tolerance seems damned stupid.'

She strode past him, pale with anger, in the dark she turned back.

'At least he's no pussyfoot.'

What did she mean? Inconceivable she could be acting like someone rejected? Had there been messages, promises, invitations, and Boyd had missed them?

TOOT FOR THE BELLEVUE

Boyd found himself carrying his placard with the others. He stood in the crowd along William Street, at the back of the old building.

Rumour had passed round that demolition would start from there, from behind.

'Usual form,' muttered Don, sparkling again with excitement. He had knocked together a couple of dozen placards and was handing the last ones round. The street had been dense with cars, lights dipping and then up full-beam, horns, arms, almost a party.

Behind Boyd a small group of punks formed a little knot. Green hair, henna tufts, a sort of London East End aggro but with suntans.

'C'mon, Mega, give it a go. Y'r chance to crack the lockup.'

'What? With this mob? They'll have me singing hymns in the cell.'

'Do ya good. Might learn a few tricks.'

'Square Dance anyone? Do-si-do?'

'C'mon c'mon. This place gives me the creeps. What sort of place is this place? What they wanta save that for, anyway?'

'Let's shift, yuz mob. No action here.'

'Stuff it, Megaton. Let's stir this mob a bit.' Cora had offered a placard.

'Jeez. Ya wanna *save* this dump?'

'Jesus Saves, Jesus saves,' chanted the one called Megaton. The henna'd one dutifully laughed. She was smaller.

'Look, Mega, it's the political heavies behind all that.' One of her skinhead pals in plastic leather reminded her, 'Not the dump itself; it's the way they dumped it.'

'Yair. Yair, power to the people! Power to the purple!' Her voice grew louder, though in the large crowd only her neighbours noticed. 'Power to the punks.'

The little group was shovelling its way out of the centre again. 'Let's hit the Curry Shop,' one of them piped.

Cora caught Boyd's eye, then shrugged. 'They're uncommitted. Fair enough. That's their choice.'

'Huh. Take that logically and you'd find *all* your ideals short-circuited.'

'Look around. We've got the numbers.'

'But not the machinery.'

There was a ten foot high wire mesh fence protecting the back area of the hotel. Inside, figures in overalls moved. Their presence prickled the crowd.

Half an hour before, Don and Cora had been joined by four of the State Parliamentarians, some of the Liberal coalition. It was said more would turn up to make their protest. Some of the younger ones. They had been intense, disgusted. It was one of them, Mr Akers who was also an architect, Cora whispered, who confirmed reports that the demolition squad would move in any moment. The contractors had been instructed by phone from the Premier's office: raze the site overnight. It could take as little as three hours.

'What was all that from the Premier about a month?' Boyd reminded the others. No one responded.

The police reinforcements arrived. Placards rose like agitated whisks against a wasp plague. In Boyd's ears sound had already become waspbuzz, close-packed bodies moved in a swarm. TOOT FOR THE BELLE VUE TOOT FOR THE BELLEVUE, and the pitch was inside him, his eyes were part of a multi-faceted focus.

Radio stations had been broadcasting the news, the bulb-flash of cameras punched light and dark. The after-theatre crowds were converging, well dressed couples, some running, they were pulled into the agitation, the common voice deciding them: this was no student rag-bag it was part of their very city making them shout with the others, 'Save the Bellevue save the Bellevue.' Some paused on the edges. Some pushed by, but most became participants. Police lights covered them with parade ground light.

Traffic was jammed. Boyd could not tell what might happen; he found himself chanting alongside the others, rhythmically, 'Save the

Bellevue save the Bellevue.' Next to him was a woman who clutched her Lurex bag and had eyes shining; her partner bellowed his chant like a footballer. He was wearing a seersucker striped suit. A small group of dark-clothed priests and nuns were just in front. Boyd caught sight of the punks, shouting in unison with others. Party time, louder than radio 4ZZZ up full volume. It was a congregation that mixed together fervour and ridicule, glee and derision, a church service blended with kids' party games and the boozy league finals. It was desperately serious. Fuse-wire, trip-wire, balancing.

Someone was pushed over.

No. An accident. The tiniest tremor, but prepared for anything. The uniformed police sent out shockwaves. Boyd was reminded of those Nazi rallies, 1930s. For an instant he imagined he saw Marie's dark head and profile in the crush across from him.

Impossible.

The figure was lost in the wave of heads, shoulders, eyes focused towards that sudden presence of dark blue uniforms. Marie? Boyd lurched towards that figure. A dark head, bobbing; long elegant neck in her characteristic uptilt. Without conscious thought he was pushing others roughly in order to find her. Eagerness, elation, surprise. For days it was possible to move in independent action, to discover new motivation, but one glimpse – hardly a glimpse, a subliminal flash of Marie's fine nose, the large brown eyes straining, the wonderful hugging cupful of black hair that framed her forehead – one moment to contact sight of her and the pulse through his head and body rocked him to immediate action. No explanations. No talking things over. Marie somewhere and Boyd must find her.

The figure was gone again. Of course he was mistaken. There was a sudden deflection and noise from the crowd, behind the backs. Six heavy trucks with two smaller vehicles pushed their way through, slowly, and with inexorable deliberation. People were pushed away, they scattered, then shoved. Placards bobbed in the ripple. The trucks forced their surly passage right up to the wired enclosure. Somewhere on the other side the figure who might be Marie had been divided from Boyd. Of course it was not her.

Electricity. Crowd tension.

Then Boyd was caught up from behind by the crush. He was rammed suddenly against wire. Like those about him he began tearing hard at it. The chant inside his head, part of his nerve-tissue, tearing. He might almost not have been shouting. But he was, throat tight as wire. A crush of policemen from the other side bumped, shoved and jarred against them through wire. Punches somewhere. High pitch of male insult. Then the outside policemen were among them, tearing coats, shirts and shoulders backward, pummelling and pulling till they forced through an entry. Boyd found his fingernails torn as his grip of the wire became ripped from him. Thwack of truncheons. He was tugged and jostled abruptly by a heavy sergeant then flung out.

The flash of anger was pure enmity. It caught Boyd by surprise with its passion. Bastard. Bastard. That one act made a foe of him. Boyd understood warfare instantly. He was pure snarling animal, savage with blood-lust. Someone tugged him gently to one side.

'Get back here. Get back there. Keep back off.' The megaphone voice butted and jarred.

For a moment the restraining grip might have been Marie. It was Don.

'Hey, Boyd; keep control, not so wild now. This has got to be peaceable.'

Boyd flushed with attrition. He caught his breath. There were TV cameramen; a radio announcer was arrested, and Boyd grew embarrassed at the spectacle he was making. He had lost sight of Marie, Cora did not exist, Don quickly dodged elsewhere. All were part, finally, of the same tide wave, but the few who lost control stood like sparks, threatening the whole momentum.

Police managed to cordon off the precinct. The groups were forced back. Some were moving off now, back along George Street into the city centre, as if the performance were over, as if they had not been part of it. Someone passed round beer cans. Someone waved at a cameraman. That glimpse of Marie – how could it be possible? Or was it really possible? Why not make the flight up to Brisbane? After all, he did. Was she there in the crowd, looking for him? She would know that this was where he must be.

Through a cardpack of faces Boyd stared anxiously, eager. Restless. They would be in this together. No need for explanations, just the act of participating. The rush to the airport. The rush to the water at Hayman. The first sharing of things together; why not this, too?

A decade vanished, just like that. Just like that? And this last week, these few days?

Boyd lurched on two uneven blocks of paving-stone, part of the ancient carriageway of the Bellevue. That sudden instant of *déjà vu*: the warm night air, almost tropical, yes, it could have been Hayman Island. Impossible; more than impossible. This sweaty crowd was full of strangers. Don was a stranger; Cora. Marie was more of a stranger than any of them. The memory was of a sudden moment of remoteness, as he and Marie had stumbled across uneven paving, one night on the honeymoon, and it had struck him with a terrible grief that this girl, this new woman, his wife, was someone he would never know, who would be distanced from him forever. He had pushed that moment out of his mind, he had laughed loudly so that he surprised her and had invented jokes. He had kept them laughing for hours, that night. And after, when they clung together, she said nothing about his sobbing, though it had racked him suddenly and seemed to open up forever. Then, just as suddenly, it had dried up. At the time he could not explain it. No need to explain everything, Marie had murmured, stroking him gently. No need to lay it all out.

To have that return, instantly, with this moment of stumbling over uneven paving stones in the darkness. In the crowd where there was nobody who could ever understand what it was Boyd had been instantly swept back towards, he realized his total alienation. And it was this realization, he had to admit, that made the one person who had actually engendered that alienation the only one capable of sharing it with him. Marie had been bound into his fibre.

It was not Marie.

Through the cardpack of faces Boyd stared anxiously, unable to account for his eagerness, unable to believe the superficiality of his responses. Don, in the mêlée, gave him a wave, as if Boyd were still the same person. Cora, up ahead with others, like a remote and different species. He had never known Marie. He had taken what he wanted of her, all he needed, and then in a sense had discarded her. What could they have said, now, after greeting and exclaiming at the noise, the excitement, the incoherence? He was an idiot. Marie here? Never.

Further back than Hayman. He was defending the ghost of the Bellevue Hotel that was part of his grandmother's precinct. He was seeking her favour, her approval. Would she never let him escape?

Boys don't cry, Boyd, big boys never cry. The night he had become engulfed in those dry, racking gulps it was not Marie but his grandmother who stopped him. He would have to destroy her entirely. He had uncovered his grandmother's tears only once. Terrible. He would never own her.

Someone behind him hissed: 'That one, look. Taking photos. He's the one, plainclothes pig; he's snapping everyone here.'

Boyd instantly thought: Marie, don't let her be photographed, tabbed, fingerprints taken, lined up for police surveillance. Unbearable. It was the 1938 Vienna of her mother etched in ghostly photographs of Nazi stormtroopers.

No, not Marie. Himself? Hell, yes, he must be counted.

On the outer edges of the crowd more people backed off; some shuffled almost guiltily, almost gleefully. Street theatre: Marie would see that.

In the gaps of space from the slackening crowd there was a tropic night breath, part of the slow moving body.

It was early morning. A lull.

SATURDAY

In the Park

The big boy led the way. He pushed through the thicket and as he shoved ahead the long canes of the clump whipped back and strapped Boyd's face. He held his arm in front to protect himself, the way he saw the bigger boy was doing. They reached a small clearing in the centre. The ground was springy, littered with fallen leaves rolled flat, as if someone had been lying there. There was hardly space for two.

The other turned round to him then, unbottoning his pants. Boyd could not help looking. The bigger one dropped his pants to the ground and kicked them into the bushes. His thing was straight out in front of him, bigger than Boyd had seen before.

'Like the look of that, eh? Show me yours.'

'No.'

'I won't hurt you. Gotta learn sometime.'

'No. You're not supposed . . . '

'Your mother tell you that? Bet your dad never did. Never had a stiffie before, betcha. Never noticed if you did. Come on.'

'I want to go back.'

'Can't go back. Not ever. Y'only come.' He was grinning with those big white teeth, but it wasn't really a smile. Boyd let him unbutton. He couldn't help it.

'What a tiny little dick. I'll make it big for y'. You're in for big surprises. Y'never tried to see how big y' could make it? Can't be that dumb.'

'No. Don't.' But Boyd's voice trembled. The other had unbuttoned him now. His rough hand began rubbing. The sun clouded over, white scuds of surf roared in Boyd's ears, he was not seeing anything. His body had become centred into touch.

'Like that? Huh? Come on, you're going to give it to me, I'll make you remember this one, if it's really the first. It really y'r first?'

Boyd did not reply.

'Didn't know you had it in you, hah!' The sound of the big boy's laughter was the hard gritty sensation of his fingers. Boyd became aware of sweat, his shirt clinging, the big boy's grubby chest and his small eyes, close to him.

He had broken through a mirror, he had burst back into the same place but it was not the same place. For an instant his body had not been his own. The big boy was working his hand on his own member now. He pushed Boyd round and tried to tug at his pants with the other hand. He was grunting gently, self-absorbed. He did not look at Boyd's face but his hand on Boyd was another hand, tough and urgent. Boyd gripped tightly at his own belt.

'Fuck you, little bastard. Get 'em right down. You give it to me now you gotta take it.'

Boyd pushed blindly through the bushes, pulling his belt in tighter. It was not until he got free and back to the path that he began to button up his front. The big boy was not following.

He ran, though, a safe distance further on and paused near the Lotus pond. He was all right, what had he been afraid of? He still felt tickled by sensations as if a new body was crawling over him, as if a new skin were being prepared, like an insect.

That big boy wasn't really a tough kid. He would not have hurt him. Would he?

From the safe open space beyond the lotus pond Boyd saw him at last push out through the thicket. He was wiping his hand on his pants. He did not look at Boyd. When he at last reached the shade of the jacaranda-tree, along the other path, he did look up. He caught Boyd's eye. Boyd was prepared to run hard. The other gave him a wink.

Boyd felt the flush scald through his face, down his neck. It had been against his will, that thing, it was the other's fault. And what that big kid had wanted to do to him, Boyd knew what it was. The sudden burst of radiance, light, the new winged creature – how could that be the same? His eyes were scalding.

Once, in the bath, his grandmother had fondled him with her soft, soapy hands, all over, every part even into all the creases. It had seemed wonderful, he had wished ever since she would bathe him like that again.

The grease mark on that boy's shoulder, the sandy rough hand. No, he was not going to let that happen again, he was not going to let anyone.

If only he could hold the good part. But he knew it was all together. 'Never want anything too hard, don't ask for too much,' grandmother was always saying.

It had happened, by surprise, he had not been ready. His knees still felt weak. It had claimed him, dragging something deep out of him, and then making it impossible and inevitable, like excrement.

Boyd

Action and reaction are equal but opposite.

That shove and jostle from the policeman: it was what had propelled Boyd into commitment. Up until that moment he had, somewhere inside, felt himself half observer, half party visitor. Until that one shove, Boyd perhaps had been only half anything.

Even now the great exhilaration of commitment washed him over with warm waves of enthusiasm. How long would it last? How easy it was. Little ironic tugs and crabsclaw sensations scuttled already beneath the tides.

Boyd accepted a can of Fourex. He was grinning at everyone. It had become a party. Cora stood beside him for a few moments, though she was fired with an internal combustion that made her seek constant movement. It was as if she might take back the fruit and deliberately lick where his lips and teeth had made contact. 'Take another bite. Good, eh?' She was off again.

Hours now. Onset of exhaustion. The last party crowd, linking arms to chant 'Save the Bellevue', had a tired festivity: arms reaching, embracing. Encounter group feelies. The urgent voltage of Cora's touch. A battery charged with all the voltage of the evening. For a moment Boyd felt like a teenager. Then he wiped his brow.

Suddenly one of the swarthy contractors started up his excavator. It cut through the drenched noise of onlookers, picketers, passing motorists, policemen: switch. Momentary hush. Some mother beast jungle-tensed at a twig crack. Energy.

Arc lights sheeted over. The shell of the old building was lit up from the rear, a sudden blanching of detail. Then precise as a documentary. Wreck of all possible salvage: the Bellevue was a hump, garbage, torn stack of cartons.

The excavator ground forward. The end had begun.

There was protest, a renewed burst of indignation. Indignation now, Boyd thought, not outrage. The fence became a playing net, opposing teams each side; not even semi-finals. The fence held. Under police direction a second trailer roared up and attempted to enter the enclosed destruction zone. This one edged too close in avoiding one little pocket of demonstrators. Cries. That sudden up-pitch of the human noise at its instant of raw shock. The lower, edgy pitch of anger. Some of the demonstrators and police had been caught, jammed up against the offside fence by the vehicle. There were injuries.

Boyd was shoving forward again. He could hear Cora, her voice stinging. Then the instant was jarred to splinters. It was not only demonstrators had been hurt. Someone was helping a policeman to his feet: one of the crowd.

So little to tilt things.

Later, when activity among the picketing group had again quieted, a subsidence more lethargic than before, Boyd rocked his heels over the gutter, cadged a cigarette. Only words meant anything at this stage, and that was too little. Could he have been caught in such entire hatred? Yes. Yes, entirely.

His cigarette butt glowed dully, merchandise.

One onslaught, one firm stand, that was the sum. The old shell was doomed. Excavators rumbled monotonously. He saw Cora deep in conversation, an older man with grey hair and suit. In profile, she could have been any age, thirty-five. She had not abandoned anything.

Some of the police on patrol began to relax. One came over to Boyd's group.

'Call it a day, now?' The sergeant rolled his own.

'Not likely. This can't go unnoticed.'

'Well. Hardly. Y'know, the wife's got a "Save the Bellevue" sticker, back of her car. We're not all on the side of the wreckers.'

'Good for you.'

'That's the way, sport.'

'She's even trying to get me to buy a big old colonial out Rosalie. Got a soft spot meself for those big airy rooms, lots of height. Grew up in one.'

'Lots of height in these ceilings – now.'

'Yeah. Now mind I don't catch up with you all back in the watch house. That's where your radio-friend got to. Y'know, that disc jockey, Wayney-poo . . . '

'Good for him!' Someone rejoined. 'Send up his ratings.'

'That's publicity for you,' the sergeant nodded. 'He'll get his headlines, though y'ask me it was hysteria.'

Post-mortems already. Boyd wandered off.

It was very late. Nothing to do but listen to the roar and grumble, occasional crunch of falling masonry. How curious he had imagined seeing Marie here. It was that feeling after tiredness, almost light-headed, when sleep has been too deeply desired. Boyd now could have stayed here till morning, the ritual seemed to demand that. She would have understood that.

In the straggling groups Cora was the all-encompassing presence, constantly moving, constantly flowing. She seemed to know everybody, to be talking with everybody. And when she caught his eye, it was if there were nobody else.

Olof came down along George Street. He had two pretty girls in tow, arms around both. He was grinning. Even with gravel rash, bruises, medication, Olof looked rakish. Energy.

'Come to join yuz. Where's the party?' He cocked his head at a new sough of machine noise. 'Not got it bulldozed yet? Hey, Cora. Cora, come here. Cora, come over here meet my new chicks.'

Where was the rancour? There must be resentments: these people had feelings didn't they? Boyd looked hard at Cora. She knew one of the girls. Soon they were laughing. Cora still had that decisiveness but there was something wider, broader; it flowed. Three a.m. Night air still warm.

Suddenly there was a new crash. Bricks, flooring, balustrading tumbled down from the third floor on Alice Street. A lot of it spewed out onto the footpath, over the barricading. Several parking meters were crushed. The street was festooned. No one, fortunately, was in that area.

The excavator itself was half buried in debris. Boyd could see its hydraulic pipes had been smashed, and the engine compartment was wrecked too. For a moment nobody did anything. Dust began to sift over.

There was movement inside the cab. The operator. A burly figure in overalls shouldered out of the pile, swearing. He was not injured.

'Hey! Hey, Halmud! Hey there, Halmud! Halmud Khan, it's me, it's Olof, Olof Ristič!'

Olof was jumping on the footpath, outrageously excited; he seemed to be springing from the shoulders of his two tittering girls. 'I know that fella. Hey, Halmud! That's Halmud Khan! Hey, I know him!'

'So what side you on?' someone interrogated.

'What's it matter? That guy went to school with my brother. How ya goin' there, Halmud?' Olof was against the wire now, thumping it gleefully, pointing and beckoning to himself. There were two large squat figures at the wrecked excavator, examining and assessing the damage, conferring together. They ignored all activity outside their wire enclosure. They had focused themselves upon immediate business.

'And that's Buddy. That's his brother. There's Stevo. It's the whole Khan family.'

'The Khans? not those ones in the papers . . . ?'

'All the same tribe, there's lots of them. Hey there, Buddy! Any jobs for a good labourer?'

'Scab!' someone hissed. Boyd recognized none of them.

But it was over; venom had been leeched away. It had all been futile. Olof attracted the Khans' attention with loud yahoos; others had begun drifting away; his two girls clung like shadows.

So this was Olof? Olof, drawn like a magnet to energy, part of the drama, making the drama. Sexuality, that was drama. It seeped from his very shadow, Olof with his power. His two girls were like flies trapped in the amber of it. Olof could secrete it. Boyd remembered a television programme: mice and rats in a laboratory; they had trained male stud rats for one purpose – sexual prowess. Anything put in with them – female rat, male rat, rat kitten, even other creatures – they would instantly hump over to mate. Olof, in this sub-tropical laboratory, seeking outlets, had one outlet, one only: energy had him wound like a top's string. He spun indiscriminately. Boyd felt the shoulder bump off him. He could not take his eyes off him. Olof's large hands gestured fully in swoops and grabbings; he thumped wire, roared his laugh with one of the younger Khans through the gate, other arm firmly meshed across the back to the buttock of one of his girls. Impossible. Without darkness.

Undirected, unfocused: give him ten years, five, nothing further, Boyd thought. Why should someone so roughly assertive be so seductive?

Cora spun differently. Hers was a cohesive world, fiercely guarded, but quite personal. In a sense, Boyd thought, she was entirely moral. She had her own order and she stuck to it. With passion. Like the Golden Orb spider she spun her whole community, and within it she let others live and make their habitation without disturbing her equilibrium. From a distance it looked a shambles, just a tangle of webs. But in its centre all was intricately ordered, a design of pure filigree. The Golden Orb was poison, Cora said to him, poison strong enough to kill a man. But they are not predators. They keep their own order and symmetry and their harvest comes to them. Perhaps the control could be dissolved, to allow some new process.

Boyd began to cough. The place was full of dust. Someone strolled to the Botanical Gardens and broke off some branches to weave a wreath. Someone else grabbed one of the old placards and wrote a sign for the wreath: 'May the Bellevue rest in pieces'.

Some chuckles. Shrugs. The six in Cora's group went off laughing. The sound of the diggers and excavators had become background drone. All the night air was dusty, gritty. Like whirls of interstellar dust.

'Let's go up to Spring Hill, look up Lev,' one of the new girls suggested.

'Who's Lev?'

'That's what we call him. You know, Lev for levitation.'

'Floating in air?' They were walking through dust particles as through a series of gauzy curtains. 'That's impossible.'

'No it's not!' Olof joined in. 'I did levitation once. So that proves it.'

'You, Olof?' Boyd punched his shoulder. 'Come off it. You're too muscle-bound, you'd be too heavy.'

'When I was twelve. One time, just after Ramadan. I used to be very religious and I'd really been fasting. That was when me dad used to take me everywhere, out to the building sites, everywhere. Said he was real proud of me. Used to show me off to his friends.'

'I know. Went to your head. You just floated.' Don was on the edges, skipping.

'Not like that!' Olof was stern. 'Tell you, this happened. I was out in the backyard, see. Under the mango-trees. And then suddenly I was about thirty feet up, above everything. Above the house even. I could look down. See everything clearly. So clear, can still almost see it. And the angle of it. You know, looking down from the top of it. Like things I had never seen before, down the ground. I could see them things clearly. I could see the rusty bit on the roof. I could see leaves in the gutter. I could even see myself. Lying there. Just in the shade of that daggy, old tree.'

'Must have been dreaming.'

'No. It was not dreaming. It had a different way; how can I say it, it was different. It had this real clearness. Real clear.'

'And when you saw yourself, down there. What did you look like? To yourself?' They laughed.

Olof stopped in his tracks. His face lifted up, turned skywards. He had a sort of grin.

'I looked – *beautiful*.'

Olof strode ahead. 'No,' he said decisively. 'Not to Lev's place. I been through that sort of thing, why should I share that sort of thing with yuz guys? No, there's that place out back of Aspley, that mud pool. That's more like all of us. This moment. Huh?'

Boyd was not surprised that they all agreed. He, too, followed.

One of the Olof girls had a car and they piled in. Out through dark suburbs. Endless. Boyd was drowned in his tiredness but swept along, also, by the spirit of momentum. Impossible, simply, to return to the flat. What could he do there? Or could he face the thought that he could do nothing?

They turned off the main road and after more meanderings where the car's lights picked out streaks of vision and dark areas that quickly were screened and discarded they bumped onto a rutted dirt track. The car stopped. Lights were snapped off.

'We walk from here.'

Boyd followed, stumbling and still enclosed. Passive, he thought, passive and simply a follower. Could he accept that? He reached Cora. Gripping her shoulder, then her arm, he was about to ask her ... what? She laughed softly at him.

They clambered through barbed wire, across cow paddocks. They entered the darker shadow of trees.

It was a sort of sliding pit. In the night he could make out the others, already stripping. Pale, naked shafts of moonlight, darting, tumbling. Soon they became mottled and were lost, or disappearing, re-emerging.

'Come on,' Cora whispered. She was already half undressed. Boyd hesitated, then shrugged. The banks of the mud pool were slippery and very cool. Otherwise the night air kept a balmy breath. Boyd slid.

Soon he was, like the others, coated in a slippery mud skin and someone pushed him further, into the pool of water at the bottom.

'No. Don't wash it off. Let it harden and then roll down again. That way the skin feels the real mystery of it.' Cora again instructing.

Other bodies were twisting and seemed to be clinging together. There was laughter, chuckles, deep murmurs but none of it directed at Boyd. Yet he was not excluded.

The hair of his body resented the pliant mud, he longed to wash it off. He longed, also, to find Cora again. Reassurance.

Olof loomed up, his nakedness undeniable. He hugged Boyd and shoved him over, laughing hugely. The contact was with mud, and with muscle. Boyd imagined the mud drying, cracking, flaking. Too much.

'Keep to yourself.'

'You really shit scared to face your own sexiness. Haven't you faced it yet? You eye off everything that moves, like you want to rip the clothes offa them, then soon as anyone wants to come on in with you, share the warm and the feel and the tickle: slam, man, you got that door shut tight as a prison. Shit man, you got problems.' But Olof rubbed his big hand through Boyd's hair with a sort of intolerable tolerance. 'Some day you gotta see the real tease you are.' Then he gurgled. 'Hell, man. I'm a nutcase meself, being taken in by you. What's the promise, what's the promise, huh? A bit of cock and a bit of tugalong? Man's crazy to get tugged in every time. You like me, Boyd? You like me, huh?'

'Olof, you're the last person who needs reassurance . . . look, you outgrow some things at thirteen, you know . . . '

'I outgrow nothin'!' Olof thumped Boyd, 'I'm going to hold on to every feeling I have. It's all you got, man. Hey man, I sorta love you man, know that?'

Mud-caked hands, hands rough and drying, exploring hands. Boyd shoved him away, almost with panic. 'Olof, you're mad. Cut it out.'

'You like it, but. Little feelies and tingles. Hey, Boyd, I could really go down on you. Tell you this, I could even take it from you, what ya say?'

The hands were hard, feeling hard round to Boyd's buttocks, tweaking, teasing, in the darkness something that a half second of delay had given licence to. Olof was rubbing his chest against Boyd now, his mouth close to his ear. 'It's all right, it's all right, man, for once in your life you don't have to prove nothing. Not with me, baby.'

The rough chin on his neck. Suddenly Olof was down on his haunches, with a little laugh. 'Beauty, baby. Proud one, what a whopper.' Boyd thrust him off. Olof, roaring and laughing, tumbled back into mud. The damp splash echoed his snorts. Olof stayed down there, a pale moon figure, on his back, laughing and mocking.

'Come on down, Boyd,' he whispered, between giggles. 'Roll in it, roll on me, roll with me, baby.'

Boyd tried to wipe the feel of saliva from his caked mouth. Olof was there, all right. His white teeth gleamed from the darkest web of his beard. Olof's body, too, was visible. He was feeling himself, now.

Boyd veered and stumbled, not saying anything. His feet struck firm sand, not mud. It was the edge of the mudpit. Overhang of trees. In the furthest darkness, another form. As it moved to him he knew it was Cora.

Had she seen? Had she heard? Before she could say anything Boyd reached out to take her wrist. His limbs were floating in the delirium of exhaustion but the resources of energy had been proved. He gripped her tight. At the instant she discovered the thrust of his embrace he felt a slight contraction; she tried to deflect herself sideways.

But it was too late. He would not be stopped now. With a cry dry from his throat, he entered her.

. . .

In the branches overhead a small bird had begun hissing *Tease tease tease*.

Cora vanished. They all had vanished. He had been on his back in the warm sand; had he been sleeping? What was that thing his grandmother had cried? No, no: but he was forced to remember.

It had been that last visit and she had never been so intimate, or so dependent. 'I do not want to die, Boyd, I do not want to lose control, I do not want them to come when I am helpless, making a mess, Boyd, the way poor Eve Bennett was writhing and dying last week, Eve Bennett full of panic. Dance of Death, Boyd, know what that is? The tormentors. They are all those who know you. Poor Eve Bennett when she did look up with her frightened eyes I could tell I was one too, part of the Dance Boyd, one of the tormentors.' His grandmother weeping. Impossible.

Why should it all come back? Boyd had escaped under the house and then out, to the bus and the Botanical Gardens. He had sought out the lotus pond and had walked into the thickets wilfully, in search of that thing which had been waiting on him, holding off, following.

Nobody.

When he returned his grandmother was her old self. But there was still a great distance.

In the distance others were splashing still. There were voices. Could it be so late? Even his body was floating off from him, clumsy and stumbling. How many others? How could he count them?

In a dream, water that had thickened into a sort of slow dance of flowing torpor Boyd washed what he could from his limbs. His body was slow and almost alongside him. Were there others there or had they all clambered uphill. Drugged voices, murmurs, of course they were nearby, just round the darkness in what was a long billabong in the creekbed. Sand underfoot, not mud. Marie's hands had a firmness he instantly recognized, she was leading him and it was not her fault that the buzzing noises of silence and the bush with its too many tiny choruses distanced them. She was saying something, he made that much out, and the sudden irruption of a shout or a laugh from one of the others only made Marie's quiet insistence somehow more urgent, more unheard. It was something about how he had been in the centre of it, and how she was behind him, why did he not turn that time, the time the whole side of the building fell, that was the time she had come closest to him, but then all the noise and the tumult once again pushed between, wasn't it always like that, but she did not mind, when he took the direction from her and moved into possession she did not mind, she did not really mind, and tonight, whose wonderful idea was it to get away from the dust and the crowd and the terrible shadow of that old building the Bellevue with its ghosts and its dust and its simple claims including the claims of Boyd's grandmother hadn't he ever been afraid of them had he never faced them or what she had done for him done to him imprisoning him but Marie would not urge she would not reprimand now she would not counter she did not have the heart any more it was all right now and Boyd could he not endeavour to hear the clear air and the lightness of the air already almost morning almost getting towards that moment towards morning when he must be prepared for the sudden drop in temperature and really it was silly to be naked then though Marie had been close to him too there somewhere and they Boyd knew it was all right and you were young and the mud did help like forgetfulness and wash it off but Boyd with his body had a debt of hair of the weight of hair that Marie was stroking now, frightened hands, and it signified a pattern of how the body protects itself and was not free and then Marie already part of the neighbouring pulse part of the deep inside rhythm and Marie had learned that much with him hadn't it always been that hadn't they always wished that?

But Cora was calling somewhere
Don and Olof
Ain't she afraid ain't she afraid toodleloo toodleloo ain't she

SUNDAY

Helena Maria Adriana

First light suffused the room and returned objects to their form, though shapes still bartered for the right of weightlessness as well as bulk.

Helena Maria Adriana at this hour was afloat in the perfect equipoise between waking and sleep, that state of lightness, unsought and therefore pure. She was curled around the tight stone of Joszef's back.

Soon enough she would become channelled again into veins, sinews, secret passages and supporting struts of bone. For as long as she could Helena Maria Adriana believed in the power of floating, of pervading the room with her presence unhindered by muscular bonds.

The inner channels were reclaiming her, though. They were storing up the cost. With a sigh that rattled like slats of a Venetian blind Helena Maria Adriana heaved her weight back onto her side of the bed, cast off the covers, making sure that Joszef's back was tucked in, and located her slippers, her dressing gown.

When she returned to the bed Joszef neatly uncoiled and was on her. His hands were like a cat's tongue, his chin bristled across her pale breast. Like retracting claws, his toenails scraped at her instep, her ankle, her calf. He pushed her back onto her pillows and sheets, the tongues of his fingers urgent now. The thin moisture of urine was flushed out and replaced by lubricant juices. Joszef was licking her ear; she wrapped her legs round him and pulled his tight buttocks with both hands.

'Igen, igen, igen,' he croaked as he centred his whole being into the world thrusting into her. Deep, deeper this time, deeper in than last night, she could feel the entire burst of his energy as it found the dreamcentre and he gasped, sobbed and gasped clutching her.

The room flooded with light, space and shape now. It was her true bedroom.

He was still absorbed in her body. The cat's tongue, white with milk, licked and fingered.

She lay on her back and imagined grapes swelling with sweet juices. The orchard was sunlight. Fruit had to be fondled and squeezed till the ripe grapes burst, sweet and tart reconciled; perfection.

Perfection. When she shuddered to climax she felt his own groin twitch and convulse with a sympathetic echo.

At 7.30 there was a knock.

'*Bitte*,' she called, and motioned Joszef to sleep on. She searched for the dressing gown, unconcerned that the daylight was wrinkling her buttocks and mottled her thighs. With her coat swathed around her she shook back her hair and could not resist finding her comb though the knocking still kept up, insistent and patient.

'We were going to look for asparagus at the Victoria Markets. That was right?' Dagmar gave her a hug and a kiss.

'But Marie is not . . . '

'I'm very cross with Marie. She might at least have contacted me before she left.'

'She is thoughtless, so selfish. Only herself, always herself only.'

'She knew the direct Melbourne–Brisbane flight was mid-afternoon. But did she bother to phone me all day? And she wasn't at work, I tried both places.'

'I will make coffee. You will at least come in.'

'We will still go on to the markets. Let's have this *Spargelfest*.'

'*Nein. Nein.* I do not know. It was Marie . . . '

'I found out yesterday that if you go early you can always buy *Spargel*, it might cost the earth but not to worry. This time of year it will be air-freight from Israel. Or Mexico.'

'I do not believe. And it is still real?'

'Fresh, you mean? It's perfection. Almost too real.'

'Ach, we live in a wonderful age; or an unreal age truly.'

'Marie, right now, is being unreal – scooting off to Brisbane. I call that unreal. I think the invention of flying made us all strange and unreal. It's like getting your own way as a kid. When you were finally handed the treat, it was never what you wanted at all. I hope Marie is having hell right now. Then she might come to herself and be satisfied with what she's got. And that might or might not include Boyd, is what I say.'

'Once she sets her mind that girl is stubborn.'

'Telling me! There was an early flight up yesterday. She could have taken that. Perhaps she really is looking at the art gallery and the Picasso.'

'Picasso? I thought they had only pineapples.'

'And tropical islands, and surfing beaches, and koala bears.'

'And of course Boyd.'

But at that moment Joszef came out, scratching his belly. He was wearing his undershorts but they hid nothing.

'Dagmar has reminded me. We are going to bring home the international *Spargel*. In your car, will you drive us?'

'You are cooking me *Spargel*?'

'We'll let you have some, if you hurry,' put in Dagmar, taking over. 'Though you weren't on the original guest list. But it seems we have a last minute vacancy.'

'Marie is without us. *Ach weh*, but we will do this together and perhaps next time I will be able to show her.'

'To share with her, you dear thing.'

Helena Maria Adriana beamed when Dagmar planted such a daughter kiss. She had forgotten entirely that the comb was still stuck in the crown of her hair.

Boyd

He must return. All through Saturday and through Saturday night Boyd slept. When he woke on Sunday he felt calm and refreshed.

Someone had brought in a mug of coffee. It had gone cold with a congealed skin on the little table drawn up beside him. Cora? Perhaps Olof?

There were newspapers. Banner headlines, photos, post mortems. Yesterday's stories.

The past does not matter.

It does matter, but it is over, the cycle moves onward, somewhere further. It was necessary to keep with it. The past is part of that centre, that core. Perhaps also the future. But to be released from it: Boyd curled and stretched and luxuriated in the body that filled and claimed and pampered him. He heaved his thick legs over the bedside. These high old beds. This one was anonymous now. The boy, Boyd Kennedy, had been absorbed entirely into the man he had become; the room and its memories were absorbed; the house, Brisbane. His grandmother.

He remembered having a long shower, with dawn light seeping in. They had all crowded in the car, half naked, clutching mud-crusted garments, lightheaded.

Let her old ghost keep its separateness. He had grown through them to his present self. It felt good. Boyd breathed deeply. He breathed out. In again. Lungsful of good air.

He must ask Marie. He would return with no presents, tokens in old games of bribery. But there would be something. Had to be something. Routine carried everyone. To break routine had been his privilege, his entirely.

The Bellevue wreckage filtered its dust around him. No; he would not go back there.

Marie. Would she have found some sense of new independence without him? Would she not need him? He thought of the way she muddled over things: lighting the gas, getting the coffee. But would she not need him?

He shrugged. He must learn to think of all things as being possible. He would have so many things to tell her. The old glass vase, the Bellevue...

Boyd padded to the clumsy old refrigerator, jerked its door open. For a moment he thought: mineral water, anything less would be impure.

Then he laughed at himself. Better watch out, he might end up a convert, bullying everyone, ripping meat from the mouths of children, reproving them; insisting on porridge-meal sandwiches, beancurd and carrot, thistle salad, cucumber peel. He might become, if he didn't watch it, the Office Guru, sandals and bedlinen, flapping through the university corridors, a sort of gingery Gandhi, with digital watch.

Flying lessons in the living-room, shoving aside the cane furniture; competing with hang-gliders on the South Coast, spotting sharks – he'd send telepathic messages to the lifesavers; giving Reg Ansett a nod as they passed above Burke Street, Reg heading for his helipad, Boyd for the Law Book Company. The Boyd Kennedy School of Energy: prospectus on application, learn your own radio wavelength, be your own solar heater, train yourself to displace the electric blanket, be an instant hotplate; become your own computer chip; 'This invention transcends television.'

Boyd's invention started to flag.

Back to the coffee and meat. Well, how could Boyd give up food? Impossible. Nothing could keep him, in the right mood, from a T-bone, done lightly with rosemary and onion rings, something green, say zucchini (never aubergine): Boyd the complete carnivore, unrepentant.

Cora. How careless he'd been, at the end. She had been quiet. Not her usual incisiveness. The Bellevue disaster must have thumped into her. She would not give it up lightly; she would remember; she would not forgive. Had he really made love to her? It was Boyd who was trivial. Flashy jokes; computerese... but this morning benignness was all. As if the chrysalis, indeed, had burst open. Clear air. The same creature but a new stage of development.

And he'd not eaten since Friday. Boyd raided the refrigerator, gobbling two tomatoes, demolishing a cheesestick and two salami beersticks, then he buttered four slices of bread, tore the wraps off the ham shoulder, sliced more tomato. Those juicy green apples.

But one really needs muesli. Damn it, that milk! He felt comfortable, companionable, the kitchen at home could be like this. He would flood Marie with cups of brisk coffee, he would smother her with little offers of tribute: toast, vegemite, something.

He found Don next door, dusting. The hallway mess had vanished. Cora spent all Saturday in a clean-up, Don explained. She had not slept. Then she went off. She was going to front up to her father. Don looked apprehensive.

'What's he like?'

'A big Dutchman, Mr van der Groeben. You heard about his wife?' Don added timidly.

'Not a thing. I know nothing about any of you. Her father. I did get that.'

'You better know. Specially as you and Cora have been eyeing each other off all week.' Not jealous. Not even curious.

'You know he raped her, right. Had it off with her. She was thirteen. Well okay you know that and of course it was in the papers. Not the name but. Though everyone at school knew about it. And then her mother suiciding . . . '

Boyd looked down, picked at his fingernails. He tore one off. 'I didn't know that. How could I know that?'

Don put down the duster. Flopped into a chair. 'Y'know. Cora said one thing about you yesterday. She said, Boyd think's he's Peter Pan; you know, the boy who never grew up. But the thing is, she said, you grew up to be someone different from what you thought you'd be. Bet Boyd's wife has been telling him all this time and he still hasn't registered; that's what Cora said.' Don thumped Boyd's arm as he got up again and resumed his chores. 'She called you a koala bear the other day, Boyd. How'ja like that? But she said it as if she liked you that way. Said how a koala looks funny in a three piece business suit.'

Cora drove up in a red Mazda. Don was astonished.

'I had it out with my dad. What you might call a heavy session.'

Boyd leaned against the old fence. After a moment Cora jumped on the rail too. She laughed, pulled back her hair.

'Well. Got to know me. All the dirt. You like the contour?' She profiled her face, upthrust.

Don was impatient, juggling three mugs. 'What did the two of you say, go on? How did you hit him with it?'

'Right in the guts, of course. As I just said, full tackle.' She accepted the mug, cupped it tightly.

'No anger?'

'None, Boyd. Not from me. Well, of course, some. Had to be some, why not? Even a slut can feel some reactions.'

'Meaning?'

'Meaning nothing at all. It was between me and my father.'

'I can just see you, Cora. Wonder he didn't go grey on the spot.'

'Wasn't like that, Don. No shouting, not at that stage.'

'Just turning the screws.'

'He said it was against his own will, what he did. I don't know, maybe that's so. Hardly matters at this distance.'

Cora looked drawn, wizened. When she made her tight half smile the skin over her cheeks stretched, parchment.

'Now it's over. Behind me.'

'You think it's that simple?'

'Yes. Yes, Boyd,' she crossed over to the car door. 'Switch off the ignition. That simple.'

'And you scored a new car out of the deal. Well, congratulations.'

'Why not? He's my father.'

'Lump sum compensation, they call it in Law circles.' Boyd tried to make it light-hearted. Somewhere there was a tight ache, contracting.

'He was my father.'

'Isn't he still?'

'We all change, Boyd. Even you. Damn it, letting him give me this car. That's a way of settling accounts isn't it? You've got to start somewhere.'

'You could start with reaching out.'

She stretched herself from against the car door and with a fallen twig began a tour of the spider territory in the front garden.

'You could start with reaching out, Boyd. But you would end with rape. Just like my father.'

'Hullo; something I didn't hear about?' Don was between them, alert.

'Nothing, Don. Nothing at all. That's what all these things are about.' Carefully she displaced a large spider from a too-close overhang and guided its whole web closer to the center of the bush.

'Anyway, I still have to work out my own feelings. Boyd would know all about that.'

'It was all strange and unreal,' he began.

'You haven't a clue how real it was.'

'What are you doing with those spiders?'

'What? Oh, just a tidy-up. I don't know.' Her laugh was crumpled. She turned quickly with the large spider held on the end of the twig. Don scampered.

She drove the stick into the ground, then stamped on the squirming spider.

'Why did I do that? I have been wanting to strike out at something for hours. It is *not* my own father. No, Boyd, don't flatter yourself. Not you either.'

Boyd had to come over. 'It's only an insect. Look, there are hundreds of them. Hey? Hey now, Cora. You need a good shoulder. Handkerchief?'

She shook her head violently. 'I should hate you all. I just don't understand myself.'

Cora insisted they take a spin in her new car. Driving created its own environment, where relationships were all relative. After an hour Cora dropped Don off at his parents' house. Sunday was his day for the home visit.

'Here we are. Overdraft Hill. See yuz all later,' Don quipped with his affectedly broad accent. That would modify, too.

'Where to now?' Boyd without asking clambered into the front seat. 'You know, this is my last day. I've decided to get back to it all.'

'To the wife. Marie. See, I remember.'

She shut her door firmly. 'Feeling replenished?'

'Yes. If you like. Feeling just that.'

They drove off. Boyd did not ask again where they were heading.

'You see,' he explained, feeling the need to hold on to some contact, 'It was a sort of retreat, this. Brisbane as Monastery. The hermits' cells of Toowong.'

'Yes? And what about Grandma?'

'Don't call her that. She's been nailed up, now, I can forget.'

'You can forget us all.' But she relented. 'You don't want that glass vase?'

'Well, I might just take it. No, it's yours really. I don't need it.'

'But you want it?'

'That's another question. It doesn't have to claim me. Even if I do take it, it would be merely as a curiosity, like something you'd buy in a tourist shop. Though it would have its own ambience – a new ambience. Nothing at all to do with my grandmother, or my boyhood. A lot to do with the thought of my being here, this time. A new cast of characters. You.'

'Well, keep it. It gave me good vibes when I uncovered it. I'll transfer them over to you.'

She had to realize there could be nothing. She must understand that. So he leaned over, then, and gave her a peck.

Later, she said, 'You shouldn't have done that.'

Foothills of the mountain range. They could be going anywhere. Boyd looked at her. 'Yes, you're the driver.'

'I'll say I am. I like this car. And there's no guilt whatever.'

217

The glare of the road was mica. A sudden hill slope of Natal grass, reddish sheen caught in the light. Into a dip, and to the left a glimpse through trees and a creekmouth onto the river. Cora turned into a dirt track. Bunya Street.

'This is it.'

'This? This is what? End of the road? End of the world?'

'It is a sort of nowhere.' It was not him she was smiling at. 'Be patient.'

'What's this called?'

'Ugly Gully.'

Boyd shut up.

'It's okay.' She led the way. 'They've replaced the ugly bits with the new road. We can smooth anything, you know.'

'I can see why they called it Ugly Gully. Fancy driving too often down this track.'

Carefully they trod down through a track to water. The noise was of rinsed light-shafts, slivers of glass crackling into smoothness among cold rocks. It was cool, leaf shady. The great gibbers lay exposed above runnels and splintered creek grating, tufts of reed, the blur of Brisbane wattle with its multipennate leaves looking for reflections of themselves in the impossibly quick water: reflections carried to the next set of ripples, then abruptly reformed in clear eddies and edges of backwater. The two intruders moved upstream balancing on dry surfaces of rock.

The pool under the huge rockcliff surprised Boyd. He had been looking downward, concentrating on his balance, to keep his shoes dry. Cora, barefoot as always, gripped his arm.

By the sandy bank of the pool was a huge water-gum, a swinging rope tied to one of its thick horizontal branches. Not, then, entirely secret property. Their own noises called back from rockface.

'Well? You like it?'

'Very nice. Like an old Tarzan movie.' He flopped down on the sand. It was warm from the sun.

Cora was already undressing. 'Well, you've got to *try* it.'

He remembered her under the hose, and the ghost shadow in moonlight and mud. The sight of her filled him with a warm pulse. Not the skin but under the skin. An old, secret hunger was eating through his nerve-ends.

But she could be admired. No territorial rights, no blackmail. Just admired for herself as she was, moving. She grinned, then. Boyd shook his head almost in disbelief.

Cora, feeling the water with her toe. Cora, clapping her left hand on the breast an instant; Cora reaching down with that hand to the water, underneath, allowing the water such closeness to her body, Cora splashing up water, the way her breast moved, the light that seemed reflected upwards, reaching upwards from the mirror. She turned round. Sunlight slid along her belly. Nipples, erectile now. The modest screen of hair, the great softness of skin at the meeting-place.

'Well, you are coming, aren't you?' Her eyes glinted. 'You aren't shy?'

'I'm hairy.'

'Why, you are shy!' She came back onto the bank. Determinedly she began undoing his shirt buttons. 'You weren't shy at the mud pool. You were all action then. Too much. Or that very first night. You didn't mind showing off your big furry body. Must have known it would turn me on.'

She had his shirt off. She was down, tugging at laces.

'Stop that.' He was genuinely disturbed, embarrassed.

'That's not slavery, that's impatience. It's true damn it. I'm sort of fond of you.'

They stumbled, pulling his trousers off.

'Over here Boyd. Let me look at you. Little surprises.' Slowly she rolled onto her back. 'No claims. No possessions.'

In the dappled shadows she smiled up at him.

'Can I touch first?'

She smiled. 'Do it properly this time,' she whispered.

Later, she propped herself up. 'It was good – wasn't it? Wasn't just me.

You can take your vase home now, Boyd, Boyd Kennedy. Fill it with creekwater.'

'And when I think: Ugly Gully. It'll be a code name for "Terrific", for "wonderful".' His hands kept stroking, 'You know there's nothing I can give you in return,' he added.

It seemed a steep climb back to the car. Cora grabbed his hand.

'Boyd. You will think of this place? That's why I brought you here. I wanted you to share it. You will think of it? Please?'

'Incessantly.' He nodded.

'That's one of the plaster-it-up words.'

'Yes. I guess, yes, I know that.'

In the Park

'Nothing. You have understood nothing. But I will forgive you. And it is not because of your age, or the genetic conspiracy.' She allowed him to hold his pace beside her. The December sun squeezed into his ears and through his angry, chunky silence. They had passed the lotus pond, he had not noticed. As they stepped into the wall of shade at the rainforest end of the gardens they were attacked by hordes of mozzies. His grandmother slapped once or twice and then led the way back to the riverside walk. 'When you were smaller you had such an open nature,' she went on, 'full of questions and curiosity. You always came to me and asked me to explain.' Slap, and again slap, her hand still attacked imaginary insects.

Yesterday, after the surge and excitement of arrival, Boyd found himself unexpectedly bored and restless. His grandmother had noticed it. You have changed, she said and it was an accusation. Everything had started wrong.

But he had gone back into the space under the house. Over the years he had explored it all. It was dusty and he was careful of his new pants.

'Boyd, I am quite prepared to forgive you for what you said about my new bob. It was honest, it came from the heart and spontaneous ignorance. What I find different – and not so forgivable – is the slyness. The sarcasm.' She reached for a twig of leaves from the overhanging weeping-fig. Illegal to do that, thought Boyd. It was her wilfulness that was unforgivable.

He stuck his hands in his pockets. He pulled out his new key ring and began fidgeting, pulling the long chrome chain through forefinger and thumb. 'I'm sorry, Grandmother. I said sorry.'

She paused and looked at him, hat tilted. 'You did, yes. And I must keep to my part of the bargain.' She was softening. From the very moment they entered the Botanical Gardens, Boyd was struck by its shabbiness, its patches of bare ground, yellowing grass, scraggy trees. It all seemed untidy, even the tidy garden beds. He had refused to follow the ritual of looking at the deer enclosure or ogling the ape cages.

'Well, I don't know what I'll do with you,' she had said with some asperity. Perhaps his grandmother had felt she was obliging *him*. To humour her because of their initial tiff he had quickly agreed to the expedition, the first of their annual ritual. Boyd led the way then, dragging her towards the lotus pond though there would be nothing to see. In their irritation with each other they had not even noticed it.

'I suppose the change is natural. Part of the process. The blood directs and we follow.' She laughed but there was no let up. 'I wish you would stop jangling those keys. You are like some châtelaine, or the caretaker.'

In his first year at Grammar, Boyd had been given the keyring for his locker. During the year he developed a craze for keys, any key. His ring was jammed with all shapes and sizes. Under the house yesterday he had at last been able to open the green tin trunk – not the first such success from his circle of tokens. He had learned to prowl through the locker room – not that he took anything but a secret knowledge of others, the things they kept stored or hidden, glimpses of private vulnerabilities like photos of sisters or parents, bottles of aniseed balls, matchbox cars. The locked green trunk contained only a few more piles of newspaper and magazines, some sheet music ('Intermezzo' from *Cavalleria Rusticana*), and a couple of old fur things. He put those to one side, on the little shelf above where the paint tins were stored. He browsed through the papers, bored with his old self that used to think this was all fascinating. When his grandmother discovered 'what he'd been up to' she became far more angry than was necessary. It had been nothing. No harm was done, and he would have discovered the pieces of fur in a day or so and put them back, no probs. She had been spying on him. Had she always been spying on him, every year, as soon as he left a room or the under-the-house, did she always come after to check out, clean up, pry? The hurt was enormous.

'I've got more keys on my ring than anyone in class,' Boyd boasted, to turn the conversation into something positive. He was not going to be bullied and he was not going to give up his keyring.

'I'm sure you have, my dear, and if you have a little patience with your cranky old grandmother I am sure I can come up with a few more that I never use. Though what good are keys without locks? Now tell me that? Collecting for the sake of collecting. I call that decadence. Still,' she smiled at last, and her sagging, cropped face hinted at the grandmother he remembered, the one with the wavy neat hair scalloped to hide all but her earlobes. This new style was too gaunt; it was horrible.

'I've been able to use these keys for all sorts of things. Dad's old bookcase cupboard, for instance. One of my keys unlocked that and Dad hadn't managed to open it for years. You never know when they'll come in handy.'

'Old grandfather time. Old busybody. Young secretive. And what was inside your father's cupboard, then? Well, not that I'm curious. I suspect it was empty.'

'How did you know?'

'I'm the boy's mother. Mr Collector of keys. I think you want to be the operator, the spy, the secret agent. Ah, you like that, don't you? I've hit the place.' She brushed his cheek with her leafy twig.

'I just like keys. They're . . . they're interesting.'

'You really do know nothing. Not even yourself. You think you are not transparent? Oh come on, Boyd, take it lightly, I am not going to have you sulk. Come along. We'll go to the Bellevue and I will buy you a soda. Or are you sipping banana cocktail and cherry brandy now you are a Grammar School man?'

She always did it; but it was new this time. He thrust his keys into the waistcoat pocket. The waistcoat was his other new craze and that, at least, his grandmother had been delighted by. In this climate, early December, he had become hot and uncomfortable but it gave him style and he was not going to abandon that, no fear.

'I am sorry if I upset you, about your hair style. I mean it.' He was not going to speak about keyrings to her, to anyone, nobody would understand.

'Of course you do. And I am not going to hold any grudges. Though how many times do I have to insist that you must learn to see beyond surfaces. Or what you think are surfaces. No, that part I insist on, Boyd. It is the one thing I perhaps can offer you, for your future.' She sat down on a bench under the largest of the poinsianas. 'I am tired. Just for a moment.' Boyd remained standing.

'You see, Boyd, I am like this city, I am the same but am settling and adjusting. Changing but not changing. It might surprise you to know that I had my hair bobbed like this for years. Decades. When the pageboy style came in back in the twenties I was the first to adopt it. And in the thirties I looked a positive swank in my siren suit and cropped hair. Because you only knew me at one stage – I became infatuated with the permanent wave – you think that was the fixed point of my career. Not a bit.'

'Your hair was not naturally wavy?' More edifices crumbled.

'Nothing in human nature is "natural". "Natural" is an unnatural word, if applied to humans. Only kangaroos and koala bears are natural, in that sense. We have potential. And that means we order our own shapes. Or in my case, during the forties and fifties, it meant waves.' She was smiling and relaxed now. Her leaf stroked along her own bare arms. She motioned Boyd to sit down beside her. 'Waves and blow jobs.'

He could see she was eyeing him with a strange slyness but what were the signals?

'You have grown so quickly, Boyd. You're a big man and yet this time last year you were, well, you were my little prince. Do you remember how I used to wash you, scrub you behind the ears in the bath? Seems almost yesterday. That thought no doubt is something to embarrass the big man with his secrets and locks.' Her leafy twig tickled the sweat at the side of his ears. He could feel his shirt clinging. He pulled at his waistcoat uncomfortably.

'You should unbutton a little, if you want to.' She threw the twig away and unbuttoned his chest. Firm fingers. 'When you first came up you had fly buttons, not zippers,' she was teasing him now. Had she heard him last night? 'You would run down the corridor naked, and I chased you.'

He could not bear her laugh. He stood up.

'Last month I decided: sixty-five is only another start. I will reinvent myself with a short, gamine, hairstyle. And it works. The juices do flow, you know, Boyd, there need not be any drying up.'

'I don't think I'm thirsty, Grandmother. Let's not go to the Bellevue.'

'Selfish. Ignorant. Self-centred. It all happens so quickly, that is the tragedy. You will escort me, Boyd, because it is I who might be thirsty.'

On the day before break-up, in the school toilets, big Bruce Patterson egged a whole group of them – six of the kids – into seeing who could come furthest, up the wall. Boyd had been startled at Bruce's openness, but was drawn into the dare. Typical Bruce: he turned everything into a competition. Boyd until that moment hoarded his sexual fervours like a secret. The others all laughed as if nothing could be more natural.

'The person you see now, Boyd dear, is the closest to whatever I am that you'll meet. You must be careful not to build images from your own wishes. You must read the maps, and the maps are constantly changing. Forests of symbols, but with new trees each season.'

Last night, when he went over to see Handley Shakespeare they had nothing in common. It was ages before they found common ground – Handley's father's book of Norman Lindsay plates for *Lysistrata*.

Shared excitement, shared sniggers.

'Even the most obvious things: the maps are not what they seem, none of them. Or we all follow the same map but pass through different territory.'

'I don't understand you.'

'Boyd, you are now in the big wild adultland, with your jangle of keys and no compass. And your parents, poor dears, are still locked in some suburban bungalow. If I don't help you, who will?'

'It's all right about the haircut, then, what I said? And about the fur things I left lying around?'

'That's why the sulks! I should have remembered. Those fur things, you might be interested to know, are koala. Yes, real koala fur. Awful, yet desirable. Did you look through the papers in the trunk, then? You think I do not remember each single item?'

'Sort of. You didn't mind? Unlocking?'

'Well, I shouldn't have, though at first I was cross. They all represented special things, special times, special people. I had a crush on young Tom . . . no, I'll not mention his name. Read the papers in there, if you wish to. No, I will tell you.'

They had reached the Bellevue. They found their old places. For the first time Boyd felt awkward, stared at by women. The soda drink was fizzy, oversweet. He did not know what he wanted.

'Those newspapers tell us one story, but there are other ways of seeing.'

'What story?'

'Oh, you haven't explored them then? 1927. It was the year the State Government decided to have its open season on furs. They were thought to have big economic potential.'

'Furs? You mean kangaroo furs?'

'Possum. Koala. They had been protected but it was decided to have an open season, one month a year. August 1927 was the first trial. The last, too, as it turned out.'

'Who'd want to shoot koalas? They just sit there, in trees. They don't hurt anyone.'

'Well, that is so, and if you will read those 1927 newspapers you will see that there was a big outcry against the Government for allowing it to happen, even before the event. A lot of people cared deeply and wanted to protect them. I was not one of them.'

'You wanted to shoot the koalas?'

'Well, not me personally, but it is true. I had a passion for furs, and the koala fur is very soft, short but soft and remarkably water resistant. Those fur things, as you call them, are muffs. I once adored them.'

'Grandma, how could you?'

'Don't call me that name. And I could, very easily. But you see, I am honest. I do not hide the truth of my persuasions, though history has, shall we say, gone against me. Or at least, the maps look simple now, and they point in one direction. Koalas are cuddly. Killing koalas is cruel.'

He did not like to hear that sneering tone. He would not look her in the eye.

'Well, there we are. In one month, August, half a million koalas were butchered in Queensland. In retrospect, we see that almost the entire population was destroyed. How to explain to you, you intolerant young, that the economic arguments were entirely plausible? Tom Foley, I remember how passionately he defended the open licence period, how he argued a fur trade as lucrative as Canada . . . '

'But if you kill them all in one go . . . '

'Who was to know? Who would have known that the lure of a quick cash turnover would come first in so many minds. Most of the people I talked to later thoroughly enjoyed the shooting. The open season was never renewed.'

'Nothing left to shoot.'

'Well, Queensland is like that. I learned after that particular excitement never to trust my friends when they became full of enthusiasms for something, especially if that something was indefensible. Well, Boyd; enough. That was in my shingle and shimmy era. My mirror era. My political period. When I believed in progress and that progress could come very speedily and have no consequences at all. Now I am back to my shingle cut and at sixty-five it will take a lot to convince me that you can hold on to anything. My koala fur muff was put down in the green tin chest because muffs went out of fashion. The fur itself is indestructible.'

So, thought Boyd at the time, are you. It was their last time together. Boyd roamed the house like a caged creature, chafing and easily sullen. When his grandmother saw him off at South Brisbane Station his good-bye kiss was perfunctory.

Marie

The phone rang. The sound was monotonous in its simulated desperation. After seventeen rings it stopped.

Two hours later the phone sounded again.

Approximately seven hours after that there was a loud thumping at the door of the unit.

'Marie, dear one. Marieee. Marie, it is your mother, Marie, will you open the door? Marie open the door, I forgot my key, the key you gave me. Marie? Are you in there Marie? I have checked with the airlines and am worried Marie. Dagmar your friend has been phoning, she is worried too, Marie. You are not still angry with me, child, you are not busy with cooking or with . . . Marie, *ach*! what is that smell? You have not been working on science experiments, *Mein Gott*, Marie! Someone! Everyone! Help me, help me open this door, someone, there is a smell, a smell of the poison gas in my daughter's flat, help me *ach Himmel*! Help!'

Pale sunlight filtered through an already leafless Lombardy Poplar into the lobby of the apartment building. Among the thin branches two currawongs were yodelling and singing. One of them grew restless and flew off. The other remained a few moments and then followed. On the footpath below, humans were gathering, there was movement, much activity, too much disturbance. They were joined by a third bird. From the safe distance of the small park with elms they began carolling again.

Postscript

Midnight 21 April 1979: Anglican Dean Ian George describing what he felt when he arrived at the scene of the Bellevue Hotel demolition: 'It made me feel the way one feels in watching one of those movies about the rise of the Nazis in Germany ... with the strange night light, the activity, military vehicles symbolically represented by the heavy moving equipment and the destruction of something precious. I was disgusted. I felt sick ... '

Also, during debate in Queensland Parliament on 24 April 1979, Liberal MLA Rob Akers, an architect by profession, graphically described his feelings: 'Just after midnight on Friday, I experienced tremendous fear for this State. When I stood on the footpath in William Street and watched the convoy of heavy trucks roar in charging into the crowd, with hundreds of police protecting them, and saw the gates being locked after them, I thought that that could happen only in a country run by somebody like Idi Amin — not in Queensland where, in the past, I had stood up for freedom and democracy. I did not think that that could happen in Queensland but it did. Every person who was near the Bellevue site on Friday night was scarred for the rest of his life by what he saw. I will never forget it — and I will not forgive.'

Ross Fitzgerald, *From 1915 to the Early 1980s: A History of Queensland* (University of Queensland Press 1984, p 456)

Floating
Nancy Corbett

'*Floating* is an elegantly written novel in the grand tradition of romance . . . a lively and vivid story.'
KYLIE TENNANT

Hannah is a young, talented and serious Sydney woman who, for money and growing notoriety, performs an erotic dance each night in a Kings Cross nightclub. Into her life comes Jack, a visiting fashion photographer from New York, who loves her and stays in Sydney longer than he intended.

Hannah begins to dream of a Japanese woman dressed in elaborate wig and beautifully decorated clothes. The woman, Komachi, is a *tayu*, a leading courtesan of eighteenth century Tokyo, who has come from the past to teach Hannah the old traditional movements of dance.

The story extends to the floating world of Yoshiwara, old Tokyo's city within a city, where Komachi, her apprentice Hanatsuma and her lover, the Kabuki actor Hangoro, live in a delicate peace for too short a time.

In Japan, they say that bonds made in one lifetime last for three. When Jack meets a young and beautiful Japanese fashion model, she brings to Hannah's life hatred, tension and rivalry connecting across time and space to ancient Japan.

'*Nancy Corbett* has fashioned a fast-moving novel engaging the reader's sympathy for characters, and not sacrificing content for what is excellent entertainment.'
THE AUSTRALIAN

0 947189 05 X
AVAILABLE APRIL 1988

AVAILABLE IN AUSTRALIA
AND NEW ZEALAND ONLY

BLACK SWAN

Black Cat, Green Field
Graeme Harper

It is the First World War. Sidney Nelson is a young artist caught up in the world of unions, sabotage and ideology. Duped by his lover, Sidney escapes to the country and the hope of solitude and work. But even life on the Manning River is not what it seems—he will discover unpleasant truths about his sister, the family she has married into and himself.

Black Cat, Green Field is the saga of a time of turmoil mirrored in the anguish of a young man battling memories of an unfinished war, embroiled in conflict between imagination and reality, searching for his true loyalties. A fascinating and highly accomplished first novel.

0 947189 14 9   AVAILABLE IN AUSTRALIA
                                 AND NEW ZEALAND ONLY

BLACK SWAN

The Vacillations of Poppy Carew
Mary Wesley

'Once again she deploys her admirably comic skill to good effect; puncturing the pompous, exposing humbug, nudging our perceptions in the direction of the absurd.'
FINANCIAL TIMES

'In Mary Wesley's book the dark sides of life are there all right, but never more weightily than is proper in light fiction. There are death (but what a marvellous funeral), desertion, but where would the plot be without them — and a potentially lethal road accident where Poppy is rescued by just the right free-range pig farmer in the nick of time. All the detail in the book is either cleverly and recognisably horrible, like the half-finished, cockroach-ridden North African hotel, or perfectly delightful, like the Italian dress in which Poppy goes to the funeral of her once-milkman father, with a genius for ladies and racecourses, who so surprisingly left her so much money. Miss Wesley's book is persistently light, ingenious, cheerful. I recommend.'
MARGHANITA LASKI

'Mary Wesley is high-spirited and inventive, and keeps her wayward plot moving forward at a spanking pace.'
DAILY TELEGRAPH

'Wesley's narration is as fast and surprising as ever; her sub-plots are well worked out and rich in detail; she has a sharp ear for the idiocies uttered by nurses in hospitals, publishers at parties and people in fish-shops. Her observations on old age are admirably forthright.'
TIMES LITERARY SUPPLEMENT

0 552 992585

BLACK SWAN